The Great Adventure

by

Kerry Jon Kirby

Table of Contents

Chapter 1 Origins

Like all great stories, this one begins not in a moment of glory but in the quiet corners of life, where friendships are forged and passions quietly grow. It's a story about history, faith, and a group of people who dared to chase the impossible. Before the adventure that would take them across the sands of Israel in search of biblical truth, there was a beginning, and like most beginnings, it was humble.

At the heart of the story is Errek Johnson, a man of many talents and an even deeper well of conviction. Just three years before the journey began, Errek was a big man in every sense standing six-foot-two and weighing nearly 275 pounds. He had spent years coaching professional basketball in Southern England, a career he had worked hard to build. That particular season, he had turned the worst team in the National Basketball League into playoff contenders. He loved the strategy, the camaraderie, and the thrill of competition. Yet, it wasn't basketball that truly defined him it was his faith and his unshakable curiosity about the past.

Errek's love for biblical history wasn't born in a classroom. It was forged in a hospital room in London when, at nineteen, he narrowly escaped death. That experience changed him. From that moment forward, the Bible was not just a book it was a calling. Though he had degrees in Biology and World History, and later went on to earn his third master's degree in Biblical History, it was the ancient world that truly fascinated him. His time in England deepened that love, especially as he wandered through cathedrals and castles and saw firsthand how history shaped the present.

While in England, Errek attended a local Baptist church where he met Bill and Penelope Amerson. That meeting was unplanned and yet, in hindsight, seemed inevitable. After a church game night, they found themselves at the same table, sharing laughter over a round of Rook, the card game Errek had taught them. From there, a friendship blossomed with remarkable speed. Bill and Penelope, or Penny as she was affectionately called, were eight years younger than Errek and eleven years younger than his older brother, Bob. He found in them the kind of friends one rarely finds past college genuine, loyal, and full of life.

Bill was a gifted computer programmer who specialized in translation software, a skill that would later prove invaluable. He was slim and agile, with an energy that could rival a spider monkey. Penny, meanwhile, was brilliant in her own right. A specialist in ancient Middle Eastern languages, she was fluent in Hebrew, Aramaic, and Greek, and worked closely with the British Museum on transcription projects. Despite their academic brilliance, they were warm, fun-loving, and athletic. They hiked, biked, swam, and ran half-marathons when they had time. They even shared Errek's love for miniature golf.

The three became nearly inseparable. Errek would visit them regularly, joining them for dinners, museum visits, and late-night card games. They, in turn, visited Errek in Tennessee every summer. Those visits became traditions exploring Smoky Mountain trails, going to Dollywood, swimming, eating local favorites, and playing Rook into the early hours. They met Errek's mother and older brother, Bob, during one of those trips, and quickly the group became a close-knit circle. Errek's mother, now in her early seventies, remained sharp and active despite the years. Though she'd always carried herself with youthful energy, the recent loss of her husband had quietly aged her in spirit.

Bob was three years older than Errek, but they were often mistaken for twins. Both were tall, big-framed men, although Bob outweighed his younger brother by a bit. He was the quieter of the two but had a sharp wit and a dry sense of humor that surfaced once he got to know you. Like Errek, he had a strong foundation in faith and a deep love for history. Though he held a master's degree and had worked in academia, he never boasted about it. He was the kind of person who would give you his last dollar and act like it was nothing.

Over the years, the four of them Errek, Bob, Bill, and Penny grew close. But by 2012, life threw Errek a curveball. He suffered a serious knee injury after practice while exploring the Old City and had to return to the States prematurely. That particular season had been one of his best. He was living at the College De LaSalle in Jerusalem, making friends with the local clergy, and coaching a team that would go on to lose in the championship without him. Leaving early was painful in more ways than one. Though injured and grieving, Errek did his best to care for his mother, often pushing himself beyond his limits. It wasn't easy, but he gave more than he received. Not long after his return, his stepfather passed away. Grief layered itself over his physical pain, and for a while, he withdrew from many of the things he loved.

Bob stepped in, helping with their mother's care and encouraging Errek to find his way back. That summer, as if on cue, Bill and Penny returned for their yearly visit. They found Errek in a rough state his weight up to 315 pounds, limping, tired, and emotionally drained. Bob was also struggling, his own weight hovering near 350. Yet, the Amerson's didn't let the gloom linger. They swam daily with the brothers, played cards, visited museums, and encouraged both men to focus on getting healthy again.

One evening, after dinner and a card game, Penny turned to Errek and said, "Why don't we all go to Israel next year? You've talked about it nonstop. Let's make it happen."

Errek was stunned. The idea of returning to Israel, not as a coach but as an explorer of history, reignited something in him. He began to see a way forward. "But I've got to get healthy," he replied. Penny, ever the optimist, smiled and said, "Then let's get to work."

Errek began treatment for his knee and underwent surgery to repair the damage. Around the same time, he developed a stomach issue that required corrective surgery, which ultimately helped him lose weight. On a medically supervised diet, he dropped nearly 80 pounds over several months. Bob, seeing his brother's transformation, joined him on the journey. By the time their next summer reunion rolled around, Errek was down to 235 and Bob was around 285. For the first time in years, they felt like themselves again.

That summer, while vacationing in Panama City, Florida, the group met up with Errek's old friend, Professor Joe Smith. Joe was no ordinary man. A high school friend of both Errek and Bob, Joe was a certified genius with an IQ over 170 and three PhDs under his belt in Electrical, Mechanical, and Computer Engineering. He was also an expert diver who had explored Civil War shipwrecks in his spare time. When Errek told him about the dream trip to Israel and the idea of exploring biblical archaeological sites, Joe's eyes lit up.

"I'm working on a sonar-enhanced metal detector," he said. "It can detect underground imperfections and hidden chambers. I'd love to come."

Errek laughed, half-expecting him to be joking, but Joe was already sketching designs on a napkin. By the end of the conversation, he was in.

The group was now five Errek, Bob, Bill, Penny, and Joe. Each brought a unique skill: Errek's leadership and knowledge of biblical history, Bob's historical curiosity and quiet strength, Bill's technical expertise and climbing skills, Penny's linguistic mastery, and Joe's engineering genius and diving experience. It was an unlikely team, but somehow it made perfect sense.

Over the next few months, the dream became a mission. Video calls turned into planning sessions. Joe sent updates on his prototype metal detector. Bill started working on a portable language translator. Penny compiled a reading list and began brushing up on her Aramaic. Bob hit the pool three times a week, while Errek, now in better shape than he'd been in a decade, enrolled in an online master's program in biblical history to deepen his knowledge. The group chat buzzed with daily milestone updates photos, ideas, and encouragement.

They needed someone to help with logistics, particularly access to protected sites in Israel. Errek reached out to Rubin Goldstein, a former basketball camp acquaintance who now worked with the Israel Antiquities Authority. Rubin remembered him fondly and agreed to help. Through his connections, Rubin arranged for their permits, organized local guides, and offered them a place to stay for the first few nights at the College De LaSalle in Jerusalem.

They also needed funding. While everyone could cover their own flights and lodging, the cost of gear, permits, and special access was significant. That's when Errek contacted Arthur Kingsley, a wealthy old friend and one of his earliest coaching mentors. Arthur, now in his early sixties, still remembered the days when Errek was just getting started, helping coach Arthur's sons. Moved by the story and impressed by the team's commitment, Arthur agreed to help.

"I'll loan you the money for equipment and expenses," he said. "You pay me back if you can, and if you find anything valuable, I get ten percent."

Errek laughed. "Deal."

With Arthur's support, things accelerated. Bill finalized the travel dates, booking business-class flights that would have all five members arriving at Tel Aviv's Ben Gurion Airport within thirty minutes of one another. Joe would fly from Florida, the Amerson's from London, and the Johnson brothers from Birmingham, Alabama. Rubin arranged for a private shuttle to collect them upon arrival, with accommodations reserved at the Hilton Jerusalem for the first few days.

Joe continued developing his advanced metal detector—a. A solar-powered, waterproof device with sonar imaging, capable of detecting non-metallic anomalies such as stone chambers or clay jars buried deep beneath desert sand or underwater terrain. He included backup batteries, USB power banks, and a protective casing that could withstand extreme temperatures. Meanwhile, Bill added layers to the language software uploading regional dialects and ancient scripts, designing an interface that could cross-reference inscriptions with biblical text databases.

Penny was compiling notes, translating fragments from the Book of Maccabees and the Copper Scroll, focusing on geographical markers that had yet to be definitively identified. She stored much of her research on an encrypted flash drive just in case they lost Wi-Fi or had to work offline. She also revisited the prophetic passages in Ezekiel and Jeremiah that some scholars believed held coded clues to the Ark's resting place.

Bob, reinvigorated by the group's momentum, surprised everyone with his steady weight loss and newfound discipline. He walked two miles every morning, swam in the evenings, and had even begun reading academic commentaries to brush up on the historical backdrop of the Second Temple period. Gone was the man who sat silently during planning meetings. Now he was sharing article links, asking questions, and volunteering to research.

Errek, too, had found his rhythm. With his weight down to 212 pounds and his energy fully restored, he immersed himself in his studies and began preparing a personal journal to document the journey. He titled it *The Great Adventure* and carried it everywhere. In it, he wrote prayers, route plans, historical facts, and personal reflections.

By May, the transformation was visible. Bob weighed in at 258 pounds, having lost nearly a hundred from his peak weight. Their cardiologists were stunned not just by the numbers, but by the stability of their vitals. Both brothers had reduced their blood pressure medication and no longer required sleep apnea machines.

For the first time in years, they were medically cleared for international travel, hiking, and light climbing.

One particularly memorable video call took place three weeks before departure. Bill and Penny were sitting in their sunlit kitchen in London, Penny's laptop open to a map of Jerusalem. Joe was outside under the Florida sun, showing off a dive mask prototype with an integrated voice communicator. Bob, now comfortably seated without back pain for the first time in years, sipped coffee while Errek flipped through pages in his journal.

"I found something," Penny said, circling a section near Qumran. "This ravine here, it's never been excavated. There's speculation it was once a holding site for sacred vessels."

Joe leaned in toward his camera. "Can we reach it on foot?"

Rubin, who had joined the call from his office in Jerusalem, replied with a grin, "If you don't mind goats and rocks, yes."

Bill chuckled. "You'll fit right in, Bob."

Bob grinned, "If a goat can do it, so can I."

They ended the call with prayer, laughter, and promises. There was a sense of gravity forming as this wasn't just a hobby trip or a fun getaway. It was becoming something more sacred. Each member of the group had a reason, a pull toward the land they would soon walk.

For Errek, it was the Ark. Not the physical artifact alone, but what it represented: the fulfillment of prophecy, the presence of God, the promise of covenant. He didn't expect to find the Ark lying unguarded in a cave, but he believed that the journey itself would draw them closer to understanding why it had vanished and what its absence meant for faith today.

For Joe, the adventure was as much about tech as treasure. He dreamed of finding scrolls, coins, anything that could be verified and preserved. He had already contacted a few universities about scanning artifacts on-site. Joe never professed deep religious belief, but he was moved by the sincerity of the group and often said he hoped to "see the fingerprints of God." in the dirt.

Bill wanted to witness faith through a scientific lens. For him, ancient languages were living proof of spiritual continuity. Translating an inscription on a shattered urn or deciphering a coded phrase on a temple wall was more than an intellectual thrill it was an act of reverence.

Penny's passion was deeply personal. She found solace in scripture during a difficult season in her life and hoped this journey would offer healing. This trip offered her both purpose and healing. She hoped that touching the stones of ancient places might renew her understanding of the sacred and remind her that life, like language, often hides meaning in broken fragments.

Bob simply wanted to belong. He had spent years on the sidelines, the loyal brother and silent supporter. Now, he was part of something. He might not speak ancient Hebrew or engineer devices, but he brought strength, loyalty, and a heart full of expectation.

And so, it was with faith, hope, and a touch of nerves that the final week of preparations arrived. They each packed light clothing that could handle heat and dust, water packs, dry-fit shirts, breathable boots, and lightweight hiking gear. Joe had a separate case for his diving equipment, which included collapsible fins, a GoPro, spear guns for safety, and underwater recording gear. Rubin had arranged optional access to Dead Sea diving zones, including a professional facility run by a man named Avi Breslin. Though none of them knew him personally, the business was reputable and would provide certified guides.

Penny packed the flash drive and her paper journals. Bill secured backups of his software and maps, storing them both online and on micro-SD cards in waterproof casings. Bob brought spare chargers, snacks, and a surprisingly detailed pocket Bible annotated with his own reflections. Errek brought his journal, a small vial of water from the Sea of Galilee gifted to him years before, and a silver pendant Penny had sent him engraved with the Hebrew word for "emet" truth.

The night before departure, the group held a final call. No planning. No logistics. Just connection. They shared prayers, memories, and laughter, recounting how far they had come. Penny teased Bob about the time he tried to pass off Nutella as ancient Israeli food. Joe promised to do a backflip off the dive boat if they found any coins. Bill, ever the clown, offered a ten-pound reward to anyone who could find him an ancient scroll with Wi-Fi passwords.

Errek's voice quieted as the call came to an end.

"Whatever we find or don't find, I just want us to walk where prophets once walked, to see what they saw, and to know we're a part of something bigger than ourselves."

Bob nodded. "Let's do it. Let's chase the impossible."

The morning of the flight, the Birmingham airport bustled with activity. Errek and Bob checked in early, carrying only their personal gear and a large shared suitcase of electronics and study materials. They passed through TSA with smiles, knowing that Penny and Bill would be wheels-up from Heathrow within the hour, and Joe would depart from Orlando just moments later.

Boarding the plane, Errek looked out the window as the engines roared to life. He reached into his bag and held the pendant in his hand, whispering a prayer he had memorized long ago.

He turned to Bob, whose eyes were already closed in anticipation of a nap.

"This is it," Errek said quietly.

Bob didn't open his eyes, but a smile crept across his face. "Let the great adventure begin."

Chapter 2: Jerusalem

It had taken over a year of planning and a series of miracles for them to arrive here, but the day had finally come. With permissions from the Israeli Antiquities Authority and access arrangements handled through the College De LaSalle, the team was officially cleared to explore. Rubin Goldstein, Errek's old friend and former basketball contact, had been instrumental. He now worked with the IAA and would be guiding their team through the legal and procedural landscapes of archaeology in Israel. As a former player turned administrator, Rubin had found his niche supporting exploratory and educational missions.

They'd managed to negotiate an agreement with both Jewish and Palestinian authorities any discoveries would be preserved and studied locally, with documentation provided to their academic institutions. The College had offered them lodging, and Rubin had insisted on providing transport and logistics. The pieces had fallen into place. It wasn't just luck it felt like destiny.

The team's flight from Atlanta to Tel Aviv was long but comfortable. Errek and Bob sat side by side, tired but quietly excited. Bob leaned back with his eyes closed, listening to his music.

Errek nudged him. "We're not going to sleep through our first glimpse of Israel, are we?"

Bob opened one eye and smirked. "Just resting. You'll want me fresh when the adventure begins."

Errek looked around the cabin and chuckled. "I swear half this flight is Rabbis. Feels like we're on a pilgrimage already."

As the plane began its descent into Tel Aviv, Errek pressed his face to the window. The coastline glimmered below, stretching eastward into hills and ancient lands. It stirred something in him excitement, reverence, a quiet fire.

Customs was tense at first. Uniformed officers eyed their bags with suspicion, especially the metal cases Joe had shipped with his equipment. But before things could escalate, Rubin appeared, confidently striding up to the checkpoint with an air of practiced ease.

"They're with me," he told the officer in Hebrew, flashing his ID badge.

The officer glanced over the forms, then back at the group. "Welcome to Israel," he said, with a half-smile before waving them through.

Outside, Rubin grinned. "I figured you might need a little help getting through."

Errek shook his hand. "Rubin, you haven't changed a bit."

"You have," Rubin replied, clapping Errek's shoulder. "Look at you. Dropped weight, got color back. Last time I saw you, you looked like someone had put you through a blender."

Bob laughed. "That was after the injury in Jerusalem. Now he's the poster child for rehab."

Rubin turned to Bob. "And you must be the big brother." I expected you to be taller."

"Same height just older and wiser," Bob replied.

Rubin then turned to the rest of the group as introductions were made. "Joe Smith, our genius engineer and part-time adventurer. And Bill and Penny Amerson, linguistic and tech wizards."

Bill offered a warm handshake while Penny smiled. "We've heard a lot about you, Rubin. Thanks for helping get everything set up."

Rubin nodded. "You've got quite the team here. Let's just keep it legal, yes?"

Errek smiled. "We're explorers, not looters."

As they walked toward the baggage claim, a familiar voice called out.

"Well, this place smells like my grandma's spice cabinet."

Everyone turned. It was Joe, just arriving after a different flight. His travel case thudded along the floor behind him, plastered with stickers from half a dozen countries. "Customs loved my sonar detector. Thought it was a torpedo."

"You made it," Bill said, offering a handshake.

Joe looked around at the group, then grinned. "The gang's all here."

Once outside, Rubin led them to a small, shaded bench to wait for their driver.

Penny passed around compact translator earpieces. "These are updated. They'll cover Hebrew, Arabic, and Aramaic. English feed comes through in real time."

Joe held one up to the light. "You really should patent these."

"They're still glitchy in noisy crowds," Bill said. "We'll keep improving them."

Bob shifted his bag. "I'm hungry. You think there's a McDonald's around?"

Rubin chuckled. "Yes, but kosher rules mean no meat and cheese together. So no cheeseburgers. But fish with cheese? That's actually a bigger no-no."

Lemuel, their driver, soon arrived with a clean, well-kept van. The drive to Jerusalem began with open highway and coastal plains, gradually giving way to rising hills and patches of stone terraces. Lemuel narrated along the way, pointing out landmarks and offering historical trivia.

"There," he said, gesturing toward the hills, "is the Valley of Ayalon, where Joshua asked the sun to stand still."

Bill recorded video while Penny took notes. Bob leaned his head against the window, eyes following the landscape.

"It's greener than I expected," he said. "I thought it'd be all sand and rock."

"Give it time," Rubin said. "You haven't seen the desert yet."

As they approached the city, Rubin turned and smiled. "Get ready. You're about to see the place that changed the world."

The van passed through a modern checkpoint, Rubin conversing in fluent Hebrew with the guard. The gate opened, and they entered the Old City through the North Gate.

The College De LaSalle stood quietly behind stone walls, just as Errek remembered. Three priests met them at the entrance Father Tobias, Father Albert, and Father Daoud. They wore simple robes and broad smiles. Errek embraced each warmly.

"Welcome back," Father Tobias said. "And welcome to all of you."

They introduced themselves formally, with Penny and Bill offering polite bows and Bob shaking hands. Joe nodded, already eyeing the building's stonework.

"We are honored to host you," Father Daoud said. "Please, come inside. We've prepared your rooms."

Errek warmly embraced his old friend. "Father Daoud, it's great to see you and the other Fathers," Errek said.

"Please call me Father David," Father Daoud replied, "that's my Christian name, Daoud is my Arabic name."

As they entered, the sounds of Jerusalem surrounded them, voices in multiple languages, the distant echo of prayer, birds darting between rooftops. The team felt it in their bones: this place was alive with something ancient.

The College courtyard was peaceful, shaded by olive trees. Inside, the rooms were simple but clean, with arched windows and cool stone floors. The Fathers gave them time to rest and freshen up before the first outing.

Later, Rubin led them out through the North Gate again. They followed the outside of the old city wall. Its towering stone ramparts that rose high above them, with grassy slopes stretching outward. As they approached Damascus Gate, the massive entrance loomed like a small castle, its steps rising to a wide, open gathering area where locals mingled. This was the main gateway to the Old City; the others, Rubin noted, were far smaller. From the open plaza, they took the main road leading away from the gate before turning down a narrow alley that dead-ended at a row of stone cubes. A huge red door marked the entrance to a private complex. Beyond the fence, just east of the Garden Tomb, lay the rock hill known as Mount Calvary or Golgotha.

Just past the market, Rubin turned down a narrow alley.

"Where are we going?" Bob asked.

"To see something you'll never forget," Rubin replied.

Errek smiled, recognizing the path. He had often come here during his coaching days to reflect. Still, it never lost its impact.

They emerged into a small park just outside the Old City walls. Before them rose the Garden Tomb believed by many Protestants to be the actual site of Jesus' burial and resurrection.

The team fell silent.

"It's beautiful," Penny whispered.

The area was serene, covered in greenery and centered around a carved tomb in the rock face. A stone channel and ancient olive press nearby gave it a sense of authenticity. A low, ornate concrete fence separated the garden from the adjacent rock hill, whose weathered caves gave it the eerie appearance of a skull the reason many call it Golgotha. Joe pulled out his drone.

"I'll get a quick scan of the caves in the cliffs. No flying over the wall, right?"

Rubin nodded. "Correct. Stay on this side of the fence."

A guide approached, greeting them with warmth and reverence. He explained the site's layout and significance, showing them the old wine press and possible crucifixion site known as Gordon's Calvary. The guide also confirmed that a few caves in the area remained unexplored. Penny arranged a special entry pass for the next morning.

They gathered near the tomb entrance, a sense of awe overtaking them. Errek knelt to touch the stone. Bob placed a hand on his shoulder.

"Think He really laid here?" Bob asked softly.

"I don't know, maybe," Errek whispered. "But something holy happened here."

They stood in silence for a few minutes longer, each absorbed in their own quiet thoughts. Penny moved slowly toward the entrance, her fingers brushing the stone as she passed through. Inside, the air was cool and still. The simple chamber was hewn from solid rock no gold, no incense, no adornments. Just rough walls and the ghost of an ancient presence.

She knelt briefly and whispered a prayer.

Joe leaned in behind her and nodded, unusually subdued. "Feels different here."

"Peaceful," Bill said. "Sacred in its simplicity."

Bob entered last, his usual light-heartedness hushed by the weight of the moment. "I'm not overly religious," he said softly, "but this... this I can feel."

Rubin stood near the entrance, watching. "This place doesn't need words," he said. "It speaks in stillness."

As they emerged into the soft glow of the fading sun, the guide pointed out landmarks visible from their vantage point. To the southeast stood the Mount of Olives, the Church of Mary Magdalene with its gleaming domes, and just beyond that, the Church of the Ascension. Penny took notes rapidly while Bill recorded a slow panoramic shot with his camera.

Joe returned his drone to its case, pleased with the data it had collected from the nearby hillside caves.

"I think we've got some uncharted cavities just west of here," he murmured to Errek. "If the angles are right, we'll take a closer look in the morning."

The guide permitted them limited exploration the next day. Only two of the team members would be allowed into the caves due to space and safety restrictions. After a quick discussion, it was agreed that Joe and Bill would go Joe for his tech, and Bill for his knack for spotting details.

The sun was dipping below the horizon as they made their way back toward the College. Along the way, Rubin stopped at a local market to pick up tea and bread. The shopkeeper recognized him and greeted him warmly in Hebrew. As they waited, Bob wandered into a nearby bakery and emerged moments later with warm pastries.

"Don't worry, I'll share," he said, offering a piece to Penny.

"I'm impressed," she said. "You found something not deep-fried."

"Hey, even I have standards."

Back at the College, the Fathers had prepared a modest but welcoming dinner in the dining hall. A long wooden table held bowls of hummus, roasted eggplant, cucumber salad, and fresh bread. There was also warm mint tea and, to Joe's delight, a carafe of local wine.

Father Albert offered a short blessing before they sat.

"May your journey be guided by truth and your hearts filled with peace. Welcome, friends."

They ate heartily. Penny and Father David discussed biblical translations, while Joe and Father Tobias bonded over mechanical engineering. Apparently, Tobias had helped install a water purification system in the school. Bob entertained the group with stories from their flight, exaggerating Joe's run-in with airport security to great comedic effect.

After dinner, Errek presented jerseys and basketballs he'd brought for the students. Father Tobias was thrilled. "The children will be overjoyed. We've been needing new gear for the summer program."

Later, the group made their way to the rooftop terrace. The city stretched before them, the golden Dome of the Rock glowing softly under the moonlight. In the distance, the Garden of Gethsemane lay in shadows, and the Church of the Holy Sepulcher stood silently amidst the cluster of rooftops.

The view left them breathless.

"Hard to believe this is real," Bill said.

Penny wrapped a shawl around her shoulders. "This feels like the center of everything."

Bob leaned on the railing. "You know, I thought I was just coming for the ride. But standing here now... it's like something's calling."

They stood in silence again, the city murmuring below them like an ancient lullaby. Errek's mind drifted back to his last visit here, before ~~the~~his injury and before the team was formed. The pain, the questions, the longing. And now he was back, but no longer alone.

As the night deepened, Rubin reminded them of the next morning's early schedule.

"Joe and Bill, you'll head to the Garden Tomb site by eight. I'll be there with the clearance forms. The rest of you can explore the nearby quarters or join us later."

"I'm going to check in with Sayid tomorrow, too," Errek said. "He used to play for the local team I coached. He promised to take us to Kamal's Fried Chicken."

Bob perked up. "Fried chicken in the Holy Land? Now you're talking my language."

Joe grinned. "Is that the same Sayid who built his own drone from scrap parts?"

"The very same," Errek nodded. "Brilliant mind. Heart like gold."

The team lingered a while longer before finally retreating to their rooms. Joe checked his gear one last time. Penny entered ~~her~~ notes into her laptop, cross-referencing Aramaic inscriptions she'd seen earlier. Bob flipped through a tourist guide, circling places he wanted to see.

Errek sat by his window, watching the moonlight dance across stone rooftops. He closed his eyes and whispered a short prayer.

"Thank You for getting us here. Guide us well."

And with that, the first day in Jerusalem came to a close. The search hadn't truly begun ~~not yet~~ but something sacred had already started to unfold.

Chapter 3: Bill, Penny, and Joe's Mini Adventure

The morning broke under a blanket of soft gray clouds. The weather was mild but overcast, casting a calm light across the hills of Jerusalem. Bill, Penny, and Joe had woken early, eager and prepared. They dressed in their hiking gear, slung backpacks filled with tools over their shoulders. Rubin just outside the gates of the College. Today, they'd be exploring the small caves near the Garden Tomb, places that had intrigued Joe and Bill since their drone survey yesterday.

The gatekeeper greeted them with a quiet nod. Penny stepped forward and addressed him in fluent Hebrew, explaining their intention to use a drone for an initial scan before physically entering any cave. He appreciated the cautious approach and waved them through.

"I'll head back to the tomb to take samples and pray," Penny said, adjusting her backpack. "Don't waste your time unless the drone shows something useful."

"Oye, dingo!" Bill exclaimed, "come on, Penny, let me have my fun."

She smiled and pointed a warning finger. "Just be careful. You're not getting much protection free-climbing that rock. It's no gym wall."

As Penny walked back toward the Garden Tomb, Bill and Joe scaled the low stone wall into a rougher part of the terrain. The slope gave way to a relatively flat stretch with a clear view of the three small caves nestled in the hillside.

Bill opened the bags and began unpacking tools, while Joe set up the drone equipment. With a soft whir, the drone lifted into the air, both men watching its feed carefully as it approached the first cave.

"The first few feet look good," Joe muttered, eyes glued to the tablet screen. "Light's dropping fast though. Hard to make out detail."

"Let's check the second one," Bill said. "Might be shallower, but it's worth scanning them all before we waste time crawling around."

"Agreed. This saves us a lot of guesswork."

The drone buzzed gently from one cave to the next. As it hovered before the second opening, Joe turned to Bill.

"So, how do you know Errek?"

Bill laughed. "Funny I was about to ask you the same."

He leaned back on a rock, his expression nostalgic. "We went to the same high school. Errek and Bob were the kind of guys who got along with everyone, nerds, athletes, it didn't matter. Smart, kind, and tough as nails. They stood up for anyone who needed it. We played basketball, board games, and even golf with my dad. We lost touch for a while after college, but the internet brought us back together."

Bill nodded. "Sounds about right. I met Errek through church, back when he was coaching pro ball. We hit it off instantly, played Rook, visited old museums. WeI introduced mehim to the Beaulieu Motor Museum, and man, he loved that place."

Joe grinned. "Yeah, Errek and Bob both have a thing for old cars. I remember Bob's Z28 and Errek's Cadillac. And then for his 19th birthday he got that beautiful 10th Anniversary Trans Am. That car and Bob's Camaro could fly."

"We used to play Dungeons and Dragons–" Joe continued. "I was the Dungeon Master, they loved the quests I made up. When Errek mentioned this trip, it reminded me of those old days. I just had to join."

"They haven't changed much," Bill added. "Still into seafood, classic cars, and solving puzzles."

Joe smiled. "Bob's the quiet one, but once he opens up, his sarcasm is golden."

"True," Bill agreed. "And Errek's more like Penny, funny, competitive, and talkative. But both are peacemakers. Never get in trouble, always dependable. They're more than friends, they're family."

"Errek says you and Penny are the smartest people he knows," Joe said, adjusting the drone controls.

Bill waved him off. "He says that about you too. Honestly, he loves all of us and I can see why. You're exactly what he described."

They turned back to the tablet.

"All right," Joe said. "Let's check this third cave."

The final cave was tucked around the curve of the knoll, harder to access, and half-hidden by the terrain. "This could be interesting," Joe muttered. "A great place to hide something."

Fifteen minutes in, and the drone had already cleared the first two caves, both of which proved shallow and uneventful. But the third?

"This one's tricky," Joe warned. "We'll have to go slow and rely on the camera. There's a blind spot."

The drone entered the cave slowly, its propellers humming as light gave way to shadow. The jagged interior passed on screen narrow, sharp, irregular.

"Whoa," Joe said. "Just hit the ceiling. Didn't see that."

"Is that a scorpion?" Bill asked, squinting at the monitor. "Or a rock?"

"Can't tell. There's almost no sunlight in this part of the cave. I'll fly in the flashlight drone."

Bill nodded. "If this place is as interesting as it looks, we're going in."

He began gathering gear. "Time to suit up."

"I'll bring the drone back," Joe said. "Grab my backpack and I'll meet you at the climb."

Bill led the way up the rock face. It was steeper than expected, the stone damp from earlier weather. A few slips reminded him to take it slow. Fortunately, he found good handholds and hauled himself steadily up to the first ledge.

Joe followed, cautiously retracing Bill's path. Halfway up, a handhold gave way beneath him. He let out a sharp yelp and began to slip.

"I got you!" Bill reached down and pulled him up just in time.

Breathing hard, Joe found his footing. "That... was close."

They entered the cave and paused.

Outside, light rain began to fall.

"We might be here awhile," Bill said. "I've got some anchor pegs we can drive in."

Flashlights revealed a rough interior with a slight reddish discoloration on one side.

"Looks like iron or rust," Joe noted. "Water's seeping through the ceiling."

"Might be an old fault line," Bill said. "Or damage from an earthquake centuries ago. Erosion probably filled it with mud over time."

He pulled out a chisel and sample kit. "I'll take some of this back for analysis."

As he moved toward a corner, he stopped. "There's something here. Shine the light."

Joe aimed his beam. Half-buried in the soil lay a deteriorated leather pouch weathered, ancient, and delicate.

"Could've been placed here hundreds of years ago," Joe said.

"I've got a mini shovel. I'll bag it carefully."

They secured it in a collection pouch for Rubin to inspect later.

"Penny can read Aramaic," Joe added. "If there's anything written, she might be able to translate."

The rain continued, steady and unrelenting. They waited out the worst of it, seated just inside the cave entrance, resting and whispering about what they might have found.

With the rain still lightly falling, Bill and Joe prepared to make their way toward the third and most elusive cave, the one partially hidden at the curve of the knoll. The climb would involve a horizontal traverse across a slippery face and then a ten-foot descent.

"You think we can make it now?" Bill asked.

"We've got the non-slip gloves," Joe replied. "Let's wait ten more minutes and take it slow."

In dry weather, it would've been a five-minute job not even fifty feet away. But the slick conditions made it a technical challenge.

Joe started the traverse, carefully placing each hand and foot. But just a few steps in, one of his handholds crumbled.

"Whoa!" he shouted as he lost balance.

The commotion echoed down the slope. Penny, who had returned from the tomb, looked up in alarm and sprinted over.

"Joe! Are you okay?" she yelled, trying to spot him through the mist.

"I'm good!" he called back. "Just a loose hold. Bill's got me."

Penny stood below with a worried expression, arms crossed tight against her chest. Bill shook his head. "You don't have to tell me to be careful twice."

"This isn't like any cliff I've climbed before," he muttered. "Gotta expect brittle spots."

They finally reached the cave ledge. Joe climbed in behind Bill, flashlight in hand.

"Keep your eyes peeled," Bill warned. "We saw something moving in here earlier, scorpion or snake."

Joe nodded. "Light's on."

A soft beam illuminated the interior. "Hey… Bill. I think we hit paydirt."

Nestled at the rear of the cave were two ancient jars, their lids still sealed. Faint marks lined their surface inscriptions, nearly worn away by the passage of time.

"Whoa," Bill whispered, crouching down. "There's something else. Look right there."

A Deathstalker scorpion skittered across the stone floor, tail raised, its movements deliberate and menacing.

Joe moved slowly, kneeling and pulling an empty jar from his backpack. He edged toward the scorpion, watching its every twitch.

Just as it struck, Joe brought the jar down, trapping it.

The sharp thunk echoed in the cave. The scorpion's tail lashed against the glass, but it was caught.

"That was close," Bill muttered, backing away. "Too close."

Joe exhaled. "One sting from that thing, and we'd be in real trouble."

As the scorpion thrashed under the jar, Bill began carefully wrapping one of the ancient vessels in cloth. But as he lifted it, he suddenly yelped in pain.

"Ahh! Something bit me!"

He dropped to one knee, cradling his hand.

"What is it?" Joe asked, rushing to him.

"Ants," Bill said through gritted teeth. "Not normal ones, these are desert fire ants."

Joe helped him unwrap the second jar while Bill winced, his skin already showing swelling from several bites. "Okay," he said, jaw clenched. "We've got what we came for. Let's go."

"You okay to climb down?" Joe asked.

"I have to be," Bill replied.

They made their way toward the exit. Bill descended first, his injured hand shaking as he reached for footholds. The pain made it hard to focus, but he gritted his teeth and kept going.

Thirty-five feet down. Then thirty. Then twenty.

At fifteen feet, he called out. "Penny!"

She rushed over again, hearing the urgency in his voice.

"I need you to take the backpack," Bill said. "Don't let it hit the ground, it's fragile."

She climbed up onto the ledge below him, took the bag as he lowered it.

"I'm going to drop," he said. "Can't hold on much longer."

"I'll catch you."

He let go, falling into her arms. The impact knocked them both to the ground, but the bag was safe.

Bill groaned in pain. "Cortisone... in my bag."

Penny opened the kit and applied cream to the swollen bites.

Rubin, who had been watching from a distance, finally stepped in. "That looks bad."

"I've been bitten several times," Bill said, breathing heavily.

"You need a shot. Come on."

He called a driver, who arrived within minutes and whisked Bill off to a nearby clinic. There, he received cortisone injections and a dose of pain medication.

Joe, meanwhile, was still inside the cave, trying to figure out how to escape without freeing the now-frantic scorpion. He waited until the creature moved slightly, then carefully lifted the jar just enough to free himself then bolted for the entrance.

The scorpion struck again, its tail slicing through air as Joe rolled out of the cave and onto the ledge.

"Made it," he whispered, breathing hard.

He followed Bill's path down the rock, slower but safer, and finally touched solid ground.

By the time the group reunited at the College De LaSalle, it was just after 11 a.m.

"Bill, what happened?" Bob asked, eyes wide as he saw his friend's wrapped hand.

"Desert fire ants," Bill said, grimacing. "But the scorpion didn't get us."

"Five bites," Penny added. "Joe got one, but he had allergy meds on hand. Helped a lot."

Joe raised his hand. "We found something though two sealed jars and a really old, worn leather pouch."

"From the time of Christ," Penny said, her voice alive with wonder. "Maybe even mid–first century AD."

"I've seen jars like those in the British Museum," she added. "This is a serious find."

Rubin nodded, carefully taking the jars and pouch from their packs. "Let's open them carefully. If there's anything inside, don't touch it. It could be extremely fragile."

With precision and patience, Rubin cracked the seals.

Scrolls.

Faint traces of parchment remained inside each jar dried, curled, but still intact.

Penny's hands trembled. "Can I read them?"

Rubin held her back. "Not yet. The Antiquities Museum has the lab and tools to handle this properly. But I'll make sure you're invited when they do."

He opened the pouch last. Ashes.

"Just ashes," he said quietly. "Could be ceremonial. Still, we'll test it."

He looked at the group with a smile. "You might have earned your vacation just with this."

They gathered for lunch, hummus, cheese, flatbread.

"I'm ready for some real food," Bob joked. "Like KFC."

That gave Errek an idea.

He pulled out his phone. "Faheem? It's Coach Errek."

A pause. "You and Sayid still around?"

"Sayid's here visiting."

"Perfect. We're at De LaSalle. You guys swing by in 30? And bring a bucket from Kamal's Fried Chicken. Enough for the Fathers and the team."

"You got it, Coach."

Errek laughed. "It's good to have connections."

Chapter 4: Touring the Old City

After lunch, Errek stood up and said, "Let's head up to the roof to get our bearings and plan the rest of the day." The group eagerly followed him to the rooftop of the college, where a panoramic view of Jerusalem unfolded before them.

"Okay," Errek began, pointing out different directions, "Bethlehem lies about eight miles to the southeast. Over on the western side of Jerusalem is the City of David. They're still doing active excavations there. Not far from that area is the Cenacle, the room where the Last Supper was held, and the place traditionally believed to be King David's tomb. Just across the way is the site where Mary is believed to have passed away."

He gestured again. "Near the Zion Gate, archaeologists are digging down toward the old wall of David. If you follow that wall south, you'll find some Roman columns and steps embedded inside the wall, leading to the Muslim bazaar. Through there, we can visit the Western Wall and the Temple Mount. The golden dome you see-," he pointed, "that's the Dome of the Rock Mosque."

Penny leaned forward, eyes wide with anticipation. "Inside the Old City, what else can we see?"

"Well," Errek continued, "Hezekiah's Tunnels are in there. Some of them are unexplored or blocked off, but we can visit them later. We've got twenty more days. Behind the college, if we walk down the cobblestone street, it winds its way to the Mosque of Omar. A short distance past that is the Church of the Holy Sepulcher, the other site believed to be where Jesus was crucified and buried. From there, we could go to Mount Zion."

Before they could make a decision, Father Albert appeared, announcing, "Lunch is ready."

Errek chuckled. "More hummus, cheese, and pita bread, I bet."

"We managed to get a bit of meat," Father Albert said. "We'll have fresh roasted lamb tomorrow your birthday, Errek. Today, it's still hummus and cheese."

"Perfect," Errek replied. "Let's save the lamb for tomorrow."

Just then, a familiar voice called out, "Coach!"

It was Faheem, one of Errek's former players, along with Sayid. They entered carrying a large bucket of fried chicken.

"I told them to bring Kamal's Fried Chicken," Errek said, grinning. "The local version of KFC."

"Thanks, guys," said Father Albert warmly. "We rarely get to enjoy this."

"Don't worry," Errek said, handing him a folded bill. "Here's a hundred dollars, buy supplies, meat, vegetables. You all deserve better meals."

Father Albert looked overwhelmed. "Thank you, my son."

"And I didn't forget," Errek added. "I brought basketball jerseys for the kids. I remembered you needed them from my last visit."

"You're always welcome here, son," Father Albert said, his voice soft with emotion.

"We'll be moving to a hotel tomorrow," Errek explained, "but maybe we can stay here the night before our flight home. It'll be easier to get to the airport."

"Absolutely," Father Albert nodded.

After lunch, the group sat down to enjoy the fried chicken. Bobby dug in with enthusiasm, devouring three pieces.

"This is real food," he said, satisfied.

Bill, still nursing a swollen hand from his earlier encounter with desert fire ants, managed a smile. He felt up to sightseeing later but admitted he'd just rest until lunch.

Penny reassured him. "Don't worry, Bill. I'll take plenty of pictures for you."

"For Bill, not being able to take pictures is pure torture," Errek joked, and they all laughed.

Father Tobias entered the room and offered to walk them down to the Church of the Holy ~~Sepulchre~~Sepulcher.

"Tomorrow," he said, "before you leave, we can drive you outside St. Stephen's Gate near the Garden of Gethsemane. From there, you could walk the Via Dolorosa to the church and back up to the college."

Penny, Bobby, and Joe loved the idea.

"Sounds like a plan," Errek said.

"You can leave your bags here," Father Tobias added. "After your walk, Abdul will drive you and Rubin to the Hilton."

"The hotel's nice," Rubin added. "Rooftop pool, fitness center, and a good restaurant. On Saturday, I'll take you all to the Dead Sea."

"That's generous, Rubin," Penny said.

"It's become my main mission," he replied. "Some say Sodom and Gomorrah were near the Dead Sea. It's so salty you float, no one's explored its depths. I've got special scuba gear, lights, and metal detectors. We're going to have some fun."

After a light meal, Father Tobias led them down the wide cobblestone street behind the school. They turned onto a broader street flanked by shops on one side and larger buildings on the other.

"Oh, silk scarves!" Penny exclaimed. "We *must* stop on the way back."

After 100 yards, they turned into a narrower pedestrian lane, lined with colorful market stalls, fruit stands, and fabrics flapping in the breeze. The smell of spices filled the air as they passed shopkeepers offering tea and trinkets, their calls echoing, "My brother, come inside!"

It felt like walking through a vibrant maze from another era.

At the end of the alleyway, a small square opened before them, dominated by the majestic Church of the Holy Sepulcher. The church sat on what Catholics believe is Mount Calvary. With its large dome and two smaller ones, the grand structure felt almost surreal.

They passed through its immense doors into a sacred quiet. Below was the Chapel of Adam, named because, during excavations, a skull believed to be Adam's was found symbolically placing the crucifixion over the tomb of the first man.

Ascending steep stairs, they reached Calvary. On one side was a depiction of the centurions; on the other, the place where Jesus was nailed to the cross. A statue of Mary stood solemnly nearby.

In the next chapel, a magnificent crucifix stood with an altar beneath. Pilgrims knelt to touch the white granite rock said to be where the cross was planted. Many crawled beneath the altar to reach the hole.

Father Tobias read Scripture aloud. They prayed silently, each deeply moved.

As they descended, they stopped at the Stone of Anointing, where Christ's body was prepared for burial. The scent of myrrh and frankincense lingered. Penny touched the stone, whispering a prayer.

Then, Tobias led Errek down to the church's oldest section, Helena's Chapel.

"Helena was Emperor Constantine's mother," Tobias explained. "She found a cave filled with old crucifixion crosses. One remained untouched by time."

"There's a story," he continued, "of a deathly ill explorer traveling with Helena. He stumbled, touched the blood-soaked cross, and was instantly healed. That's believed to be Jesus' cross."

"They brought back nails and a large piece of the cross to Turkey," Errek added. "That's where Constantine founded the Holy Roman Empire."

Rubin looked impressed. "You really know your history."

"Helena sent word to Constantine," Tobias nodded. "He ordered a church built over this spot and any other sacred places she found."

They moved toward the Aedicule, the small structure over the empty tomb. Only a few people could enter at once. The atmosphere was reverent, heavy with history and faith. Pilgrims wept, prayed, and knelt.

"It's up to each person to decide which tomb is the true one," Tobias said softly. "But both are powerful."

After leaving the Aedicule, Rubin guided the group out into the bustling streets once more. "You've seen some of the most sacred spaces in Christianity," he said. "Now, let's explore more of Jerusalem's unique neighborhoods and hidden gems."

The old city buzzed with activity. Children played in the alleys, shopkeepers called out to passing tourists, and the scent of spices mingled with the aroma of grilled meats. The city allowed no cars within the walls, so the group walked though. Bobby was beginning to feel the strain.

"It's amazing how so many different communities coexist here," Penny observed.

"Yes," Rubin nodded. "Here, everyone calls you 'brother.' They'll invite you in for chamomile tea, offer you trinkets or souvenirs... and then comes the hard sell. It's all part of the charm."

"I've learned my lesson," Errek said, chuckling. "The last time, I ended up buying three rugs I didn't need just to get out of a store."

The cobblestone streets proved tricky. Many steps were uneven and nearly invisible in the sunlight, reflecting the golden hue of the stones. Errek stumbled more than once and rubbed his knee. "It's easy to get disoriented in this labyrinth," he muttered.

This time, he had come prepared. He handed out snacks to some of the kids, earning smiles and friendly chatter in return. The group made their way down the Via Dolorosa this time in reverse passing the Stations of the Cross and echoing arches. They briefly admired the Church of the Flagellation and St. Anne's Church but chose not to enter.

"We'll come back later," Tobias reassured them.

Soon, they reached the Pools of Bethesda. Two ancient pools, now dry, lay about 15 to 20 feet below street level, surrounded by crumbling Roman columns.

"It's hard to believe this was once a healing center," Joe said.

Rubin nodded. "This place was revered. People believed that when an angel stirred the waters, the first person to enter would be healed."

"Think we could find coins or pottery in the mud below?" Bill asked.

"It's possible," Rubin replied. "Bethesda became a Roman spa later on. Coins from Christ's time through the third century might still be there."

"I'd love to come back with the metal detector," Joe said, his eyes lighting up.

Bill, despite the pain in his hand, remained upbeat. "Let's push on to the Garden of Gethsemane," he said. "I'll just need a fizzy drink so I can take another pain pill."

Penny offered to carry his camera bag. "I'll take pictures for you."

The group passed through St. Stephen's Gate, just fifty meters ahead. Named for the first Christian martyr, it opened to a peaceful grove of ancient olive trees Gethsemane.

They entered a fenced area and were immediately awed by the serenity. Ahead of them stood a majestic Byzantine-style church with a mosaic front and three Corinthian-arched doorways. Above were four statues representing the Gospel writers set against a golden triangular façade.

"That's the Church of All Nations," Rubin said. "Built by contributions from many countries."

Inside, the lighting was subdued. The stained-glass windows cast deep blue hues across the vaulted, domed ceiling. Twelve small domes formed the roof, giving the space a sacred symmetry. No artificial lighting was used, adding to the solemn atmosphere.

At the center of the sanctuary lay a large piece of exposed bedrock, surrounded by a one-foot-tall gilded fence shaped like a crown of thorns.

"This is where Jesus prayed before His arrest," Tobias whispered.

Pilgrims knelt, many weeping. The gang joined Bill, who had found a seat in the pews near a mosaic of Judas betraying Jesus with a kiss. The walls depicted scenes of Christ's arrest and sorrow.

They sat in silence, letting the spiritual weight of the place wash over them. Bill took his pain pills, hopeful they'd help him make it through the day.

After some time, Father Tobias offered to guide them through the garden paths outside. "Some of these olive trees," he said softly, "have stood here since the time of Christ."

Penny took dozens of photos of the trees, the domes, the statues. "Bill, I have more than fifty already," she said, trying to ease his frustration at being unable to take photographs himself.

Up the hill, Rubin pointed to another domed structure. "That's St. Mary Magdalene's Church Russian Orthodox. You can see the onion domes from all over the Mount of Olives. And above that dome see it? That's the Dome of the Ascension."

"Is that where Jesus ascended to Heaven?" Joe asked.

"Yes," Rubin replied. "Inside, there are scorched footprints in stone. A supernatural event had to cause it."

"Can we see it?" Penny asked.

"Not today. It's closed. But we can still try to reach St. Mary's."

Errek, Joe, Penny, and Bill followed Rubin up the hill. Bobby and Tobias, meanwhile, decided to take a break and walk back toward the Church of the Flagellation.

As the others climbed, Rubin explained, "St. Mary Magdalene's Church was built by Tsar Alexander II in honor of his mother, Maria, and Mary Magdalene. It's mostly run by nuns."

The white façade, gold-topped domes, and towering structure stunned the group. As they neared, Rubin pointed out statues and tombs.

"Grand Duchess Elizabeth Feodorovna, her companion Nun Varvara, and Princess Alice of Battenberg Prince Phillip's mother are all buried here."

"Wow," Penny whispered. "We had no idea."

Unfortunately, a notice on the gate stated that the church was closed to visitors, open only on Tuesdays and Thursdays. Penny still managed to take plenty of photos for Bill.

"Let's head back," Rubin said. "Gethsemane might be closed by now."

They began their descent, planning to take the Kidron Valley path back toward St. Stephen's Gate and then retrace their steps to the college.

As the main group made their descent from the Mount of Olives, Bobby and Father Tobias were already enjoying a peaceful rest at the Church of the Flagellation. Inside the quiet chapel, they sat near a statue of Jesus being whipped by Roman soldiers.

"This place..." Bobby whispered, "it makes me realize how much Christ endured. It's humbling."

Father Tobias nodded. "Yes, being here brings His suffering closer to the heart. Every step of this city reminds us of His sacrifice."

Refreshed, they stood and began walking again, weaving through the tight alleyways and buzzing bazaar. Everywhere they went, shopkeepers called out in warm tones.

"Come, brother! I have something for you. Sit, have tea!"

Tobias smiled knowingly. "Get ready for the sales pitch," he said.

Bobby paused at a small silver shop and noticed a ~~cross necklace~~ ~~a~~ large Jerusalem Cross necklace with greenish stones set into the sterling silver.

"What's this one?" he asked the vendor.

"Ah, my brother! This is the Jerusalem Cross. The large cross at the center represents our Lord. The four smaller crosses around it? They stand for Jerusalem, Judea, Samaria, and the uttermost parts of the world."

"And these stones?" Bobby asked, intrigued.

"Solomon stones! Very rare," the man boasted. "Just $100, special price."

Bobby chuckled. "Silver's worth maybe $30 here. I'll give you $40."

"No, no, my friend, it is handmade, you see? I can do $80. That's a blessing."

"$50, with tea included," Bobby countered.

The vendor laughed and quickly poured chamomile tea. "Sit, sit, enjoy, my brother. What is $70 among brothers?"

Trying to escape the negotiation, Bobby started walking away with a laugh. "Okay, $60 and a soda."

"Deal!" the vendor shouted. "You are hard but fair."

With the necklace in his pocket and a soda in hand, Bobby and Tobias reached Damascus Gate, its ancient steps rising dramatically toward the skyline. As they stepped out into the small square just beyond the gate, Bobby spotted a resting camel and an Arab man approaching with a wide grin.

"Would you like a camel ride, my friend?" the man asked.

Bobby's eyes lit up. "Absolutely. That's been on my bucket list!"

Father Tobias raised an eyebrow. "Be careful. They rise in stages rear legs first so you must lean back."

Bobby confidently climbed aboard, swinging into the saddle with gusto. The camel grunted beneath him. As the animal rose, Bobby leaned a little too far forward, causing him to lurch awkwardly and wrap his arms around the camel's neck.

"Whoa! Whoa!" he cried.

"Just relax," the owner advised, grabbing the lead rope. But Bobby misunderstood and shouted, "Giddy up, Clyde!"

To everyone's surprise, the camel took off, galloping through the square like a racehorse. Bobby bounced wildly in the saddle, hollering like Yosemite Sam. Tourists and vendors scattered as the beast barreled toward a fruit cart filled with grapes, bananas, and pomegranates.

"Whoa! Stop!" Bobby screamed.

The camel skidded to a halt, bumping into the cart. Bobby flew forward, rolled down the camel's neck, and landed in a heap covered in fruit.

"Are you okay?" Father Tobias called out, running up.

"Yeah," Bobby muttered, brushing himself off and picking grapes out of his hair. "Not doing that again."

He handed the fruit vendor $20 to pay for damages and scooped up the remaining produce. "Might as well take it back for the Fathers," he said sheepishly.

The camel owner scowled but accepted the apology. "You surprised the camel," he said. "He was not expecting spurs!"

Together, Bobby and Father Tobias walked back through the North Gate checkpoint and into the De La Salle College campus. Bobby dropped off the fruit in the kitchen, where the cook gratefully turned it into a fresh salad. He joined Father ~~Daoud~~David in the lounge where a soccer match between Morocco and Egypt was playing on TV.

"Would you like some tea while we wait for the others?" Father ~~Daoud~~David asked.

Bobby nodded. "That was enough adventure for one afternoon."

Not long after, the rest of the group returned. "What was that noise by Damascus Gate?" Joe asked.

"That," Bobby said, smirking, "was me on a wild camel ride."

"No way!" Penny laughed. "I wish we'd seen it. That would've made the photo album for sure."

As laughter filled the room, Father ~~Daoud~~David arrived and greeted the group. "I heard about your adventure. Welcome back!"

Errek introduced him. "Father ~~Daoud~~David is an old friend. ~~If it is easier you can call him Father David. Daoud is Arabic for David.~~ He's also from Bethlehem, and he's offered to take us there tomorrow for my birthday."

"Oh, it's your birthday?" Bobby asked.

"Yep. Tomorrow's the big day."

"We'll celebrate properly," Father Tobias added. "We're having a special dinner tonight."

Plans began forming for the next day: a trip to Bethlehem, including Shepherd's Field, the Herodium, and lunch near the Church of the Nativity. Father ~~Daoud~~David agreed to drive them and meet his sister, Marium,- at Manger Square later for lunch.

"We're also moving to the Hilton in New Jerusalem tomorrow," Errek said. "A little more comfortable for the rest of the trip."

"And we'll be using a 10-passenger Mercedes van, modified for our equipment," Joe added.

"Sounds like this expedition is gaining momentum," Rubin observed.

That evening, the group gathered for a hearty lamb shank stew served with hummus, cheese, pita bread, and the fruit from Bobby's wild ride. Spirits were high, and conversation lively.

"This lamb stew is incredible," Joe said, digging in.

"Definitely better than just hummus and cheese," Bill added, with a grin.

After dinner, the group headed to the lounge for a night of games and fun. Joe, Penny, and Bill engaged in a fierce Scrabble showdown. Joe edged out Penny 3–1 and Bill 3–2, but together, the couple beat Joe in a best-of-five final.

They also played Rook, pairing up in different teams, and laughed at Penny's live commentary of "Tom and Jerry" playing on TV in Arabic.

Later that night, Father Albert asked, "What time should I wake you in the morning?"

"Let's do 8 a.m.," Bill said. "We'd like to check into the hotel by 9:30."

"No problem," the Father replied. "We'll be ready."

Bill and Penny nodded in agreement. "We haven't even unpacked, so we'll be ready."

As the evening wound down, the friends reflected on a day filled with sacred encounters, ancient wonders, and unforgettable moments from holy ground to runaway camels. Tomorrow, a new adventure awaited in Bethlehem.

Chapter 5: Errek's Birthday and Bethlehem
– A New Day

The morning sun crept through the curtains, casting a soft golden hue over the room. While Errek still slept soundly, the others were already up and bustling about. Bob, Joe, Penny, and Bill moved swiftly and quietly, loading the luggage and equipment into the van before returning inside.

At 8:30 a.m., Penny playfully leaned over the staircase and called out, "Wake up, sleepyhead! You overslept!"

Errek stirred, groaning and rubbing his eyes. "Where's the luggage?" he asked, groggily sitting up.

"We packed the van for you," Joe grinned, holding up a mug of tea. "Breakfast is on the table."

Downstairs, a spread of freshly fried eggs awaited, alongside aromatic muffins infused with chamomile, cardamom, and pomegranate. Rubin, smiling behind his glasses, had brought them in from the market earlier that morning

"You shouldn't have," Errek said, genuinely touched as he bit into a muffin. "This is amazing."

The group gathered around him, and even the Fathers came by to wish him a heartfelt "Happy 38th Birthday!"

"Today's your day," Bill said. "But remember, we still need to check in at the hotel and make our way to Bethlehem."

"Right," Errek replied, glancing at the clock. "It's 9 a.m., we better get moving."

As Joe loaded one of his sonar metal detectors into the van, Errek paused to admire it. "Wow," he said, running his hand along the polished grip. "It looks like a mop handle but clearly not your average mop."

Joe laughed. "I wanted it to be light. This can withstand saltwater, freshwater, heavy pressure, and even mild impacts. It's battery-powered, solar-charged, and can detect metals up to six feet underground."

"What about material type?" Errek asked.

"Custom frequency detection for silver, copper, bronze, and gold. It even picks up soil density changes, so if there's a buried object or chamber, we'll know. Think treasure chests, ancient pots, even sealed rooms."

Errek blinked. "You've outdone yourself, buddy. This is incredible. What's it weigh?"

"Just under four pounds," Joe said proudly. "Perfect for fieldwork."

"Let's bring one detector with us and leave the rest at the hotel," Bill suggested.

"Agreed," Errek nodded. "How's the hand, Bill?"

"I still can't close it, but it's better than yesterday. Maybe I'll be able to dive in a couple days."

Rubin, already seated in the van, nodded. "The Dead Sea will help the swelling. Two more days and it'll be back to normal."

By 9:15 a.m., the van was packed. They added an igloo cooler with drinks and snacks, and left De La Salle College, heading toward Bethlehem.

As they drove, Bill glanced out the window at the growing number of concrete barriers and security checkpoints.

"Why all the heavy fortification?" he asked.

"Well," Rubin began, "after the Six-Day War, Israel annexed some Palestinian territory around Jerusalem, including this area. Bethlehem is Palestinian-run, but the road we're on leading to Rachel's Tomb is controlled by Israel. This road is considered 'safe' for all faiths, but it's heavily protected."

"So Rachel's Tomb is actually in Jerusalem?" Penny asked.

"Technically, yes," Rubin replied. "But it's right at the border, which makes it complicated."

Soon they approached Checkpoint 300, just beyond a towering 30-foot wall on one side and a shorter wall on the other. Israeli Defense Forces approached their vehicle. Rubin and Father David stepped out, presenting documentation from the Antiquities Authority.

"We're clear," Rubin announced upon returning. "They're cautious, but respectful."

Ahead, the field opened up. An ancient olive tree, gnarled with age, cast a gentle shadow over the otherwise stony courtyard. "That one's probably over 200 years old," Rubin noted. "Not quite as old as the ones in Gethsemane."

They parked and walked toward the tomb.

The Tomb of Rachel, enclosed within a square, white-stone structure topped with a dome, resembled a jewel box. Attached to it was a more recent square building: a Muslim prayer chamber.

"There are separate areas for men and women to view the tomb," Rubin said.

"Why?" Joe asked.

"In traditional synagogues, spaces were divided, men, women, and gentiles in different courts," Rubin explained. "This tradition continues here."

As they entered, an air of quiet reverence enveloped the group. The tomb of Jacob's beloved wife, who died giving birth to Benjamin, had been a pilgrimage site since the 4th century AD though its significance dates back much further.

They took a few moments to pray, take photographs, and reflect.

Bill whispered, "It's humbling, to stand here. The mother of Israel's tribes, laid to rest on the road to Bethlehem."

Penny nodded. "This whole journey… It's starting to feel like something more than just an adventure."

"We need to leave soon if we want to make our 1:00 p.m. meeting at Manger Square," Penny reminded them. "Let's aim to leave the Herodium by 12:15."

"I suggest we skip Shepherd's Field for now and go after lunch," Rubin added. "That'll give us time to do justice to the Herodium."

Driving through a landscape of rolling hills and ancient ruins, they soon reached the Herodium, a massive fortress-palace built by King Herod the Great.

They parked, purchased tickets, and stopped by a 15-minute documentary playing in the visitor center.

"This'll help us plan our route," Errek said as they watched footage of the upper and lower palaces, baths, and Herod's tomb.

"Let's start with the tomb," Rubin suggested.

They climbed halfway up the artificial hill, facing west toward Jerusalem and Bethlehem. Even in its ruined state, the tomb monument, a square base with columns and a conical rotunda, was imposing.

"The original structure stood at least 25 meters high," Rubin explained. "It's inspired by Absalom's Pillar. This reconstruction is a small replica. The real thing was destroyed, but Professor Ehud Netzer uncovered much of this before his untimely death here during excavation."

"Is this where they found the broken sarcophagi?" Joe asked.

Rubin nodded. "Three were discovered shattered, no bones inside. Some think Herod's remains were removed. Others think they were never buried here."

Bill pointed. "Look at that massive stairway climbing toward the upper palace."

"It narrows into a tunnel halfway up," Penny added. "Incredible engineering."

Joe, noticing the ongoing work by archaeologists near the stairway, wandered over with curiosity. Through Bill's interpreter software, he asked what they were doing. The workers explained they were sifting soil for possible artifacts, scanning the rubble inch by inch. Joe held up the sonar-assisted metal detector. "Mind if I try something?"

At first, the workers looked skeptical, but he powered the device, swept it over the ground, and it emitted a sharp beep. The archaeologists leaned in. Following the detector's signal, they began to dig and, to everyone's surprise, unearthed a pair of ancient coins one gold, the other silver.

Their eyes widened. Joe shrugged, grinning. "My invention."

The site manager, stunned, asked about purchasing the technology. "I have four prototypes," Joe said. "But I'm here with permission from the Antiquities Authority. Talk to Rubin."

Rubin nodded in support. "This is exactly where Professor Netzer found the three sarcophagi."

"Still no bones?" Errek asked.

"No," Rubin replied. "Either removed or never placed there. In Judaism, contact with the dead requires ritual cleansing, so it's always complicated."

Joe glanced around. "What if I adjust the detector to search for calcium and iron? Could help locate bones."

Rubin lit up. "That might work. But first, let's explore the rest. The baths and amphitheater are still ahead."

Their path led to the amphitheater, carved into the slope, modest in size but rich in detail. Though it seated only about 450, it held grandeur in its preservation. At the top sat the loggia, Herod's private viewing area. The walls bore frescoes animals, landscapes, vibrant scenes painstakingly preserved, pigments mixed into the plaster in true Roman style.

"Marcus Agrippa designed this," Rubin added. "Yes, that Agrippa. His son appears in Acts."

They climbed back up to the upper palace, a network of rooms and arches still somewhat intact. From the top, the panoramic view stunned everyone, Jerusalem to the north, Bethlehem to the west, the Dead Sea glimmering to the east, and Hebron far to the south.

Bill stood still, gazing into the distance. "This is where Herod built his personal monument," he said quietly. "He removed two hills to encase his palace inside a man-made mountain. A funeral mound, built for one man."

"This is nuts," Joe said. "It's like a Roman coliseum on a mountain. Overkill, even for a king."

They moved into the bathhouse complex, beginning with the caldarium, a large hot bath room nearly 6 by 9 meters with barrel vaults and seated alcoves. The adjacent tepidarium featured a natural open dome reminiscent of the Pantheon. The final chamber, the frigidarium, even included a Jewish mikveh, a purification pool suggesting Herod's close ties to Jewish advisors.

In a dimly lit corridor, a small sign caught Bill's eye: "Pontius Pilate Ring Found Here."

"Joe, can you fire up that detector again?" he asked.

They had already spent an hour, and time was tight, but Joe powered it on. Though no new finds emerged, the potential was obvious.

The group exited through the ancient reception hall, now converted into one of Israel's oldest synagogues. Rubin pointed toward the two exit paths: either retrace their steps through the tomb and the royal stairway, or take the Jewish resistance tunnels, built during the Great Revolt.

"Fifteen-minute walk through tunnels, comes out near the tomb," Rubin said. "What do you think?"

"Let's go through the tunnels," Bill replied. "We can climb the rim afterward."

They followed him to the narrow entrance, descending into the man-made tunnels. Cool, dark, and cramped in places, these were carved by Jewish rebels hiding from Roman legions. Along the way, they passed old water cisterns where Herod had once diverted mountain springs. Agrippa's genius was on display everywhere.

"This place is more than ancient architecture," Joe whispered, "It's history alive."

The group emerged from the tunnels, blinking against the afternoon sun. After a short walk, they reached the van around 12:10 p.m., just as planned.

"I'm exhausted," Bobby whined, collapsing into a seat.

"You'll thank me later," Errek laughed. "Next stop, Shepherd's Field."

"It's literally all downhill," Bill smirked.

A five-minute drive brought them to the Shepherd's Field, a lush valley unexpectedly green in a region of rocky hills. They passed under an arch reading *"In Excelsis Deo."*

The Roman Catholic Church of the Shepherds, designed like a shepherd's tent, stood modestly at the edge of the field. Inside, three large frescoes depicted the Nativity story: shepherds in the field, angels announcing Christ's birth, and the shepherds adoring the baby Jesus. The translucent dome above created a soft glow, enhancing the atmosphere.

"It's moving," Penny said, voice catching. "Simple. Beautiful. Honest."

Below the church, a large shepherds' cave had been expanded into a worship space. Rows of pews lined the chambers, with dioramas of the Nativity story nestled into alcoves. In another part of the cave, ancient pottery bowls, cups, even oil lamps spoke of millennia of history.

Outside, they spotted Bedouins herding sheep, just as shepherds had done for thousands of years. In the distance stood the Greek Orthodox Church, far larger than the Catholic sanctuary. Though plain outside, inside it dazzled. Murals covered every inch, columns, ceilings, domes, even the chandelier bore artwork, a colossal twenty-foot dome adorned with the Twelve Apostles.

"Who paints murals on chandeliers?" Joe asked, spinning slowly in awe.

"Let's get some group pictures," Penny said, pulling out the camera.

They snapped photos beneath the magnificent dome, then strolled back to the fountain, resting and chatting.

"Look at the valley," Errek whispered. "Boaz and Ruth's field is just beyond that hill. Bethlehem behind us. Herodium on the horizon. And shepherds still out there… It all feels so real."

Bill nodded. "Biblical stories don't feel ancient here. They feel… present."

Bobby, holding a cold soda, stretched his arms. "Okay, this was worth the walk."

Rubin smiled. "We still have one more stop before lunch: Manger Square."

As they entered Manger Square, the bustle of pilgrims and locals filled the air with anticipation. Errek spotted a familiar hand waving. "That's her, David's sister!" he said.

Introductions were quick and warm, and they made their way down a side road to a small restaurant David had recommended. The group slid into booths after placing orders for falafel, hummus, lamb kabobs, and soft drinks, with special requests for Dr Pepper. As they waited for the food, Penny chatted with David's sister in Arabic and Aramaic, beaming with joy at the chance to use her language skills. Joe activated the instant translator, allowing them all to understand the conversation in real time. The technology worked like magic, translating and transmitting dialogue in both directions without delay.

The food arrived, warm and fragrant. The falafel reminded Bobby of Mediterranean hushpuppies, crispy on the outside and soft within. The hummus was fresh, creamy, and brightened by a hint of lemon, while the lamb kebobs melted in the mouth. "This is the perfect birthday meal," Errek said between bites, his face glowing with contentment.

After about an hour of rest and rich conversation, they returned to Nativity Square. Errek pointed toward a large sandy-colored rectangular building. "That's the Church of the Nativity," he explained.

Bob tilted his head. "It doesn't look like much from the outside."

"No, but it's what's beneath it that matters," Father David replied.

They approached the small doorway, the Door of Humility, through which pilgrims for centuries had bent low to enter. Inside, the group descended narrow stone steps into the Grotto of the Nativity. The space opened up to reveal the birthplace of Jesus, marked by a 14-point silver star embedded in marble, surrounded by red embroidered cloths. People knelt reverently, some weeping, some silent in awe.

"The Savior of the World was born right here," Rubin whispered.

Silence filled the air, heavy with meaning.

They moved next to St. Catherine's Church, connected by underground tunnels. One tunnel led to St. Jerome's Cave, where the scholar had translated the Vulgate, much of the Old and New Testaments, from Hebrew and Greek into Latin. The space was bare but filled with a quiet reverence. Oil lamps and a wooden table gave a glimpse into a scholar's life nearly two millennia ago.

They continued through a second passage to a darker, colder cave. "This is the Cave of the Innocents," Father David said solemnly. "It was here that bodies of infants were found, slaughtered during Herod's massacre after the birth of Jesus."

Joe's hand tightened around his camera, now hanging unused by his side. "So much cruelty in contrast to so much hope."

"Herod was brilliant… and terrifying," Rubin replied.

Back in the main square, David gestured toward another path. "There's one last place you must see. About a hundred yards away, the Milk Grotto."

The path led to a white cave, unlike anything they had seen. Inside were three small chapels, tended by the red-and-white-robed Nuns of Perpetual Adoration, who prayed around the clock for world peace. Statues of Mary breastfeeding Jesus, Joseph, and infant Christ were scattered throughout.

"Legend says a drop of Mary's milk turned the cave white," Father ~~Daoud~~David explained. "That's why the entire space glows like alabaster."

"This is otherworldly," Penny murmured. "I've never seen anything like it."

The cave's chambers offered a rare calm. In one section, people knelt, praying silently. In another, visitors lit candles beneath ancient frescoes. The walls sparkled, reflecting light like crystals.

Back in the van, the group sat in silence for a few minutes, each digesting the depth of the day.

"I could live in that cave," Bobby said finally. "It felt… peaceful. Not just sacred. Peaceful."

"We've walked through history today," Bill added. "Biblical stories aren't just stories here. They're… tangible."

Father David glanced at the clock. "Still time for one more quick stop, Mount Zion, just outside Zion Gate. We can drive past the Church of the Dormition, the Upper Room, and King David's tomb."

They passed by the Dormition Abbey and stopped near St. Peter in Gallicantu, perched on the slope of Mount Zion. It is noticeable for it's~~its~~ rooster on the steeple. From there, they walked down to the Roman steps leading to the Kidron Valley and Gethsemane.

"These are the steps Jesus was led up after his arrest," David said. "And somewhere down there… Peter denied Him three times then the rooster crowed."

The group descended the steps in reverent silence. At the bottom stood a statue depicting Peter's denial, a fire pit nearby where Roman soldiers once warmed themselves. Inside the church, they descended to the prison chambers, hollowed from solid bedrock. Each room carried a somber story, tiny cells, a punishment room with ancient stone hooks, and one central slab that had once held prisoners in place for flogging.

Penny touched the stone. "It still feels like pain lingers here."

David nodded. "The current church was built later, but these cells were in use well before Jesus' time… and after."

They climbed back into the van, weary yet filled. "Let's swing by the College," Errek suggested. "I want to see if Father Tobias and Father Albert can join us for dinner."

David agreed. The Fathers were thrilled by the invitation but unsure about Sabbath restrictions. Meanwhile, Joe made a quick call to the Dead Sea Dive Company to confirm gear and scheduling.

"We're pushing the dive to Sunday or Monday," he explained. "They'll bring wetsuits and gear tonight. We'll train in the pool eight feet deep should be enough."

He rattled off everyone's sizes and weights, ensuring proper suits and weight belts were available. "The suits are tight," the man on the phone warned. "But we've got what you need. We'll bring it tonight."

As they reached the Jerusalem Hilton, Errek called Arthur. "Today was wild," he said. "Herodium, Shepherd's Field, Nativity Square my birthday was unforgettable."

"Well," Arthur replied, "I'm sending you another $5,000 for your treasure hunt. Call it a loan. And happy birthday again."

"Thanks, man. Really."

They checked into their rooms, spacious, modern, and comfortingly familiar. "This bed is perfect," Bob said, flopping down. "Wake me for dinner."

Errek called the front desk. "Is the pool open late?"

"Until ten, sir."

"Can we practice diving in our wetsuits?"

"As long as you don't disturb other guests, feel free."

Errek smiled, glancing at the gear being delivered. "Looks like training starts tonight."

Chapter 6: Preparing for the Dead Sea and the Via Delarosa

The evening began with a relaxed game of Rook while Bob caught up on rest. At six, we woke him, and soon we were all heading downstairs to meet Father ~~Daoud~~David, Father Tobias, and Father Albert. They were already waiting for us, smiling warmly.

"Glad you all could make it," Father ~~Daoud~~David said with a playful glint in his eye. "Well, we did take a vow of poverty, but it says nothing about gifts from friends," he added with a laugh.

We decided on the hotel's main restaurant, its warm lighting and rich aromas promising a good meal. Joe, the Fathers, and I ordered red mullet with latkes and hummus. Bob and Penny opted for prime rib with potatoes. The plates arrived, steaming and fragrant, and conversation drifted easily between laughter, light teasing, and bits of shared history.

Just as we were leaning back in satisfaction, the waiter appeared, wheeling out a large birthday cake. "For Errek," he announced. Avi, the owner of Dead Sea Divers, stepped forward with a smile. "Sit, have birthday cake with us," he urged. The gesture caught me off guard, and I thanked him sincerely.

As we shared the cake, Avi reminded us of our meeting with him ~~after~~in two days. "I'll see you at Ein Bokek ~~in two days~~," he said. "And enjoy the cake, it's from all of us." His enthusiasm was genuine, a perfect mix of professionalism and friendliness.

After the meal, we lingered for a short while, speaking of the next day's plans and the possibility of arranging a trip with Ahmed for a three-day journey to the Sea of Galilee and Acre. Eventually, we said our goodbyes, promising to stop by if time allowed before our departure north.

Back in the lounge, Joe's eyes were alight. "The dive suits and tanks are here," he announced, already thinking ahead. The 5 mm full dive suits, full masks, and tanks sat ready at the front desk. His excitement was infectious. "Let's meet at the pool at 8:30. That'll give us an hour to digest dinner before we train."

Joe began explaining what made the Dead Sea unique. "The water's density is near thirty-five percent; normal seawater is barely three and a half percent denser than fresh water. That means you'll need about forty to forty-five percent extra weight to sink. And every movement must be slow, deliberate. Pressure builds fast, that's why we'll use full masks. Even at the surface, it's like swimming in nine meters of water."

He went on to describe the geography: the Southern Basin, shallower and smaller, and the Northern Basin, nearly thirty miles long and up to 9.5 miles wide. The Southern Basin rarely reached more than 150 meters in depth and would be easier for our dives. The Northern Basin was more rugged, with underwater cliffs and freshwater springs. "We'll stay within two to three hundred meters of shore, where the depths are between thirty and a hundred meters," Joe explained.

He described Ein Gedi, a natural oasis where King David once hid from Saul, with archaeological finds ranging from Neolithic tools to synagogue ruins with ancient inscriptions. "We'll start in the Southern Basin at Ein Bokek," Joe said. "Then move north to Kalia the next day. Avi recommends rinsing thoroughly after each dive and resting for a couple of hours, preferably at a local hotel. And drink water, lots of it. Dehydration happens fast out there."

When we gathered at the pool, the suits proved challenging for some. Bob struggled the most, grunting as he finally managed to zip up. "I feel like a beached whale," he declared. Joe grinned. "You'll be adding about 115 pounds of lead for the Dead Sea dive."

He inspected each tank, ensuring the oxygen flow was steady, then gave the thumbs-up.

"Start by practicing breathing in and out of your mask," Joe instructed. "Get used to it for a few minutes before we walk around the deep end."

Penny considered sitting out. "Maybe I'll just monitor and chill with a mineral mud mask," she said.

Joe shook his head. "If you do go in the Dead Sea, always stay on your back. Face-down floating can be dangerous, it's hard to turn over."

We stepped into the pool, breathing steadily through our masks. Walking across the bottom was oddly fun, the weight holding us down in slow-motion balance. Bob and Penny eventually exited, Penny's mask fogging and Bob muttering about a bathroom break. Bill, Joe, and I stayed longer, testing movements and exchanging underwater gestures.

Afterwards, we gathered poolside. "First time in suits, you all did well," Joe said. "The Dead Sea will be denser, and those weights will feel heavy until you're submerged. Adjust slowly." Penny admitted she'd prefer the Sea of Galilee or Mediterranean dives but was willing to give this one a try. Bob, on the other hand, was eager: "Maybe we'll find remains of Sodom on the sea floor or even a cave."

We wrapped up the session, storing our suits and agreeing on one more practice in the morning.

The next morning, the air in Jerusalem carried the hum of weekend life. We woke later than usual, around ten, and grabbed a quick breakfast at the American Diner downstairs before arranging for the hotel car to drop us at Damascus Gate. The descent to the gate was framed by steep stone steps and a narrow driveway bustling with small trucks unloading fruit and goods for the day's trade.

Inside, the gate opened into a maze of stone-paved streets that quickly narrowed into the heart of the market. Vendors called out from every stall, some waving us closer, eager to show their wares, brass lamps, silk scarves, fragrant spices, and jars of sweets glistening in the morning sun. The aromas of fresh bread, cumin, and roasting meat tangled in the air.

We turned left into the route of the Via Delarosa, the Way of Suffering. The path was layered with history and devotion, each stone step bearing centuries of pilgrims' footsteps. Near the Ecce Homo Arch, we paused. This ancient Roman structure, its name meaning "Behold the Man," marks the place where Pontius Pilate presented Jesus to the crowd. Just beyond stood St. Anne's Church, serene and echoing, said to be built over the home of the Virgin Mary's mother. Behind it lay the Pools of Bethesda, quiet and still now, but once the site where Jesus healed a paralyzed man.

We moved slowly, each station of the cross bringing us closer to the events we had studied for years. At the Chapel of the Condemnation and the Church of the Flagellation, the walls seemed to absorb the silence of contemplation, their age visible in every weathered stone. Turning deeper into the Old City, the route climbed gradually, punctuated by steep steps and narrow corners.

At the third station, tradition holds that Jesus fell for the first time. At the fourth, he met his mother. Here, faint etchings in the stone were said to be the imprints of his footsteps. Market noise dimmed in my ears as I took in the moment. The street bent upward at the point where Simon of Cyrene was compelled to carry the cross. Further along, Veronica's act of compassion was marked, where she wiped his brow.

The ascent steepened as we passed the Greek Orthodox Monastery, then reached the spot where Jesus comforted the women of Jerusalem. Finally, the last climb took us into the Coptic Chapel at the top corner of the Church of the Holy Sepulcher. Inside, stations ten through fourteen unfolded in solemn beauty, the nailing to the cross, the crucifixion, the laying in the tomb.

The gold cross above the altar shimmered in the dim light, and near it, a crevice split the rock, said to have been caused by the earthquake at the moment of Jesus death. Encased in glass, the fissure seemed to run with rust-colored veins, like a trace of blood absorbed into the stone.

We descended into the lower chambers, where the story of Helena, mother of Constantine the Great, was retold. Legend says she found the true cross here, identifying it when a sick companion touched it and was healed instantly. The Holy Sepulcher itself was a space of reverence, a two-chambered tomb with the Angel Stone in the first, the burial slab in the second. The space was small, almost intimate, its stillness thick with history.

Though I leaned toward the belief that the Garden Tomb might be the actual burial place, the power of this place was undeniable. Both locations stirred something deep, a reverence that words barely held. We explored St. Vartan's Chapel and the old treasury before making our way back toward the College de La Salle. Penny couldn't resist a shop along the way, emerging with seven silk scarves bought at a fraction of what they'd cost back home. "You can't have too many embroidered scarves," she said with a grin.

At the college, Fathers Tobias and Albert welcomed us again, offering a light lunch. Over coffee, Father Tobias suggested we walk with them toward the Zion Gate and the Church of the Dormition. The streets wound between weathered stone buildings, the light softening as clouds drifted in. We passed the Church of St.

James, its arches echoing with history, and nearby, St. Mark's, considered by some to be the oldest Christian church still standing.

Approaching Zion Gate, the massive stones bore scars from centuries of conflict. Just beyond lay excavations revealing the original city wall, and then the road to Mount Zion. The Church of the Dormition rose ahead, round and stately, marking the traditional site of Mary's passing. Inside, a sculpted figure of Mary lay in serene repose, framed by murals and gold filigree, a dome overhead casting gentle light on her face.

Across the street, David's Tomb awaited, its entrance marked by a statue of the king with his harp. Upstairs, the Cenacle, also known as the Upper Room, spread out in vaulted arches, evoking the Last Supper and the descent of the Holy Spirit at Pentecost. Downstairs, the tomb itself drew quiet reverence, men covering their heads before entering.

By mid-afternoon, we returned to the hotel, the day's walk still in our legs. Joe reminded us we had one last pool session before the real dive. This time, the practice felt more natural, breathing steady, movements smooth, our small circle gliding through the deep end without interruption.

Penny's mask stayed clear after Joe adjusted the fit, and even Bob seemed more at ease. We clocked over an hour in the water before climbing out, peeling off suits with far less struggle than before. Sitting in the evening air, we all felt it, tomorrow's dive was no longer just a plan; it was real, and it was close.

After the evening pool session, we returned to our rooms to clean up and rest before dinner. The air carried that mix of anticipation and fatigue you get before a big day, each of us was already half in the Dead Sea in our minds.

We decided to eat at the smaller American restaurant in the hotel, keeping the meal light. Burgers for most of us, pomegranate salads for Bill and Penny. Between bites, the conversation drifted toward the dive again, as if none of us could help ourselves. Joe mentioned his plan to attend morning Mass at the Church of the Holy Sepulcher before meeting Rubin at the North Gate. "How often do you get to worship at the cross?" he asked, almost rhetorically. The others nodded, whatever our denominations, the significance was the same.

Rubin's call came just after we'd finished. He'd agreed to accompany us to Ein Bokek, partly as our advisor and partly just for the joy of being out of the office. The plan was set: Mass in the morning, then back to the hotel to collect scuba gear, hiking clothes, overnight bags, and at least a gallon of water each. Rubin would meet us at the North Gate at 11 a.m., and we'd drive together to the southern basin of the Dead Sea.

The conversation naturally turned to logistics. Joe explained that Ein Bokek was perfect for our first dive, it lay in the shallower southern basin, with a maximum depth around 100 meters. The proximity to where the Dead Sea's two pools were now separated meant unusual underwater formations, and even the potential to spot brimstone deposits thought to be linked to the destruction of Sodom.

Errek mused about visiting Lot's pillar of salt, visible from a distance with binoculars. "It's not much of a climb, but the view alone would be worth a quick side trip," he said. Joe added that plenty of resorts lined the shore, some with spas and hot pools perfect for decompressing.

We all agreed it made sense to stay overnight rather than make the long return to Jerusalem after a dive. En Gedi emerged as the favored option, a desert oasis almost midway between Ein Bokek and Kalia, the northern basin dive site for the following day. The hotel there, according to the front desk clerk, had everything from standard rooms to family suites, plus its own pool and spa. The surrounding reserve held caves, fresh springs, and Wadi David, an area steeped in biblical history.

The clerk promised to call a friend at En Gedi Hotel to secure us a good rate. Meanwhile, Joe discussed the metal detectors he had brought ~~two.~~ Two would be coming with us, their sonar and sensors sealed for underwater conditions. The detectors could scan up to six feet below the surface, and the sonar could even help locate caves or chambers beneath the seabed. Bob shook his head in mock disbelief. "You're a genius, Joe," he said. Joe grinned. "Yes, yes I am."

When Rubin called back later, he was as enthusiastic as we were. "This has been the most fun I've had in ages," he said. "If my boss agrees, I might even join you for the Galilee and Haifa leg." He mentioned that the wrecks off Acre and Caesarea were of particular interest to the Antiquities Authority, places where Joe's detectors might uncover something truly remarkable.

With the calls made and the plans in place, the rest of the night was about quiet readiness. We double-checked gear, packed extra water and snacks, and laid out clothes for the morning. The thought of ~~the dive of~~diving the unique, dense waters of the Dead Sea and the history resting beneath them lingered as we drifted to sleep.

Tomorrow, the real adventure would begin.

Chapter 7: On to the Dead Sea

The morning in Jerusalem began with the familiar scent of fresh coffee drifting from the hotel's American restaurant. The group stirred to life one by one, gathering in the dining area where a modest continental breakfast was laid out, eggs, pastries, fresh fruit, and the ever-reliable toast with jam. Errek and Bob had decided to keep their room for later in the week, while the others checked out and rebooked their rooms for Tuesday. It was a simple task, but Rubin's insistence on punctuality had everyone moving with purpose. By the time the last receipt was signed, the air in the lobby was already warm, sunlight spilling across the tiled floor as the city outside began to hum with activity.

At precisely 9:30, a hotel driver dropped them at the North Gate. The old stone steps that led to the College were cool in the morning shade, and as they climbed, they spotted familiar faces Father, Fathers Tobias, Albert, and DaoudDavid were already waiting. "Ahh, you're early," Father Tobias remarked with a smile. "The bells will start in about fifteen minutes."

"Bells?" Joe asked.

"Oh yes, always before worship. A tradition here," the Father explained, motioning for them to follow. "Come, let's not linger."

Joe, ever practical, asked about timing. "How long will the service be? We're supposed to meet Rubin at the gate around eleven."

"Forty-five minutes to an hour at most," Tobias reassured him. "Plenty of time."

The path curved gently toward the square before the Church of the Holy Sepulcher. By the time they reached the open space, the first rich tones of the bells rang out, reverberating across the stone walls and cobblestones. The sound seemed to still the air, drawing pilgrims and tourists alike toward the entrances. Clusters of Greek Orthodox faithful gathered on one side, Roman Catholics on the other, their separate traditions converging in this singular holy place.

Today, the agreement was for the Greeks to gather near the Edicule, the shrine built over the tomb while the Catholics assembled below the cross. Joe's eyes glistened; as a devout Catholic, the reality of standing here, ready to worship at the very place of Christ's crucifixion and resurrection, was overwhelming. The others shared his quiet awe, sensing that this was not merely a tourist's stop, but a profoundly spiritual moment.

They listened to the Latin liturgy through discreet earpieces, the translation flowing in real time thanks to Bill's compact translator device. The sermon was brief but powerful, speaking of the privilege of worshipping at the cross, the victory of the empty tomb, and the weight of Christ's sacrifice. No lengthy explanations were needed, the message resonated without embellishment. When the service ended, they lingered for a moment, absorbing the solemnity, before retracing their steps to the College.

Rubin appeared five minutes later, punctual as always. "Well, gentlemen and lady," he greeted warmly, "time to load up. If we're lucky, we can reach Ein Bokek by one. Maybe even fit in a short detour."

The group moved quickly, changing into travel clothes at the hotel. Shorts, light tan shirts, sturdy hiking shoes practical for both the desert heat and any spontaneous adventure Rubin might spring on them. They packed swimsuits, an extra change of clothes, and their diving gear into travel bags, along with cases of chilled water for the large cooler in the van.

As they pulled away from Jerusalem, Rubin's route took them southward. "This road will take us close to Bethlehem," he explained. "From there, we pass Hebron, then on to Highway 90 along the Dead Sea."

The mention of Hebron sparked interest. "Isn't that where Caleb settled?" Errek asked.

"Yes," Rubin confirmed. "And it's also where the Cave of Machpelah is the Tomb of the Patriarchs and Matriarchs. Abraham and Sarah, Isaac and Rebekah, Jacob and Leah. It's the most important site for us Jews."

Intrigued, they agreed to a brief stop. Passing Rachel's Tomb and the distant Herodium, they approached Hebron by late morning. Rubin explained that the city had a layered history of Jewish and Muslim control. Before the Six Day War, Jews were allowed only limited access to the site, confined to seven steps outside. Now, access alternated between full control by each faith for ten-day periods, with neutral times allowing both sides partial access.

When they reached the massive structure, Bill was the first to notice its scale. "What is that?"

"That," Rubin said, "is the Tomb of the Patriarchs. Built by Herod with the same massive stones as the Western Wall, some of the base stones are twenty-four feet long."

Inside, the Jewish section was stark and solemn. Green-barred gates marked Abraham's tomb, while Jacob and Leah's markers stood nearby. The Muslim section, Rubin noted, was far more ornate, housing Isaac and Rebekah's graves. They weren't allowed to cross over, but a Muslim caretaker agreed to take photos on their behalf, a gesture they appreciated.

Rubin shared stories of ancient explorations, of steps leading to lower caves where bones were believed to rest, and even of legends suggesting Adam and Eve might have been buried there. Whether fact or myth, the sense of standing above millennia of history was undeniable.

By early afternoon, they were back on the road, passing an ancient oak said to be where Abraham welcomed the Lord and two angels. The heat intensified as they descended toward the Dead Sea basin, now hundreds of meters below sea level. Penny wavered briefly, torn between diving and visiting the En Gedi oasis, but the group's encouragement tipped the balance so she would join the first dive after all.

By the time the van began its descent from Hebron toward the shimmering expanse of the Dead Sea basin, the sun had risen high enough to make the desert glow with an almost metallic brilliance. The thermometer on Rubin's dashboard read a searing 39°C, but the group's excitement kept any thought of heat at bay. Chatter filled the vehicle, Penny debating whether she should do the dive today or wait until they reached the next site, Joe joking about how the Dead Sea was "probably the only place where even he could float without sinking," and Bill marveling at the arid, moonlike landscape outside his window.

Rubin's voice carried over the hum of the van's air conditioning. "In about forty minutes, we'll reach En Gedi. But first—," he glanced over his shoulder with a conspiratorial smile, "we'll take the scenic road. You might catch sight of the ancient oak at Mamre."

True to his word, just a mile or so before the turnoff, he slowed the van, pointing toward a gnarled, impossibly broad tree. "Some say this is the very oak where Abraham pitched his tent and welcomed the Lord and two angels. That would make it over 4,000 years old, older even than the olive trees in Gethsemane."

The sight drew a collective murmur. Even in the shimmering haze of midday, there was something commanding about that ancient tree, standing alone against the vastness. Cameras clicked, but soon they were back on the move, the road winding between ridges of rock and salt-encrusted earth as it snaked toward the lowest point on earth.

By 1:30 pm the van rolled into the quiet oasis of En Gedi. The lush greenery of date palms and flowering shrubs was a startling contrast to the surrounding desert. The resort's main building, though less opulent than the Hilton in Jerusalem, was modern and comfortable. Rubin and Joe shared a room, while the others spread out across the remaining accommodations.

"We'll have time for a quick rest before heading to Ein Bokek for the dive," Rubin advised. "Change into your swimsuits, but keep your shorts and shirts for the ride. Bring your travel bags and detectors, we won't be coming back here until late evening."

Suiting up for the dive was its own ritual. They donned lightweight walking shorts over their swimsuits, made sure they had their best hiking shoes in case they visited En Gedi's nature reserve, and double-checked their equipment bags: buoyancy control devices (BCDs), regulators, masks, flippers, gloves, weight belts, and the prized sonar-capable metal detectors. A large Igloo cooler filled with bottles of chilled water was secured in the van, Rubin's constant reminder to "drink before you're thirsty" ringing in everyone's ears.

The road south along Highway 90 hugged the edge of the Dead Sea, its surface a surreal patchwork of deep turquoise and pale mineral crusts. Fifteen minutes into the drive, they slowed to take in the view of Masada, its imposing plateau silhouetted against the blinding sky. Joe, ever the photographer, pulled out his deep-sea diving camera.

"I'm telling you, this thing will get more action on land than under the water," he joked, snapping shots of the fortress from multiple angles.

Bill flexed his recovering hand and gave a satisfied nod. "Feels better already. Maybe the Dead Sea really will finish the healing."

"Good," Penny teased, "that way you can take 100 photos instead of 50."

By the time they reached Ein Bokek at 3:30, the excitement in the van was palpable. Avi, their dive master for the day, greeted them warmly. "So, all five of you will be diving? Even you, Penny?"

"For today only," she confirmed, "but I want to experience it."

The group gathered for a safety briefing under a shaded awning. Avi began by holding up a BCD. "This is your best friend today. We've calibrated them for a target depth of 20 meters. Press this button to add air and ascend; release to descend. Remember, at 430 meters below sea level, your gauges will read differently than at sea level. Adjust accordingly."

Joe raised his hand. "Besides me, who here has scuba experience?"

Bill admitted to "a couple of lessons and a lot of snorkeling." Penny, Bobby, and Errek had only basic underwater swimming experience. Avi nodded, assigning Joe and Bill to dive with him, while his assistant Zachariah would accompany Penny, Bobby, and Errek.

Then came the unveiling of the detectors: sleek, broom-like devices equipped with sonar capabilities. "These work at great depths," Avi explained. "Perfect for finding metal and anomalies on the seabed. What are we hunting for?"

Joe grinned. "Oh, just Sodom and Gomorrah."

Avi chuckled. "Well, you never know."

Weight belts were distributed according to each diver's build Bob's at a hefty 115 pounds, Errek's at just under 100, Joe's at 80, Bill's at 65, and Penny's at 67. Avi warned them about the dense, oily feel of the water, the slow movements required to avoid exhaustion, and the sharp salt crystals littering the seabed. "Wear gloves," he urged, "and drink another liter of water now. Dehydration will creep up on you fast."

The entry into the water was almost ceremonial. First the flippers, then the weighted belts, then the BCDs, each addition making them feel heavier until the moment they submerged and the weight seemed to dissolve into buoyancy. Penny gasped at the warmth of the water; Errek likened the resistance to "walking through thick soup."

From the shore, they advanced slowly, following Avi's lead. Joe and Bill kept pace easily, while the others adapted to the peculiar drag of the dense saltwater. The sun, refracting through the ripples, lit the salt crystals on the seabed like scattered diamonds. They passed a towering pillar of salt, eight feet high, its sides gleaming. Joe broke off a small piece for a keepsake, while Avi checked the depth 8.5 meters, 300 yards from shore.

The group split according to plan. Avi led Joe, Bill and Errek northwest, skimming the seabed with the detector, while Zachariah guided Penny and Bobby along a shallower coastal path. Finds came sporadically, a yellowish sphere of brimstone here, a corroded coin there, and what might have been a shard of ancient pottery. At one point, Joe and Avi unearthed a fragment that resembled a charred jar, bagging it for later inspection.

Penny, meanwhile, struck gold literally when her detector pinged just 15 yards from shore. Digging carefully into the salt-crusted floor, she pulled free a gold and diamond ring, its luster dulled but unmistakable. "Didn't anyone tell them not to wear jewelry in the Dead Sea?" she laughed through her earpiece.

After nearly two hours, the two groups converged on the beach, exhaustion visible in every movement. Avi's team had pushed farther, returning last, their bags filled with brimstone balls, pottery fragments, and corroded coins. Penny proudly displayed her ring, and Rubin examined each piece with growing interest. "This… could be from Sodom's time," he murmured over the brimstone spheres. "And the pottery possibly Neolithic."

Even Avi, a seasoned diver, admitted, "I've never used a detector like this before. You've found things I've never come across here."

The gear was rinsed, the bags were packed, and the divers were sprawled in the shaded hut, each clutching a cold bottle of water. A faint hum of exhaustion and satisfaction hung over the group. Rubin was inspecting the day's haul spread across a low table: brimstone spheres, pottery shards, corroded coins, a fragment of what might have been a flint knife, and Penny's glittering gold ring.

"This," Rubin said, holding up one of the larger yellow spheres, "is brimstone of a type rarely found outside the region associated with Sodom and Gomorrah. If this really came from where you say it did, it could be extraordinary."

Avi crouched beside him, his own expression somewhere between curiosity and admiration. "You've got better results in one dive than I've had in some seasons. These detectors are something else, I'd like one myself."

Joe grinned. "I'll put in an order for twenty."

They laughed, but beneath the humor there was an unspoken awareness that the artifacts, if authenticated, could be of real archaeological interest. Still, for now, the priority was recovery.

Avi clapped his hands lightly. "Enough treasure talk. You all need food."

They piled back into the van, muscles stiff, and drove a short distance to Avi's favorite restaurant, a modest building of stone and wood, with an open terrace facing the water. Inside, the cool air carried the scent of fresh bread and grilled meats. The group settled into a long table, ordering falafel, hummus, warm pita, lamb skewers, fresh salads, and tall glasses of mint lemonade.

For the next half hour, conversation flowed easily recapping the dive, laughing about small mishaps, marveling at the strange, dense feel of the Dead Sea's waters. Joe recounted how the salt pillar they'd seen looked like "a frozen column of diamonds," while Penny described the thrill of finding the ring so close to shore. Avi listened, occasionally interjecting with local lore or his own diving anecdotes.

When the plates were cleared, Avi leaned forward. "So, about tomorrow. You mentioned wanting three dives, Joe. After today's effort, are you sure?"

Joe leaned back, glancing around the table. "Honestly, I could settle for one last dive if it's a good one."

Avi nodded. "Then I suggest Kalia Beach. It's near the northernmost point of the Dead Sea, only about seven miles from Jerusalem. The water is deeper there, but we'll have a flat-bottom boat so you can explore near the mouth of the Jordan River. There are caves, too, and it's much less trafficked than here. You'll see things you can't see anywhere else."

Rubin agreed. "Kalia's a great spot. And it's an easy drive back afterward."

They discussed logistics. The plan was to spend the morning exploring En Gedi's nature reserve, its waterfalls, ibexes, and freshwater pools before heading north. They'd meet Avi's team near Avnat, just off Highway 90, and follow them to the Kalia dive base. Avi even offered a partial refund for the reduced dive schedule, a gesture that was met with appreciative nods.

By the time they left the restaurant, the heat had softened into the golden warmth of early evening. The van rolled north along Highway 90, the desert cliffs glowing in the slanting light. Ten minutes in, Rubin slowed for another view of Masada, this time with the sun setting behind it, the sky awash in amber and rose. Cameras came out once more, and for a few quiet moments, the group stood by the roadside, taking in the view of the fortress silhouetted against the fading day.

From there, it was a short drive into En Gedi. The kibbutz's northern end housed their hotel for the night, a comfortable, green-shaded enclave that felt worlds away from the harsh desert just beyond its perimeter.

Though tired, hunger stirred again, and they decided to stop at the small restaurant near the lobby rather than trek to the larger one at the resort's southern end. They ordered falafels, hummus, and chilled drinks, talking easily about the day's discoveries and the adventure yet to come.

Tomorrow would bring a different kind of dive: deeper, more challenging, and potentially more revealing. But for tonight, the group was content to rest, rehydrate, and let the strange magic of the Dead Sea linger in their minds.

Chapter 8: En Gedi Desert with Living Water

The morning began with the group gathered at the hotel's front desk, the faint hum of the air conditioning doing little to mask the anticipation in the air. Errek leaned casually against the counter while Bob studied the map that the receptionist unfolded before them.

"There are quite a few trails," the man said, tapping the glossy surface with his pen. "The easiest one starts at the main entrance, passes the Old Synagogue, follows the Wadi David Stream to David Falls, then loops back to where you began. It's a pleasant walk with plenty to see."

Joe, always looking for something more adventurous, raised an eyebrow. "And the harder ones?"

The receptionist smiled knowingly. "From the falls, there's a direct trail up to a Neolithic temple, and also to Dodim Cave. That trail is more challenging, rockier and with a fair bit of climbing but worth it. The cave is spectacular, with little pools inside, a waterfall within and without, and several chambers. Some of them are rarely visited. It's said King David refreshed himself at Dodim often when he hid in the area."

The thought of unexplored caves made Joe perk up. "Any caves that haven't been mapped yet?"

"A few," the man admitted. "But they aren't on the tourist routes. Still, there's plenty to see even on the main trails."

Errek leaned over the map. "So, what's the landscape like?"

The man gestured to the sprawling expanse on the paper. "En Gedi is a beautiful oasis, but don't let that fool you it also has crags, gorges, and areas that look like a miniature Grand Canyon."

"Sounds like my kind of place," Penny said.

They asked if there was a guide available for the morning, from 9:30 until about 1:00.

"I'll check," the man replied. "If so, he can take you to the Synagogue, which is fascinating there's. There's writing on the tiled mosaic floor and then up to Dodim Cave. You'd be back in time for lunch."

"That would be perfect," said Bill. "Oh, and do you serve breakfast for guests?"

"Yes, from 6:00 to 9:00."

"Great," Bob chimed in. "Give us an 8:15 wake-up call. Can't give up a free meal."

The conversation drifted into casual banter about playing five-handed Rummy before bed. Before heading up to their rooms, they also inquired about staying their second night at the company's sister resort in Kalia.

The night manager checked availability. "As luck has it, there are several rooms open since it's a weekday. I'll arrange the transfer while you're out hiking."

Morning came early, and the smell of freshly brewed coffee drifted from the dining area. They shuffled into the breakfast hall, still half-asleep but brightening at the sight of eggs, cereal, muffins, Danish pastries, milk, orange juice, and fresh pomegranate juice. Halfway through their plates, a young man approached their table.

"Are you the ones looking for a guide?"

"Yes," Joe answered, brushing crumbs from his shirt.

"My name is Simon. I'll take you first to David Falls an easy walk. There's a cave on the way. From there, the climb to Dodim Cave is moderate but rugged at times. It's a lot harder than the Old Synagogue path, but it's worth the effort."

"Sounds good," Penny said.

Simon outlined the route, pointing to a folded trail map. "The main trail is shaped like a horseshoe, connecting the main sites. There's also a circular 1.5-mile connector trail, and another longer one rarely used that's extremely difficult. The left-hand route from the entrance goes along a narrow ledge, but there are handrails where it gets rough."

Joe grinned. "We'll need about ten minutes to grab our backpacks, canteens, and my metal detector."

"And my little hand pick," he added with a wink.

"You'll also need hiking boots," Simon advised. "It's going to be hot like an Alabama summer day, around 90 degrees, though the heat is drier here. There are places to wade in pools and streams, so be prepared."

They returned a few minutes later geared up_with_ gym shorts, waterproof hiking boots, safari hats, sunglasses, and the air of people ready for an adventure. Penny wore a one-piece swimsuit under walking shorts, planning ahead for any tempting pools along the way.

Crossing the street to the reserve, they passed a stone wall running along the outer perimeter. Further north was a second entrance by the research school, but they headed to the main gate.

Inside the visitor center, Simon recommended they buy the park book. "It's full of maps and history, it will make you appreciate what you're seeing even more."

They learned about the botanical gardens along the Arugot River and Wadi, home to over 600 plant species, including rare balsam trees. Simon explained how most of the balsam groves were destroyed first during the time of Masada, then by invading forces in the mid-7th century.

"They've managed to bring some back," he said. "In ancient times, En Gedi was famous for producing Arfarsimmon perfume. The name means persimmon, but the plant is different from the tree we think of. It was rare and incredibly valuable, worth as much as gold."

The group followed Simon toward a detour, the Ancient Synagogue.

The synagogue stood beneath a massive white tent, its dimensions like a triple big-top circus tent. Just behind it lay the excavated ruins of the old town.

Before entering, Simon pointed toward the restrooms. "Last chance on this side of the trail. After this, there's nothing until much later."

Penny smirked. "And we wouldn't want Bob or Errek to defile the pools."

"Not fair," Errek laughed. "Try getting out of a wetsuit fast enough for a restroom break."

They took care of necessities and followed Simon toward the tent. The synagogue's stone doorway still showed where the original door had been.

"This was burned down around 630 AD," Simon explained. "En Gedi once had balsam trees and spice production that the Romans valued so much, they essentially contracted the whole town to make it. Some say the holy incense used in the Temple came from spices here. When the Jewish revolt erupted, rebels from Masada destroyed the town's balsam groves to spite the Romans. The Masada rebels didn't survive long after that."

He led them to the ruins of the women's gallery on the second floor, explaining that men worshipped on the ground level. Burn marks were still visible on the mosaics.

The floor was intricate, reddish geometric designs forming a honeycomb pattern, a central square with the Star of David, two peacocks symbolizing resilience and divine unity, and two geese representing the feeding of the multitude.

In one section, ancient Aramaic or Hebrew inscriptions recorded genealogies from Adam to Noah, Hebrew calendar horoscope signs, and even the names Shadrach, Meshach, and Abednego.

"That's unusual," Bill said. "Maybe they were from here originally?"

Simon shrugged. "Could be."

Then came the long curse inscription, its wording a mix of admonition and divine threat:

Penny translated, "Anyone causing controversy between a man and his friend, slandering before gentiles, stealing from a friend, or revealing the secrets of the town will be cursed. He whose eyes view the whole world will set his face against that man and curse him and his offspring forever."

Penny nodded appreciatively. "It's a fascinating piece of social history."

Joe grinned. "Penny's amazing in her field."

"Hey, we all are," Bill added. "Errek's our Biblical history expert. Bob's the guy who can think outside the box. Joe's a mechanical genius. I'm the tech wizard. And Errek is the coach who brought us together."

Simon chuckled. "Well, you certainly make a colorful group."

They took a quick detour to glance over the ruins of the ancient city before returning to the main trail.

The sun was already biting at their shoulders as they continued toward David Falls. Errek's watch read 91°F and it wasn't even 10:15 yet. The group spotted an ibex on a ridge, a marmot-like creature that Simon identified as a hyrax, and several birds Tristan Grackles with their loud, cheeky calls, Arabian Babblers chattering in the brush, and even a sand partridge.

They passed through a tunnel of vines, moss, and ferns, emerging at a small pool and waterfall. Bob, already flushed from the heat, kicked off his shoes and stepped in.

"This water is amazing," he sighed, standing under the falls. The rest followed suit to various degrees, some ankle-deep, others filling canteens with the cool flow before moving on.

The path wound through another green tunnel before opening onto a breathtaking sight, David Falls. The main cascade plunged 120 meters, flanked by two smaller falls about 15 meters each. Spray shimmered in the sunlight, and the sound filled the canyon.

Simon pointed upward. "Dodim Cave is beyond that ridge, hidden behind another fall. The climb is treacherous, but there are handrails."

They paused to take in the scene, knowing the hardest part of their hike still lay ahead.

The roar of David Falls still echoed in their ears as the group gathered near the base of the trail that would take them up to Dodim Cave. Simon motioned toward a narrow path that seemed to wind upward into the sheer cliff face.

"From here," he explained, "we begin our upward trek. It's not overly long, but the incline is steep, and there are sections where only one person can pass at a time. Don't worry, there are handrails at the trickiest points."

Bob eyed the climb warily. "So… no guard rails on the easy parts, just the dangerous ones?"

"That's right," Simon said, with a grin. "Keeps you focused."

They started upward. The heat pressed in from all sides, the sun bouncing off the pale rock, but the group kept a steady pace. Every so often, Simon would stop and point out an unusual rock formation or a glimpse of the green ribbon of vegetation that snaked along the valley floor far below.

Errek kept his eyes fixed on the rock in front of him. "Don't look down, don't look down," he muttered under his breath.

Bill chuckled from behind him. "You're fine, Errek. Just think of it as a stairmaster with better scenery."

After about twenty minutes of climbing, they reached a small plateau with the Shulamite Spring trickling from a rock face into a shallow pool. They all took turns filling canteens and splashing their faces. The water was cold and sweet, a stark contrast to the baking air around them.

From here, Simon explained, the trail forked ~~one.~~ One branch led to the Chalcolithic temple ruins, the other continued toward Dodim Cave.

"Let's take a quick detour to the temple," Joe suggested, adjusting the strap of his backpack where the metal detector hung. "Never know what we might find."

The detour was short, and soon they were standing among the low stone walls of the ancient site. The rectangular structure was weathered but still held traces of its original layout. Near one corner, a circular stone well hinted at the life that had once thrived here.

Joe swept the metal detector over the ground, its quiet hum breaking the silence. A sharp ping made everyone look up. Kneeling, he began to dig with his hand pick, uncovering a small copper object. "Looks like a coin," he said, tucking it carefully into his pack.

With the find secured, they retraced their steps to the main trail and began the final push toward Dodim Cave. The path narrowed considerably, at times forcing them to shuffle sideways along ledges with only a slim railing between them and the sheer drop.

Errek glanced down once and immediately regretted it. "Yeah… that's enough sightseeing for me," he muttered, gripping the rail tighter.

"Focus on the trail, not the drop," Simon encouraged. "We're almost there ~~see.~~ See these hand grips, they go down 30 feet to the ridge and the cave."

After leaving the temple, they followed the mountain trail to its peak and then climbed down about 14 meters using handrails to reach a lower ridge. From there, they descended further, rounded a bend, and finally the entrance to Dodim Cave came into view. A curtain of moss and trailing vines framed the opening, and beyond, the cool sound of falling water beckoned.

The first step inside was like crossing into another world. The temperature dropped noticeably, and the air smelled of damp stone and fresh water. A shallow pool, clear as glass, stretched across the floor, reflecting the light that filtered in through the foliage.

"It's like something out of a movie," Penny whispered, wading in ankle-deep.

Small waterfalls trickled down the walls, their streams catching the light in sparkling arcs. The sound was both soothing and invigorating. Further back, the main waterfall thundered into a deeper pool, sending a fine mist through the cavern.

Joe, of course, wasted no time in pulling out the metal detector. The beeps came quickly from loose change scattered in the shallows, likely dropped by previous visitors. He collected about twelve shekels, some foreign coins, and then, in the dimmer light near the back, the device gave a stronger, deeper signal.

With careful digging, he uncovered a half-decayed spear, its shaft long gone but the metal head still intact. The find drew a low whistle from Simon. "That's not something you see every day."

Bill and Errek took turns cupping water from the falls to drink, their hands chilled instantly by the fresh flow. Bob, now stripped to gym shorts, sat waist-deep in the pool, leaning back against a rock with a contented sigh.

They lingered for about fifteen minutes, savoring the rare combination of beauty, history, and cool relief. But eventually Simon gave the signal, it was time to head back.

The return trip was faster, though the rocky terrain and narrow ledges demanded the same careful attention. By the time they reached David Falls again, the sun was high overhead. The descent from there to the park entrance was easier, and soon they were back at the hotel, clocking in just over three hours since they'd set out.

After quick showers and a change into fresh clothes, they packed their bags for the transfer to Kalia Resort. Lunch was a simple but satisfying affair, accompanied by several refills of cold water. The afternoon's adventure would require as much hydration as they could manage.

By mid-afternoon, they were driving along the coastal road toward Avnat. The cliffs rose steeply on one side, the shimmering expanse of the Dead Sea on the other. The conversation turned to Qumran and its caves as they passed the turnoff. Rubin, at the wheel, promised to try and arrange a visit for the following day.

At Avnat, they met Avi, the dive leader. He briefed them on the plan: they would head by boat to a spot near the mouth of the Jordan River, about half a mile offshore. The depth there would be no more than fifty meters, shallowing gradually toward the river's mouth.

"Stay aware of the springs," he warned. "Freshwater vents from the seabed can make the water less dense, if you're not careful, you'll sink faster than you expect. Swim past them slowly, and you'll be fine."

Bill, Joe, and Errek suited up in wetsuits and gear, while Bob and Penny opted to stay behind, looking forward to a leisurely float in the Dead Sea instead.

The boat ride was short, the pale green shoreline always in sight. Once anchored, Avi fitted them with GPS trackers and they slipped into the water, adjusting their buoyancy controls as they descended.

The underwater world was surreal, towering salt pillars in bizarre, almost alien shapes, some like cathedral spires, others like jagged crystal cacti. Shafts of sunlight pierced the blue-green water, turning the formations into gleaming sculptures.

They swam north toward the river mouth, the depth decreasing as the minutes passed. Joe zigzagged with the metal detector, its pings drawing them to small finds, a tarnished metal cup, a flint-and-metal knife, a flat stone the size of a notebook page.

The shallows yielded more: bits of ancient utensils, a coin, and then, buried just under the silt, the broken half of a Roman sword. Avi helped dig it free, handling it with the care of someone who knew exactly how rare such a find was.

Finally, they waded up onto the shoreline itself, stepping briefly into Jordanian territory before crossing back. They high-fived at the symbolic crossing, their grins visible even through their masks.

The swim back to the boat felt longer than the way out, but the satisfaction of their finds buoyed them. Back on deck, they stripped off gear and shared quick congratulations. The ride to the dock was quiet, each of them lost in thought about the day's events.

Rubin met them at the dive center, curious about what they'd found. When Penny examined the inscribed stone, her eyes widened. "This could be significant," she said.

Talk turned to tomorrow's plan, Qumran in the morning, Masada in the afternoon. Rubin had already spoken to the site director, who was intrigued by Joe's detector and willing to allow supervised scans in certain caves.

By the time they reached the resort, the sun was setting, painting the cliffs in gold and rose. Dinner was a relaxed affair, the conversation weaving between the day's triumphs and the promise of tomorrow's exploration. Some planned to visit the mineral pools or float in the Dead Sea before bed, determined not to miss the experience in its most traditional form.

Chapter 9: Qumran and Masada

The next morning, we rose early, the promise of the day already pulling us from our beds. By 8 a.m., we were stepping out onto the shores of the Dead Sea, the air heavy with salt and minerals, carrying that faint, metallic tang unique to this ancient body of water. The sun had already begun its slow climb, bathing the surface in shimmering silver. Without hesitation, we covered ourselves in the thick, black mineral mud the locals swear by, a natural spa treatment that's been used for centuries. The sensation was both cool and gritty against the skin, and as we let it dry under the morning warmth, the world seemed to slow.

Then came the moment everyone looks forward to at the Dead Sea: we waded into the calm, warm water. It embraced us instantly, lifting our bodies effortlessly. The buoyancy was so complete that trying to sink was laughably impossible. We floated like corks, arms stretched, gazing up at the cloudless sky. Bob grinned from ear to ear, announcing that his leg, still sore from the earlier part of our trip, was feeling "better than it had in days." Whether it was the minerals, the relaxation, or a mix of both, we all felt renewed.

After thirty minutes, our skin soft and smooth from the treatment, we reluctantly headed to the showers to rinse off the salty residue. The cold spray was refreshing, but the call of the resort's pool was too tempting to resist. We slipped into the cool, clear water, letting it wash away the last traces of salt and mud. No one wanted to leave, but Rubin appeared at the poolside, his expression equal parts amused and practical.

"Guys, it's 9:20," he called. "Time to get moving if we're going to stay on schedule."

Groans followed, but we knew he was right. We climbed out, changed back into our hiking clothes, still dusty from the day before, checked out of the hotel, and made our way to the van.

Rubin took the wheel, guiding us south down Highway 90 once again. The desert stretched endlessly on either side, a mixture of gold and pale stone, dotted here and there with scrub and the occasional acacia tree.

After about twenty minutes, we turned off the main road toward our next destination: the ancient site of Qumran.

Rubin explained as we approached, "Today, we'll meet Dr. Benjamin bar Remuel, the Director of the IAA overseeing the Qumran archaeological projects. He's agreed to show you some of the recent museum finds and even give you special access to certain areas. There are thirteen known caves here that have been explored, with a few more still under investigation. Some, like Cave 12, are infamous looted before archaeologists could fully examine them."

We passed through the front gate and soon found ourselves shaking hands with Benjamin himself, a man in his late forties with an energy that radiated both intellect and passion for his work. His dark hair was peppered with grey, and his sharp eyes seemed to assess us quickly, perhaps measuring our potential as collaborators in his carefully guarded site.

After greetings, Joe wasted no time introducing the reason for our visit. "Dr. Benjamin, has the IAA ever tried using high-sensitivity metal detection or ground-penetrating sonar in these caves?"

Benjamin frowned slightly. "Why would we? Most of the important finds the Dead Sea Scrolls, for instance were preserved in leather satchels or stored in clay jars. Metal has rarely been part of these discoveries."

Joe nodded, expecting the skepticism. "I understand. But these detectors aren't ordinary. They're about ten times more sensitive than standard field models. They don't just look for metal they can detect areas in the ground where density changes, where something has been buried, even as deep as six feet. It's a way of spotting irregularities that the naked eye might miss."

Benjamin's curiosity was piqued now. "Interesting… though I must remind you this is a protected area."

"We're not here to dig without permission," Joe assured him. "If the detector pings, we mark the spot. Then your team decides whether to excavate. It's your site; we're just offering the tool."

Benjamin considered this for a moment, then smiled. "Very well. But I'll require you to work in coordination with Rubin and my staff."

With that settled, Benjamin called over three of his archaeologists to help facilitate the day's work. Among them was a young woman named Inna a striking figure at about five-foot-seven, athletic, with intelligent eyes that hinted at both knowledge and humor. She introduced herself in flawless English, explaining she was completing her postgraduate internship here, drawn by her love of both archaeology and biblical history.

Bob leaned toward Errek with a grin and whispered, "I think we got the better end of this deal."

Errek smirked. "No arguments here."

It was quickly decided to split into two teams. The "easy-access" group Bob, Errek, and Inna would handle the caves that were less treacherous, numbers 4, 5, and 7 through 10. The "advanced" group Bill, Penny, and Joe would take on the more challenging climbs.

Bob's team started with Cave 7, one of the larger and more significant sites near the front gate, where Greek documents and fragments from the Book of Jeremiah had been found in the past. The walls bore marks of earlier excavations, the floor littered with dust and small stones. They swept the metal detector across the ground with nothing.

From there, they moved to Cave 10. This time, the device pinged almost immediately. The sound was enough to send a ripple of excitement through the group. Inna radioed Benjamin. "We have a shallow detection in Cave 10, near where the carved stone was found."

Benjamin's voice crackled back: "You have permission to excavate."

Within minutes, they uncovered a clay jar, its lid still intact. Inside was a partial scroll of Lamentations its parchment fragile but legible. Carefully, they secured it for transport. Not long after, they found another signal, this one about two feet deep. They marked the spot, agreeing to return with Benjamin after lunch for a controlled excavation.

Meanwhile, the advanced group was making its way into Cave 3, scaling its narrow entrance with practiced ease. The inside was cool and dim, the walls closing in toward the far end. As they swept the detector, a sharp, steady beep filled the air. They began to dig gently in the corner where the signal was strongest. After only a foot and a half, something metallic gleamed beneath the dust a combination of copper and silver.

Benjamin, who had joined them, knelt beside Bill. Together they uncovered a small leather pouch containing ten silver coins, the designs still faintly visible despite the tarnish. Near it lay a scroll jar. Carefully prying it from the earth, they discovered two delicate scrolls inside, one in better condition than the other.

"This is an incredible find," Benjamin said quietly. He called the front office on his radio. "Send Thomas and Barnabus to Cave 3 immediately. This is priority transport to my office."

Ten minutes later, the assistants arrived with gloves and archival bags. The items were carefully sealed and carried away.

From there, the group pushed on to Cave 11, about 200 meters southwest. The air grew warmer in the midday sun, the trail winding along the rocky hillside. Benjamin explained that Cave 11 had been one of the last major caves discovered, along with 12 and 13 farther southeast.

Inside Cave 11, the detector picked up two distinct irregularities. Benjamin marked both spots for later excavation, but one shallow find was too tempting for him to leave. He knelt down, digging slowly until his trowel struck something solid a jar, its surface rough and ancient. He smiled. "You'll get credit for this find. The coins are between you and Rubin, but by IAA rules, the jars belong to us."

The camaraderie was genuine; the success of one group was shared by all. Over the radio, Penny's voice came through, reporting that her group had entered Cave 6 after a tricky descent to an upper trail. Inside, they'd found a small, decayed leather bag containing four well-preserved Roman coins bearing the likeness of Nero.

By now, it was close to noon. As both teams converged near Cave 12, the air buzzed with the anticipation of one final search before lunch. Benjamin, standing at the mouth of the cave, oversaw as Bobby ran the detector across the floor. The device pinged, and they began to dig. Just below the surface lay a scroll jar and a small leather satchel, its contents later revealed to be fragments of a copper scroll.

Benjamin examined the items with visible satisfaction. "Whoever buried this was afraid likely someone hiding in the cave, planning to return but never did."

With the finds secured, he suggested they all head back to his office and then on to lunch.

The mention of food lit up Bob's face. "Did you say buffet?" he shouted.

Benjamin chuckled. "Yes. Twelve dollars. All you can eat."

"That's all I needed to hear," Bob grinned. "I'm in." Errek raised his hand. "Count me in, too." The rest of us laughed and nodded.

Back at the base, the buffet spread awaited a comforting mix of fresh salads, warm pita, hummus, grilled meats, and local specialties. Over plates piled high, Rubin and Benjamin reflected on the day.

"These detectors… I underestimated them," Benjamin admitted. "We usually focus on jars lying in plain sight. It never occurred to me that items could be buried deeper within the caves."

Rubin leaned in. "These guys are remarkable. They each bring something different to the table skills that complement each other. After almost a week with them, I'd hire them in a heartbeat."

Benjamin nodded. "I agree."

Penny smiled when Benjamin asked her to help translate any scrolls once they were unrolled by specialists in Tel Aviv or Jerusalem. "It would be an honor," she said.

The meal stretched on, conversations flowing easily, the excitement of the morning's discoveries still fresh in everyone's minds. And though we were sated and content, the day was far from over.

When the last plates were cleared from the buffet table, Rubin leaned back in his chair and looked at the group. "So, where to next? We still have daylight left."

The answer was almost unanimous: "Masada."

The name itself carried a certain weight equal parts history, tragedy, and pride. Rubin grinned. "Then Masada it is. And don't worry, Bob, there's a cable car on the east side. It'll save us time and spare your leg."

Leaving Qumran behind, we climbed back into the van, the midday sun now casting sharp shadows across the desert slopes.

We drove south along the shimmering expanse of the Dead Sea, the pale blue water framed by Jordan's hazy mountains in the distance. After about twenty minutes, we passed the oasis of En Gedi its palm trees and springs looking almost out of place amid the stark beige cliffs. We paused briefly for cold drinks and snacks before continuing on.

Another fifteen minutes brought signs for Masada, directing us off the highway toward the parking area at the base of the eastern approach. The mountain rose ahead like an immense sandstone ship, its flat top a stark silhouette against the endless sky.

Rubin parked, and we walked toward the cable car station. The east-side approach was steep much steeper than the west and the climb by foot would have been grueling in the heat. "On the west side, you can hike up the old Roman siege ramp," Rubin explained. "But that's easier in winter. This time of year, it's a furnace."

The cable car ride was short but dramatic. As we ascended, the land fell away beneath us, revealing sweeping views over the Dead Sea basin. The blue-green water stretched far to the north and south, the salt crystals gleaming white where they clustered near the shore.

Stepping out onto the summit, we were immediately struck by the size of the plateau. Rubin gestured toward the far end. "Masada's longest point is about 500 meters, its width around 200. From here, you can see both its strength as a fortress and its vulnerability."

Benjamin, who had joined us for the tour, took over the explanation. "Herod the Great built this as one of his desert fortresses six in total. But this one… this one is the crown jewel."

He led us toward the northern palace, its three terraces clinging to the cliff edge as though suspended in midair. "The upper terrace held the royal apartments and gardens," he explained. "Fifteen meters below, connected by stairs, is the middle terrace Herod's reception hall and library. And twenty meters below that, almost hanging over the cliff, is the lowest terrace, with dining areas and baths."

Walking through the remnants, we could still see sections of the mosaic floors, intricate geometric patterns preserved through two millennia. The air was dry, carrying the faint scent of stone warmed by the sun. It was easy to imagine the palace in its prime vines trailing from balconies, the sound of water trickling into baths, servants moving quietly through shadowed corridors.

We moved next to the massive cistern system. "Ten meters deep, six meters wide," Benjamin said, peering down into the darkness. "Water was channeled here from the rock faces during the rainy season. Five layers of plaster made it completely watertight."

Herod's penchant for luxury was evident everywhere the remains of a swimming pool, steam baths, and saunas, all improbably situated atop this desert plateau. It was a striking contrast: on one side, the harsh, lifeless cliffs; on the other, a vision of Roman opulence.

Rubin paused beside a stretch of wall. "Masada means 'fortress' in Hebrew. And it lived up to that name until the revolt."

Benjamin nodded, his voice dropping slightly. "In 66 AD, during the Jewish revolt against Rome, a group of rebels took refuge here. By 70 AD, Jerusalem had fallen, but Masada held out. Three years later, the Roman Tenth Legion about six thousand troops under General Flavius Silva came to finish the job."

We followed the path toward the western side, where the remains of the siege ramp were still visible. "They built this ramp over six months," Benjamin continued. "Layer upon layer of rock and earth, hauled up in baskets, all under enemy fire."

From the top, you could see the Roman camps below, their outlines still etched into the desert floor. The ramp stretched upward to the fortress wall a testament to Roman persistence. "When the ramp was complete, they brought up siege towers and battering rams. The night before Passover, the defenders knew the end was near."

Benjamin stopped, looking out toward the desert horizon. "They had three choices: fight and be slaughtered, surrender and be enslaved, or die free. They chose the third. Lots were drawn. The men who drew them killed the others, then themselves. When the Romans breached the walls the next morning, they found nearly a thousand bodies."

A silence settled over our group. It was hard to imagine such a decision, but in that moment, the weight of it was tangible. Errek finally spoke. "I can't say I'd do the same, but I can understand why they did."

Benjamin went on to explain that the site remained untouched for centuries. It wasn't until 1959 that explorers rediscovered the human remains and artifacts, including the lots used in the final decision. In 1960, the 970 defenders were given a formal burial here, with full honors.

We wandered the rest of the site, stopping often to take in the views the Dead Sea glistening far below, the Judean Desert stretching endlessly to the west. Eventually, we took the large cable car back down to the base.

By now, the afternoon was waning, but Rubin suggested a short detour on the return journey: Bethany, atop the Mount of Olives. "It's not far," he said. "And worth the stop."

The road wound upward through olive groves and small houses until we reached the modest entrance to the Church of Mary, Martha, and Lazarus. Inside, the cool air was scented faintly with incense. A verse from the Gospel of John was inscribed near the altar: *I am the resurrection and the life; he that believeth in me, though he were dead, yet shall he live.*

Outside, a Muslim officer approached us politely. "Would you like to see the tomb of Lazarus?" he asked. We agreed, paying him a small fee for his time. He led us through narrow lanes to a stairway descending deep into the rock. The steps were uneven, worn smooth by centuries of feet. The chamber at the bottom was dim, the air cool and slightly musty. Standing there, it was easy to picture the moment Lazarus emerged, still wrapped in burial cloths, at Jesus' command.

Bob looked around the chamber. "He would've had to really work to climb these steps in that condition."

We thanked the officer and returned to the van. Rubin smiled. "I thought you'd appreciate that. Only takes a few minutes, but it's worth seeing."

The sky was beginning to soften into evening as we drove the short distance back to the hotel. Rubin accepted our invitation to join us for supper. "Why not?" he said. "Feels like I'm part of the group now."

"You are," Joe replied. "Without you, none of this would've been possible."

Talk over dinner turned to plans for the next day. Rubin warned that the Church of the Ascension would be closed by now, but we could visit tomorrow along with the Pools of Bethesda. "I've already spoken to the local authorities," he added. "You'll have permission to use the detectors there. A Muslim officer will meet you rarely anyone's around, so it shouldn't take long."

As we were finishing, Errek's phone buzzed with a message from Father Tobias. He read it quickly, then looked at Bob. "Two of the coaches are sick. He wants me to run Wednesday's practice maybe even a full day camp. Kids from all backgrounds Palestinian, Christian, Jewish. You in?"

Bob grinned. "Always. Basketball's universal."

Joe leaned back in his chair. "I enjoyed today. Still can't believe no one thought to metal detect those caves before."

Rubin smiled knowingly. "You've made an impression. To the IAA, you're heroes. You've got full access for Acre and the rest of the trip and we'll pick up your hotels and most expenses. We know there's treasure there, and you're going to find it for us."

"Sounds like a deal," Joe said.

Rubin's eyes twinkled. "Oh, and in Acre, you'll be staying at the Del Carmel Resort. First class. You've earned it."

The promise of new adventures hung in the air as we finished the meal. Tomorrow would be a quieter day, but beyond that lay the lure of Acre and whatever history was waiting to be uncovered there.

Chapter 10: Bethesda and Basketball

Morning came early, the faint glow of Jerusalem's dawn spilling through the curtains and painting the room in soft gold. The city was already stirring outside the distant hum of traffic, snippets of conversation in Hebrew and Arabic, and the echo of church bells faintly mingling with the muezzin's call. Bob and Errek were up before most of the others, fueled by the quiet excitement of the day ahead. This was not just another morning in the Holy Land; today promised a blend of two worlds that Errek loved deeply history and basketball.

They ate breakfast quickly, exchanging light banter over coffee and bread rolls, then called for a cab to take them toward the North Gate. Their destination was the College De La Salle, where the courts were already alive with the sound of bouncing basketballs and the playful shouts of teenagers. By the time the taxi pulled up, the clock read 8:55 a.m., and the courtyard was a swirl of energy.

As they stepped onto the court, a familiar voice called out.

"Sayid, is that you?" Errek asked, his tone half-surprised, half-delighted.

"Coach! How are you?" Sayid, the gentile giant standing almost 6'8 and 260 pounds" jogged over, beaming, his stride confident, his presence more athletic than before. "Oh, much better now," he said. "You look great like you've dropped a hundred pounds since I last saw you."

Errek laughed. "It's called running from airports, buses, and archaeological digs. Keeps a man young."

The reunion was brief but warm. Within moments, they were already talking shop. "Alright," Errek said, his coaching tone kicking in, "let's set up stations. Bob you take post moves. Sayid cover rebounding and passing. I'll handle shooting for the first thirty minutes. Then we'll rotate Bob and I will cover basic defense, you take offense. We'll finish with scrimmages, five-on-five, until lunch."

Sayid nodded. "Sounds perfect, Coach."

While the morning drills began to take shape under the warming sun, elsewhere in Jerusalem, Bill, Rubin, Joe, and Penny were stepping out of their vehicle near St. Stephen's Gate. The streets here were quieter, narrower, with the pale limestone walls casting sharp shadows in the morning light. A short walk brought them to their target the Pools of Bethesda, a site woven deeply into Biblical history and local legend.

Bill and Joe carried metal detectors, the sunlight glinting off the equipment as they adjusted the settings. Rubin reminded them to tread lightly. "Be as delicate as you can. Replace the divots so it looks untouched. We're here to preserve, not disturb."

They quickly divided the search zones. "Bill," Rubin instructed, "you take the north pool. Joe, the south pool and the perimeter. We'll meet at the well."

The site carried a weight of history. Once a place where Jews gathered for healing waters, it had been transformed ~~int8o~~into Roman-style baths in the third century and, in later centuries, adapted for Muslim purposes. The air was still, save for the occasional echo of voices from the nearby street. Every stone seemed to hold a story.

Bill moved slowly, sweeping the detector along the edge of the pool, the faint hum of the machine occasionally breaking into a sharper beep. He crouched when the detector pulsed, brushing away dust to reveal a worn bronze coin. A few meters away, Joe worked methodically around the south pool, his eyes scanning the ground, mind imagining what these stones had witnessed over the millennia.

By the time they regrouped at the well, the finds were impressive. Fifty coins in total some still clinging to dirt, others shining faintly. Ten of those coins had been recovered from the well itself, their surfaces damp and encrusted. Even more intriguing was Bill's find: a silver necklace, delicate yet sturdy, with an intricate clasp. Rubin's eyes narrowed with recognition it had to be the same object that distracted Errek years ago, leading to his memorable fall during a past visit.

As they stood admiring the morning's work, a tall man approached the appointed Muslim advisor for the site, Mohammed. Dressed simply, with a calm and courteous demeanor, he examined the collection carefully. Selecting around twenty coins most of them ancient along with five newer ones, he nodded in approval. "These will go for preservation," he said, thanking them for their service before departing.

Joe looked at what remained in their collection. "Well," he said, turning the coins over in his palm, "we've still got seven Roman pieces from the first and second century, one fifth-century Arabic coin, and the rest are modern. Not a bad morning's work."

"Not bad at all," Rubin agreed, smiling. "Let's go check on Bob and Errek. I think they'll be ready for a break by now."

Back at the College, the morning session had just wrapped up when the group arrived. The air inside the gym was thick with the scent of sweat, determination, and polished wood. Sayed was still animatedly talking to a cluster of kids when he spotted them. "Hey, Coach," he called out to Errek, "how about we pick up some KFC for lunch?"

Laughing, Errek replied, "Sounds like a plan."

Sayed's expression shifted to a more serious note. "Oh, and Coach… the afternoon isn't exactly what you think."

"Oh?" Errek raised an eyebrow.

"You'll see," Sayed said, his smile returning.

Bob and Errek exchanged glances, but didn't press further. "Alright," Errek said, "we'll be back in twenty minutes."

They left to grab lunch, the smell of fried chicken quickly filling the air as they returned with a couple of big buckets. The group sat in the shade outside the gym, peeling back wrappers and digging in. Between bites, the truth about the afternoon came out.

"So, what's going on?" Joe asked.

"Well," Errek said, "apparently some of the better players are coming in for the afternoon. I thought it was just more drills, but..." He motioned to Sayed.

The young coach grinned. "We've got a friendly match against Bethlehem our archrivals at 3:30. The full team will be here. You're going to help coach us since our coach is sick. And..." Sayed's smile widened, "we're running your offense."

Errek blinked, then laughed. "Well, I can't be mad about that. I'm honored you'd keep teaching it."

Sayed shook his head. "You coach. I'll assist."

"No," Errek said firmly, "you coach. I'll be your assistant. This is your team. I'm just here to help."

The plan came together quickly. They would divide responsibilities Sayed taking the starting five to work on defense, Errek working with the second group on offense. Then they would switch, with Errek introducing a "wrinkle" to the existing plays and a variation on the defense.

The offensive tweak was simple in concept but dangerous in execution. "We'll keep Flat 1 and Flat 2," Errek explained, sketching in the air with his fingers. "But after the guard runs through the two screens, the double screeners will peel off the weakside post will screen for the guard on the opposite side, then flash to the free-throw line. That forces the defense to choose leave the shooter open or leave the post open."

Sayid's eyes lit up. "That's brilliant. More movement, more balance. And with the right timing, they won't know who to guard."

"Exactly," Errek said. "Multiple scoring options all from the same set. Keep them guessing."

On defense, Errek proposed a hybrid approach. "We'll disguise the 2-3 zone so it looks like man-to-man. One guard pressures the ball at half-court, forcing them toward the wing into a trap. That pass to the free-throw line? We cut it off with the second guard stepping in for the steal."

Simon, the team's quick-footed point guard, overheard this and grinned. "Coach, that's going to drive them crazy."

The afternoon practice ran like a well-oiled machine. Drills flowed seamlessly, players picking up the new concepts with surprising speed. The first scrimmage showed just how quickly they had adapted the hybrid defense created turnovers, the new offensive wrinkle generated open looks. Sayed watched his players execute with quiet pride, while Errek nodded in approval from the sideline.

By the time they called for a water break, the team was buzzing with energy. The Bethlehem match was no longer just another friendly; it was a chance to put something new to the test and, perhaps, to surprise their rivals.

By mid-afternoon, the gym was buzzing again, but this time the energy had shifted. The casual chatter of morning drills had been replaced by a sharper edge the anticipation of competition. The sound of sneakers squeaking on the polished wood, the rhythmic bounce of basketballs, and the occasional laughter blended into a kind of pre-game symphony.

The Bethlehem team arrived at 3:45 p.m., their warm-up routine brisk and focused. As Errek scanned their lineup, his eyes caught on a familiar figure. Mozell. A friend from years past, and a man he respected but also a coach whose style he knew inside and out.

"Mozell," Errek called with a grin as they crossed the court.

"Man, Coach, I can't believe it's you," Mozell said, breaking into a wide smile. "Last time I saw you was at that FIBA camp in Latvia. You won the whole thing. And if I remember right, four years ago you were here… leaving in a wheelchair."

"Oh yes," Errek said with a chuckle. "That was a trip. But I'm much better now. On vacation, doing some exploring. They pulled me in last-minute because the local coach was sick."

Mozell raised an eyebrow. "Well, looks like we've got a game on our hands."

The whistle blew, and the game began. Errek decided to open with man-to-man defense, wanting to feel out Bethlehem's offensive flow. The first quarter was a battle of small margins both sides trading baskets, the score close. Bethlehem edged ahead by three points at the buzzer.

Between quarters, Errek gathered his players. "We're switching to the 2-3 zone," he said, his tone calm but deliberate. "Surprise them. Force turnovers."

The change worked. The traps at the wings forced hurried passes, and Simon intercepted two in quick succession, converting both into layups. By halftime, Jerusalem led 28–26, and the home crowd small but vocal was on its feet.

In the third quarter, Bethlehem adjusted, slipping past the zone and hitting a few outside shots. They regained a three-point lead. Errek called time-out, eyes scanning his players. "Alright, triangle-and-two," he said. "Shut down their best shooters."

It was a risk, but the players bought in. They fought their way back to a tie heading into the final quarter.

Now came the move Errek had been saving. "Do you remember the disguised man-to-2-3 we worked on?" he asked, looking directly at Simon and Abdul.

Simon nodded. "We run it now?"

"Yes. All the way to the buzzer."

The effect was immediate. Bethlehem's guards hesitated at the half-court trap, their passes disrupted by Simon's quick hands. Abdul dominated inside, pulling down rebounds and scoring twice on fast breaks. The offensive wrinkle worked like a charm the defense was confused, unsure whether to guard the perimeter or collapse inside.

When the final whistle blew, the scoreboard read 67–57. Jerusalem had not only won, they had done so convincingly the first victory over Bethlehem in years.

From the sidelines, Father David, Father Tobias, and Father Albert clapped and cheered. As the teams shook hands, a distinguished man approached Errek. "Coach, I'm Peter," he said warmly. "Simon's father. I watched how you worked with these boys you've done wonders in just one day."

"Your son's a natural," Errek replied. "I just gave him the tools; he did the rest."

Peter introduced himself further. "I'm also the team doctor for the Jerusalem Super League and our Division 1 team. We're in need of a new Division 1 coach our last one moved to a Super League club. My brother Paul, one of the directors, is here too. We both watched the game. You're unpredictable, adaptive… and you clearly understand how to build a team."

Paul stepped forward. "First time in years we've beaten Bethlehem," he said. "Mozell's a good coach, but you out-thought him. We've heard about your record coaching in the US, England, Ireland, even beating the Chinese National Team on tour. Rubin's told us about you as well. You'd be a strong candidate for the job."

Errek hesitated, caught between curiosity and humility. "That's quite an offer. I'd need to think about it. But I'll admit the idea of coaching here is tempting."

Peter outlined the details: a seven-month season, good pay, housing provided, bonuses for winning and for youth program work. "It's rare we get American coaches over here," he said. "You could bring one assistant from home, plus a local coach. Sayid would be an excellent option he's talented, and the players respect him."

Bob, listening nearby, whistled. "That's not bad at all."

Errek promised to send his résumé, but made no commitments. "I'd like to see more maybe some game footage from the top teams, both Division 1 and Super League, so I know what I'd be working with. You can't aim for the middle; you've got to aim for the top."

Paul grinned. "I like the way you think."

The conversation drifted to shared basketball stories, mutual acquaintances, and the possibilities ahead. Before leaving, Mozell approached. "Coach, you've still got it. Maybe more than before. You're calmer now. More precise."

Sayid beamed. "Thanks, Coach. You made a huge difference today. I meant what I said you were my favorite coach."

By the time the group left the gym, the late afternoon sun was casting long shadows across the streets. They returned to the hotel briefly, only to head out again for an early evening walk. Rubin drove them past familiar landmarks before stopping at a modest hilltop site the Church of the Ascension on the Mount of Olives.

The structure was small, hexagonal in shape, with a domed upper level. Inside, there was little decoration just candles, a donation box, and a patch of bare ground where footprints seemed burned into the stone. The air was still, reverent. Together, the friends dropped fifty shekels into the box and lingered in silence for a few moments.

From there, they visited the nearby Church of Mary Magdalene and Mary, the Mother of the Russian Tsar. Its white façade gleamed in the fading light, the gold domes glowing like fire against the sky. "Now that," Bob said, "is beautiful."

They continued toward St. Stephen's Gate, wandering the bustling lanes toward Damascus Gate. Penny and Bill paused at a bazaar, bartering for souvenirs a small painting of Jesus, some handcrafted trinkets. The narrow streets smelled of spices and fresh bread, the sound of merchants calling out in multiple languages filling the air.

Their final stop was the Garden Tomb. The site was peaceful, the greenery softening the stone paths. They walked slowly, pausing at Golgotha, then entering the empty tomb itself. The stillness here was different not silent, but filled with a quiet hum of reverence. They stayed for nearly an hour, reading scripture, letting the moment settle into memory.

Before heading back, they stopped by the Fathers' residence once again. After a round of chamomile tea and friendly conversation, Errek discreetly pressed a couple of hundred dollars into Father Albert's hand. "For supplies whatever you need," he said.

The Father's eyes softened. "You're a good man, Errek, even if you're not Catholic."

Errek laughed. "That's one of the kindest compliments I've had in a while."

As they left, Father Albert mentioned that Ahmed, an old acquaintance of Errek's, would be picking them up in the morning in a blue Mercedes van to serve as their driver for the next leg of the trip.

Back at the hotel, the group took a swim, followed by a leisurely dinner at the nicer restaurant downstairs. They played cards until the food settled, the conversation drifting between archaeology, basketball, and the next few days' plans. Tomorrow would be a rest day, then they'd be off to explore Galilee, Haifa, and Acre with some diving in the Mediterranean for good measure.

Looking out from the pool area, the skyline of Jerusalem stretched before them ancient on one side, modern on the other. It was a fitting view for the day they'd had: history and the present, side by side, both alive in their own ways.

For Errek, the thought lingered perhaps this wasn't just a vacation. Perhaps this was a door opening to something he hadn't dared imagine in years. But for now, he let the thought rest. Tomorrow was for relaxation, and the road ahead would be waiting when the time was right.

Chapter 11: The Sea of Galilee and the Surrounding Area

The morning sun rose softly over Jerusalem, casting a golden hue across the Hilton's polished windows. After a hearty breakfast, the group gathered in the lobby, luggage pared down to small carry-ons packed for three days. The larger suitcases remained in Errek and Bob's hotel room until Sunday. Just then, Ahmed pulled up in the sleek Mercedes van, stepping out with a polite smile to help load their bags.

"Morning, my friends," Ahmed greeted warmly, stacking the cases neatly in the back. "Three days on the road you'll see the Galilee, Acre, Haifa. Everything is set."

Joe, always precise, leaned against the van. "Avi's in on the plan. I called him last night. We'll be staying at the Hotel Del Carmel in Haifa. He's bringing the tanks, diving gear, and a couple of spearguns. I reserved him a room."

Ahmed nodded approvingly. With that, they climbed into the comfortable van and pulled away from the bustle of the city, heading north.

The ride was smooth, the landscape unfolding in layers of stone and scrub before opening to wide valleys. After about fifteen minutes, they left the main Tel Aviv route and veered right, following the ancient road northward.

Ahmed gestured out the window. "Ahead lies Shechem, between Mount Gerizim and Mount Ebal. Do you know the story?"

Errek's eyes lit up; his love for biblical history was boundless. "Of course. Joshua gathered the tribes here. Half stood on one mountain, declaring the curses if Israel disobeyed the Lord. The other half stood on the opposite mountain, proclaiming the blessings. A covenant carved into the very landscape."

The van grew quiet for a moment, each reflecting on the solemnity of the story. They stopped briefly at a roadside café for coffee and a quick snack, then pressed on.

Before long, the terrain gave way to the wide, fertile Plains of Jezreel, stretching out like a green triangle beneath the morning sky.

"This is Megiddo," Ahmed said gravely. "You know it as Armageddon the valley where the Book of Revelation says the final battle will be fought."

The group stared out across the plain, imagining the armies of prophecy. The valley was broad, triangular, hemmed in by rising ridges. To the northwest loomed Mount Carmel, and further east, a lone bowl-shaped mountain rose from the horizon.

"That's Mount Tabor," Ahmed continued. "Some believe it's the Mount of Transfiguration where Peter, James, and John saw Jesus in his glory, speaking with Moses and Elijah."

Straight ahead, nestled in the hills, sat Nazareth.

The van climbed the winding road toward Nazareth, the city sprawling across a ridge that climbed higher into Upper Nazareth. At its heart gleamed a striking cathedral with a conical dome, standing like a crown over the town.

They parked about a hundred meters downhill at a parking structure unlike any they had seen. Not only did it house cars, but attendants offered detailing and cleaning services. The group chuckled at the thought a medieval pilgrimage site with modern car wash convenience.

Together they walked the hill, the city's narrow streets lined with shops and small cafés. Ahmed led them toward the Basilica of the Annunciation.

Inside, the air was cool and reverent. The great wooden doors carved with intricate designs opened into a soaring sanctuary. The group moved quietly through, pausing at mosaics and paintings donated by churches from across the world. Down below, reached by narrow stairs, lay the ruins of what was believed to be Joseph and Mary's home. They peered into the cave-like dwelling, its stone walls enclosing what appeared to be a carpenter's bench still etched with the marks of ancient work.

"In most towns back then," Ahmed explained, "there would be only one carpenter's shop, sometimes none at all. This could very well be the place where Jesus grew up, watching Joseph work."

The group lingered in silence, absorbing the weight of history. Outside, the square overlooked the Jezreel Valley. From the cliffs, one could see for miles even Megiddo lay visible in the distance.

"Imagine," Penny whispered, "Jesus could have stood here as a boy, gazing down at the plain, knowing it would one day be the site of the final battle."

The thought sent a shiver through them all. They returned to the van, pausing only to buy postcards and souvenirs while waiting for the car to be retrieved.

Just three miles away lay Cana, a modest town built on the slope of a lower hill. The van wound its way up, arriving at the Church of the Wedding. Inside, stone walls enclosed what was once an ancient banquet hall, where tradition held that Jesus performed his first miracle, turning water into wine.

On display were ceremonial goblets and wedding utensils from the period, their craftsmanship delicate and timeless. At a counter, samples of Cana Wedding Wine were offered. The group sipped the sweet, low-alcohol vintage.

Joe's face lit up. "This is too good to pass up. I'm buying a case."

Bob laughed. "Three bottles for me as souvenirs," though his grin betrayed his eagerness to taste them again later. Errek nodded and added his own purchase.

Back in the van, they marveled at the landscape. The road wound past lush orchards and fields bursting with life.

"Now I see why they called it the land flowing with milk and honey," Bill said. "Look banana groves, orange trees, fig orchards, date palms. Fertile, green, abundant."

Penny pointed out the contrast. "Amazing how just south, near Bethlehem and along the Jordan to the Dead Sea, it turns to barren desert. This little country holds every landscape in miniature."

The group nodded in agreement, each gazing out at the richness of the Galilee.

Finally, they crested a ridge and the Sea of Galilee spread out before them. Smaller than some had imagined, it stretched about seven miles across at its widest and twenty miles long, with the Golan Heights clearly visible across the water.

"It looks like a great lake," Bob observed. "Hard to believe so many miracles happened here."

Their first stop was Magdala, hometown of Mary Magdalene. They glanced briefly at the church there, then continued north to Tabgha. The area was alive with pilgrims and tourists, the air buzzing with quiet reverence.

At Tabgha's visitor center, they browsed maps and souvenirs, grabbing a coke and candy bars. Tabgha or Heptapegon, "seven springs" was known as the place where Jesus fed the four thousand.

Just beyond the information center, a gentle slope led them to the Church of the Multiplication. Inside, mosaics depicted loaves and fishes, eternal reminders of abundance. Outside, sandy banks gave way to pebbly stretches of shoreline, dotted with fishing boats rocking in the breeze.

Ahmed guided them to a small bay. "Here the Apostles would set off in their boats. And there," he pointed to a simple stone grill-like structure, "they could cook their catch."

Nearby stood another church, built over the spot where tradition said the risen Jesus cooked fish for his disciples and reinstated Peter.

"Peter, do you love me? Feed my sheep." The words echoed in their minds, and Joe whispered them aloud. All fell silent, humbled by the reminder.

They climbed another gentle hill, where the Church of the Beatitudes overlooked the sea. Its stained-glass windows shone with verses of blessing. Outside, a great stone stood, believed to be the very place where Jesus sat to deliver the Sermon on the Mount.

Errek sat quietly in one of the pews, eyes closed, imagining the multitude spread across the hillside, Jesus' voice carrying on the wind.

"Blessed are the poor in spirit…"

When he opened his eyes, he found Penny smiling softly at him. "You look like you could sit here forever."

"I almost could," he admitted. "This is the heart of the Gospel right here."

Leaving the church, they descended back toward the shoreline. Rolling up their pants, they waded knee-deep into the waters of Galilee. Warm and gentle, the lake lapped around them as they looked out across its expanse.

Joe spoke first. "Imagine Jesus walking on this water."

"Or calming the storm when the disciples feared for their lives," Bill added.

"Or Peter leaping out of the boat, splashing toward him," Penny said with a quiet smile.

They stood in silence, letting the moment wash over them. The Sea of Galilee was no longer just a name in scripture it was alive, under their feet, wrapping them in its story.

The group left the Hill of the Beatitudes behind them, descending once again toward the shimmering shoreline. Their next destination was Capernaum, the fishing village that had once been the hub of Jesus' ministry. As the van rolled along the narrow road, excitement hummed among them.

They stepped out into the ruins of Capernaum, where the foundations of stone houses stretched in neat lines, as if the village had only just been abandoned. The air smelled faintly of dust and the sea breeze drifting inland.

"It's incredible," Penny whispered, kneeling to touch the stones. "These are the very outlines of homes from two thousand years ago."

Near the heart of the site rose the remains of the synagogue. Its broad white limestone foundation stood in stark contrast to the black basalt used in the village houses. A placard showed a rendering of how the synagogue would have looked, its walls rising proudly above the fishing village.

Joe, unable to resist, pulled out his compact detector. "Just a quick scan," he said, grinning like a boy caught sneaking candy.

"Joe," Penny scolded gently, "we're supposed to be respectful here."

"I am," he replied. "And look ten coins already. From Jesus' time up through late Roman occupation. This place was bustling."

Bill bent low to study the coins as Joe carefully bagged them. "It's amazing to hold something in your hand that a fisherman or merchant might have dropped two thousand years ago."

Near the shoreline stood an octagonal foundation covered by a protective modern structure. Ahmed pointed toward it. "That is said to be Peter's house the place where Jesus healed his mother-in-law and likely taught many times."

"To think this was home base for the ministry," Errek said softly, eyes tracing the outline of the ancient walls. "From here, the message spread across the world."

A short walk away lay a simple but moving site the Church of the Primacy of Peter, built over the spot where tradition held that the risen Jesus cooked fish for his disciples and reinstated Peter.

The group entered quietly. Inside, a blackened stone slab, believed to be the very rock on which Jesus had prepared the meal, remained untouched. Ancient carvings of fish adorned the floor, symbols of the earliest Christians.

Joe whispered, "Here is where Jesus asked Peter three times, 'Do you love me?' And told him to feed his sheep. Amazing to stand where forgiveness and mission were joined together."

Penny nodded. "It shows us that failure doesn't define you. Grace restores you."

The others stood in silent agreement, the sound of the waves outside echoing faintly in the small stone church.

By mid-afternoon, the van carried them south toward Tiberias. Just outside the city, they came upon a small dock where an ancient-styled wooden boat waited. Its owner, a tanned man with a lined face, greeted them with a broad smile.

"No fishing today," he said apologetically. "It is spawning season. But you can dive and swim if you wish."

Joe's face fell slightly, but he shrugged. "Well, then I'll save my spearfishing energy for the Mediterranean tomorrow."

They quickly changed into swimsuits from their carry-on bags, storing their clothes in the dock's small changing rooms. Soon, they boarded the weathered boat, which carried them two hundred yards out into the lake.

When the call came, they leapt into the water. It was warm, refreshing, and impossibly clear. Errek surfaced with a grin. "This… this is amazing."

Beneath them, schools of St. Peter's fish large tilapia darted in flashes of silver. Red mullet glided past in small groups. The divers marveled at the variety, diving and surfacing, laughing like children at play.

"I could spend all day here," Joe said wistfully, bobbing in the water. "A field day for a diver. The clarity, the life it's perfect."

Ahmed laughed from the boat. "Enjoy it, my friends. You are swimming in the same waters where miracles unfolded."

After twenty minutes, they reluctantly climbed back aboard, dripping and exhilarated. As the boat turned toward shore, Errek leaned close to Joe. "Don't worry. We've got an Arabian feast waiting next."

Bob perked up. "Now you're speaking my language."

Back on land, they dressed quickly and piled into the van. Ahmed steered them south of Tiberias to a restaurant he had visited with Errek years earlier. The time was nearing four o'clock when they arrived, and the dining room filled with the smell of spices, grilled fish, and baked bread.

Plates began to arrive one after another: seafood salad, hummus with olive oil, red mullet fingers, St. Peter's fish grilled whole, tuna salad, seafood soup, and a host of smaller dishes whose names they didn't know but enjoyed all the same.

Bob bit into a piece of red mullet and closed his eyes. "Heavenly. This is heavenly."

Joe raised a fork of St. Peter's fish. "Don't worry, Bob. Tomorrow I'll spear some for us in the Mediterranean."

Bobby laughed. "Aye aye, Captain."

They lingered over the meal, savoring each dish, sipping water and juice until they were filled but happy. The feast seemed endless, a reflection of the land's bounty.

Leaving the restaurant, they drove south along the narrowing shoreline. Soon they reached the place where the Jordan River flows out of the Sea of Galilee. The water here was calm and green, shaded by trees and gardens. A quiet hush lay over the spot, as if it had been waiting for them.

They stepped out, taking photos and gazing across the placid surface.

"This is where John the Baptist may have baptized," Ahmed said quietly. "A peaceful place. A fitting place."

The group nodded, awed by the tranquility. The sound of birds mingled with the gentle ripple of water, and for a moment they simply breathed in the peace.

Back in the van, as the highway carried them westward, conversation turned reflective. The Jezreel Valley opened again before them as they passed Megiddo.

Errek gestured toward the valley. "Imagine Jesus as a boy in Nazareth, looking down on this plain the place Revelation says will be the final battleground. He grew up with that view every day."

The thought lingered in the air as they drove. The van wound north along the coast, passing Caesarea Maritima.

"There will be wrecks there," Rubin remarked. "Ships sunk near the harbor. Tomorrow, perhaps."

Farther along the road, the conversation shifted toward Acre ancient Ptolemais. Ahmed described the walled peninsula jutting into the sea, the last stronghold of the Crusaders before they were driven out.

"Some say a third escaped by sea," he said. "Others carried treasure with them, only to sink as catapults rained down."

Joe's eyes gleamed. "Treasure. That's what I like to hear. I'm bringing my detectors."

"Best to keep them subtle," Errek cautioned. "Use them in the tunnels or underwater. The old city is bustling with shops and tourists."

Joe grinned. "I'll figure something out."

By evening, the van rolled into Haifa. The slopes of Mount Carmel rose above the coastal city, its lights glittering as the sun set. The Hotel Del Carmel loomed ahead, grand and elegant.

"Wow," Penny breathed. "This place is even more luxurious than the Hilton."

Inside, the lobby gleamed with polished marble and golden light. A manager stepped forward, greeting them warmly.

"Mr. Johnson, welcome. Your stay has been arranged and paid for by the Israeli government and the IAA. You are our honored guests."

The group exchanged astonished looks. Rooms were assigned, bags delivered, and soon they were unpacking and resting. The promise of the pool called, and they changed into swimsuits.

Down by the poolside, a commotion was stirring. Photographers clustered at the far end, snapping shots of a woman poised elegantly against the setting sun. Bodyguards flanked her as assistants adjusted lights.

Curious, Errek walked closer, only to be stopped by the guards. He squinted and then recognition hit him.

"Emily! Emily, it's me Errek!" he called.

The woman pulled down her sunglasses, her face lighting up. "Errek? My goodness, it's been years!"

She strode over, ignoring the protests of her handlers. "You look wonderful leaner, healthier, with just the right touch of gray. What brings you here?"

"Exploring," Errek said with a smile. "Working with the IAA on some digs and dives. And you? Modeling, I see."

"Finishing my swimsuit calendar, then a speech in Haifa," she replied. "But diving tomorrow? Count me in. I love scuba."

She glanced around at the group, who were staring in awe. "Introduce me?"

Errek laughed, gesturing. "My brother Bob, my friends Joe, Bill, and Penny. Everyone this is Emily Wycliff."

Joe nearly dropped his drink. "You're serious? You actually know her?"

Bob leaned in and whispered, "I want her autograph."

Emily laughed. "Of course, darling. I'll get you all signed pictures."

The group burst into laughter, the tension breaking. They spent the next hour in the pool and hot tub, talking easily. Emily was as down-to-earth as she was glamorous.

She promised to join them for the next day's trip to Acre, with one bodyguard at her side. For now, she slipped away to finish her shoot, leaving the group buzzing with disbelief.

The group awoke to sunlight streaming through the tall windows of the Hotel Del Carmel. Breakfast was leisurely, the kind that combined fruit platters with omelets, breads, and endless coffee. Emily joined them at the table, dressed casually in walking shorts, a blue blouse, and a wide sunhat. Two bodyguards trailed discreetly behind her Tom, tall and lean, and Chuck, a towering man who looked more suited to football than bodyguard duty.

"Ready for Acre?" she asked, sipping her juice.

"We've been waiting," Joe grinned. "Treasure and history the perfect combination."

By nine o'clock, they were in the van, driving northward along the coast. The Mediterranean shimmered bright blue to their left, while modern suburbs sprawled inland to the right. Soon the ancient city of Acre Akko, or Ptolemais as it had once been called came into view. Its walled peninsula jutted into the sea like a stone fortress still daring the centuries to defy it.

Ahmed parked near the southern gate, just outside the towering stone walls. The group stepped out into the bustle of modern life surrounding the old city. Fishmongers called from stalls, spice vendors spread their fragrant wares, and the smell of saltwater mingled with grilled bread from the bazaar.

Emily shaded her eyes and looked around in wonder. "It feels like stepping into another century. How much of this is original?"

Errek pointed toward the walls. "Much of it. The Crusaders fortified Acre in the twelfth century, and though the palace was destroyed later, much of the fortress, the citadel, and the city's core remain intact. UNESCO made sure it's protected."

Bob nudged Joe, who was staring toward the sea. "Treasure, right?"

"Always treasure," Joe replied, grinning. "Ships sunk right out there during the final siege. The trick is finding what's left."

They passed through the southern gate into narrow streets lined with shops. The air was alive with voices in Hebrew, Arabic, and

English, and the clash of modern life against medieval walls gave Acre its unique energy.

The group's first stop was the Crusader citadel, a massive complex of thick walls, arches, and vaulted halls. A local guide pointed out the towers, each built by different nations that had contributed to the Crusader cause.

"This was the stronghold of the Knights Hospitaller," he explained. "They turned it into a fortress-palace, complete with halls for dining, sleeping quarters, and dungeons. Later, the Ottomans repurposed it as a prison."

Inside, dim corridors led to reconstructed rooms. They stopped at a chamber where life-size mannequins depicted guards handing clothes to prisoners.

"Here they prepared them before sending them to the gallows," the guide said gravely.

"That's grim," Emily whispered, her brow furrowing.

"Eight Jewish rebels were hanged here in the 1940s," Errek added, recalling his studies. "They had escaped with the help of compatriots who set a fire as a distraction. Only eight were caught, and they were executed here."

Bob shivered. "This place feels heavy with history. You can almost hear the echoes."

The gallows room still had its wooden beam, dark with age. Everyone stood silently, imagining the defiance and despair of those who had stood beneath it.

From the citadel, they wandered into a nearby mosque, its walls adorned with intricate geometric patterns. A bronze fountain sat at its center, corroded but still elegant. Light filtered through high windows, painting the stone floor with shifting shadows.

Penny admired the craftsmanship. "Even in conquest, people left behind beauty."

Outside, the bazaar stretched in a colorful sprawl of fabrics, spices, sweets, and trinkets. Emily and Penny immediately gravitated toward a row of scarves and blouses.

"Oh, I have to try this hat," Emily laughed, setting a wide-brimmed woven piece atop her head.

Chuck obediently carried armfuls of bags while Tom lingered nearby, amused.

Emily leaned close to Penny. "So tell me what's the story with Errek? He seems… different."

Penny smirked. "Different? He's always been the same generous, kind, brilliant in his own way. But yes, he likes you. A lot."

Emily's expression softened. "I thought so. He's been such a good friend through our letters. My mother always said I should find someone like him."

Penny lowered her voice. "Don't tell him I said this, but he's shy under all that leadership confidence. He's been let down before. I think he's afraid to risk it again."

Emily's smile was wistful. "Maybe I'll give him a little nudge."

Meanwhile, the men sampled Turkish delights at a pastry stall. Bob declared them "worth the calories," while Bill snapped photos of the clock tower rising above the square. Joe kept glancing toward the shoreline, mind already on the dives ahead.

At the citadel's far side, a tour guide named Ezra pointed the way to the hidden Crusader tunnel.

"It was rediscovered in the 1990s," Ezra explained. "A merchant heard water rushing beneath his shop, and excavations revealed this passage. It runs nearly 200 meters, from the citadel to a hidden harbor. The Crusaders likely smuggled weapons and treasure through here during sieges."

The group followed him down into a musty corridor lit by dim bulbs. The stone walls dripped with moisture, and the air was thick with the smell of age.

Joe pulled out his compact detector, its telescoping arm unfolding like a strange staff. As they walked, the device began to ping insistently.

"We've got hits already," Joe said, kneeling with his flashlight. "Silver, corroded but intact. Probably coins."

Ezra nodded approvingly. "Your instrument is powerful. It confirms what we suspected that objects were hidden beneath the planks."

The detector chimed again, and again. Joe marked the floor with red chalk at each signal. By the time they reached the tunnel's end, he had left nearly forty marks.

"There's treasure under there," he said quietly. "Gold, silver, maybe weapons. Enough to prove this was an escape route."

Emily's eyes widened. "You're telling me this floor is hiding hoards of Crusader treasure?"

"Potentially," Joe said. "But excavation must be done carefully. That's for the IAA."

When they emerged into sunlight, Ezra gestured toward the sea. "See those three walls extending into the water? That was the palace, destroyed after the Crusaders fell. The hidden harbor lay just there, where royalty and knights fled. Ships were sunk within sight of safety."

Bob shielded his eyes, staring at the waves. "And tomorrow, we're diving right where it happened."

Their stomachs growled as they followed Ezra's directions to the Buri Buri restaurant, perched near the harbor with its whitewashed walls gleaming in the sun. Inside, the staff ushered them into a private room, recognizing Emily instantly.

The maître d' smiled. "It is our honor. The meal is on the house for Miss Wycliff. The rest, on the Antiquities Association's account."

They settled around a long table. Platters arrived quickly red mullet appetizers, smoked mackerel dip, fresh bread, olives, and then larger plates of snapper and grouper.

Joe groaned in delight. "This is superb. Better than any seafood I've had back home."

Chuck, usually stoic, nearly devoured his share. Tom laughed. "You don't feed us like this on duty," he teased Emily.

She grinned. "Consider it a perk of guarding me today."

Ahmad arrived midway, settling happily with a plate of snapper. "This," he declared, "is living."

They ate for over an hour, laughter mingling with the clink of glasses. The guards relaxed, Joe kept marveling at the food, and Penny leaned back, smiling at how normal the moment felt despite the centuries of history outside.

By the time they rose from the table, the sun was already dipping toward afternoon. Their next stop the harbor, where Avi awaited with dive gear and the promise of underwater discovery.

The Mediterranean breeze carried the salty tang of the sea as the group walked from the restaurant toward Acre's harbor. The sun gleamed off the water, dazzling the surface in a thousand shifting diamonds. Seagulls circled overhead, squawking and diving for scraps from fishing boats pulling in with their morning catch.

A black Jeep stood out amid the rows of small cars Avi's Dead Sea Diving vehicle, plastered with faded stickers from past expeditions. Its back hatch was open, revealing tanks, wetsuits, and other diving gear stacked neatly.

"There he is," Joe said, waving.

Avi strode forward, tanned and energetic, his grin wide as ever. "My favorite treasure hunters! And today, I bring gifts gear for everyone, even a celebrity."

He bowed theatrically toward Emily, who blushed and adjusted her sunglasses. "It's an honor, Miss Wycliff. My kids adore you."

Emily laughed lightly. "Thank you. I'm here as just Emily today. And yes, I do dive."

"Of course you do," Avi said approvingly. "I brought a suit your size. And for one of your guards men's extra-large. Safety first."

Tom raised his hand. "I'll go with her. Chuck doesn't swim."

Chuck grunted his agreement. "I'll stay on deck and keep an eye out."

The group gathered around the gear. Avi handed out wetsuits, fins, masks, and buoyancy control devices. Joe checked over the specialized sonar metal detector, making sure its settings were calibrated for saltwater.

"We're going to start at the wreck just a couple hundred yards out," Avi explained. "It's shallow by Mediterranean standards thirty to forty meters. Good visibility today, maybe twenty meters. Perfect conditions."

Errek helped Emily into her wetsuit. She laughed at how snug it felt. "I always forget how flattering and unflattering these are."

Bob smirked. "Trust me, you look better than any of us in one."

Emily rolled her eyes, but her smile betrayed amusement.

Errek tested the straps on his tank, then turned serious. "Same safety rules as before: stay with your buddy, check your gauges often, and signal clearly. Emily, you and Tom stick with Avi. Joe, you and I can handle the detector. Bill and Penny, cover the midline."

Penny raised her hand playfully. "I'm just here for pictures and maybe coins."

"And that's important," Joe said, patting the waterproof case of his Nikon. "Document everything."

They boarded a modest 35-foot fishing boat, captained by one of Avi's friends. The craft chugged out of the harbor, passing under the shadow of Acre's sea walls. Beyond the breakwaters, the water deepened to a rich, impossible blue.

Avi pointed ahead. "There see where the surface changes slightly? That's the wreck. Burned and sunk as the Crusaders fled. It rests like a skeleton, ribs of wood and stone ballast still visible."

Excitement buzzed through the group. Joe slipped on his mask and BCD, then nodded. "Let's do this."

One by one, they plunged into the water. It was cool but not frigid, the density less oppressive than the Dead Sea but still buoyant enough to feel different than a freshwater dive.

Bubbles rose in shimmering trails as they descended slowly, following the anchor line into the blue.

The outline of the ship emerged below a dark shape half-buried in sand, timbers jutting like bones, stone blocks scattered across the seabed. Fish darted through gaps, schools of silvery mullet flashing in the sunlight.

Emily's voice crackled faintly through her comm unit. "This is incredible. It feels like swimming back through time."

Avi gestured to Joe, who extended the detector. Its soft hum filled the water, growing louder as it swept over the wreck's remains. Almost immediately, it pinged.

Joe signaled, and Errek swam closer. Together they brushed away silt to reveal a small corroded object a bronze buckle.

Bill 's camera flashed, capturing the find. "First artifact," he said through the comm. "Not bad."

The detector buzzed again, this time stronger. Joe marked the spot, and with careful gloved hands, Penny dug into the sand. She surfaced with a small copper coin, faint markings barely visible.

"Roman, maybe?" Penny wondered aloud. "Could be Crusader."

Avi's voice was filled with awe. "You've barely started, and already found something. This is going to be good."

Emily swam alongside Tom, her movements surprisingly graceful. She spotted something glinting beneath a broken timber. Tugging gently, she pulled free a silver ring, its band encrusted but its shape unmistakable.

She held it up triumphantly. "Look at this!"

Tom chuckled. "Leave it to you to find jewelry."

Errek swam over, eyes widening behind his mask. He gave her a thumbs-up. Emily's grin shone even through her mask.

"Maybe treasure hunting really is my calling," she said.

"Not bad for your first dive with us," Errek replied.

They ventured toward the stern, where the detector pinged more frequently. Joe motioned for caution; parts of the wreck were unstable, beams collapsing inward.

Together, they unearthed a small ceramic jar, sealed but cracked. Inside, faint outlines suggested grains or dried material, long fossilized.

Bill whispered in awe, "Supplies. They left in such haste they never unloaded."

Penny translated markings etched faintly on the clay. "Greek letters. This ship carried mixed cargo probably provisions for knights."

Nearby, another ping revealed a cluster of iron arrowheads, fused together by rust but still sharp.

Bob whistled. "Weapons cache. Just like the tunnel evidence."

Suddenly, Tom's voice cut in. "Movement on the edge!"

A shadow loomed a massive grouper, easily three feet long, gliding past. Its mottled body looked prehistoric, and its jaw snapped at smaller fish.

Emily stiffened, clutching Tom's arm.

Avi swam calmly toward it, spreading his hands. "Don't worry. They look meaner than they are. Just don't corner it."

The grouper drifted away lazily, uninterested. Still, everyone's heart rate spiked.

"Adds excitement, doesn't it?" Joe quipped, though his laugh sounded nervous even over comms.

They continued another twenty minutes, the detector guiding them to several more objects:

- A corroded dagger hilt, green with patina.

- Fragments of chainmail links.

- A handful of coins, some barely legible, others with faint crosses.

Emily, still buzzing from her find, whispered, "Every object feels like a voice from the past."

Errek nodded. "Each one tells a story. Fear, escape, hope all frozen here."

At last, Avi signaled time. Air gauges were dipping low. They slowly ascended, pausing for a safety stop before surfacing.

The boat rocked gently as they hauled themselves aboard, dripping and exhilarated. Chuck handed out towels, eyes widening at the ring Emily placed in his palm.

"You found that?" he asked.

"Yes," she said proudly. "My first treasure."

Joe laid the artifacts carefully on a cloth coins, buckle, dagger hilt, arrowheads, and the ceramic jar.

Avi shook his head in wonder. "In one dive, you've recovered more than some teams find in months. Tomorrow, with the IAA's official boat, we'll explore deeper. But today this was history."

Emily looked at Errek, her eyes shining. "Thank you for letting me be part of this. It's everything I imagined and more."

Errek smiled softly. "You belong here with us, Emily. Adventure suits you."

She held his gaze a moment longer, the sea breeze tugging at her damp hair, before looking back at the artifacts laid out like treasure on the deck.

The van hummed softly as Ahmed steered it back toward Haifa. The group, still damp-haired and sun-warmed from their dive, sat in companionable exhaustion. Salt clung faintly to their skin, and the tang of the Mediterranean seemed to linger even inside the enclosed vehicle.

Chuck, wedged comfortably in the back, rumbled in his deep voice. "That was something else. I've guarded her on film sets, concerts, red carpets… but never on the bottom of the sea."

Emily laughed, leaning forward between the seats. "You looked more nervous than I did when that grouper swam past."

Tom snorted. "I wasn't nervous. Just… cautious."

Joe shook his head, grinning. "That thing could swallow a football. I'd say cautious was the smart move."

The van broke free of the coastal road, climbing the hillside toward the shining bulk of the Hotel Del Carmel. Its terraces gleamed in the golden light of early evening, glass windows reflecting the sea below. As they pulled into the circular drive, doormen in crisp uniforms hurried to assist.

"Back to luxury," Bob murmured. "We're living two lives ancient explorers by day, pampered tourists by night."

The group spilled into the marble lobby, all polished stone and chandeliers. A fountain burbled gently at the center, casting shifting reflections across the high ceiling. Emily removed her sunglasses and adjusted her new hat, drawing quick, hushed recognition from a few guests who tried and failed to be discreet.

She leaned close to Errek as they waited for the elevators. "This place… it's beautiful. Almost too much."

"It suits you," he replied simply.

Her smile lingered even after she turned away.

Upstairs, they retreated to their respective rooms. For an hour, the group showered, changed, and rested. Salt gave way to soap, wetsuits to linen shirts and sundresses. By seven, they reconvened in the hotel's kosher restaurant, lured by the scent of baked bread and roasted meats.

A long wooden table accommodated the nine of them, including Ahmed and the bodyguards, whom Emily insisted join as equals. Platters soon arrived roasted lamb, spiced couscous, fresh vegetables, and baskets of pita with creamy hummus. A bottle of champagne stood unopened in a silver bucket, while bottles of Coke and Dr. Pepper circled the table for those who abstained.

Joe raised his glass of soda. "To treasure, history, and not getting eaten by grouper."

Laughter rang around the table as glasses clinked.

Penny leaned forward, eyes bright. "I can't stop thinking about the ring you found, Emily. It's remarkable."

Emily twirled the silver band between her fingers. "It feels… personal. Like someone wore this, loved it, lost it. And now, centuries later, it's in my hand."

Bill nodded thoughtfully. "Every artifact has a story. Some we can read, others we can only imagine."

Avi, seated at the end, leaned in. "Tomorrow's site might hold more. Caesarea Maritimais full of wrecks, some deeper, some shallower. With Joe's detector, we may uncover things no one has touched in centuries."

"Then we'd better rest well tonight," Bob said, patting his stomach. "Though with food like this, that might be difficult."

Later, as dessert arrived a tray of honey-drenched baklava and fresh fruit Emily rose quietly and motioned to Errek. They stepped out onto the restaurant's balcony, overlooking the Mediterranean where the city lights shimmered across the waves.

For a moment, neither spoke. The sound of the sea carried up faintly, mingled with laughter from diners inside.

Emily rested her hands on the railing. "I meant what I said earlier. Today was one of the most thrilling days I've ever had. And… it wasn't just the artifacts."

Errek glanced at her, cautious. "What do you mean?"

She smiled, her eyes catching the soft glow of the lamps. "I mean, you. You've changed since I last saw you stronger, lighter. And yet, you're still the same man who wrote letters about faith and history and basketball, who made me laugh even when I was filming twelve-hour days. You grounded me when everything else felt unreal."

He looked away briefly, steadying himself. "Emily, you're… you're a star. A world knows you. I'm just"

"Stop," she said firmly, turning to face him. "Don't reduce yourself. You're the reason I wanted to come today. You've always seen me as just Emily, not as someone on posters. That means more than you know."

A silence stretched between them, filled with unspoken weight. Finally, Errek managed a smile. "Well, for what it's worth, I'm glad you came. You made the dive brighter."

Her laugh was soft, almost shy. "Then maybe I'll stay a little longer."

When they returned, the group was finishing the last bites of dessert. Avi spread a map across the table, smoothing it with his hands.

"Here Caesarea Maritima. Built by Herod the Great, once one of the greatest ports in the empire. Wrecks litter the coast from centuries of trade and war. Tomorrow, the IAA has granted us their boat. We'll have more time, more range."

Joe traced a line along the map. "We start near the old breakwater. Sonar shows anomalies possible ballast piles, maybe even treasure chests if we're lucky."

Penny raised an eyebrow. "Treasure chests? Really?"

"Why not?" Joe grinned. "Stranger things have happened. We already pulled scrolls from Qumran."

Bill tapped another spot. "What about the deeper wrecks?"

"Those come later," Avi replied. "We'll start moderate. Emily, if you want to dive again, it will be safe twenty to twenty-five meters."

Emily nodded without hesitation. "I'm in."

Tom leaned back. "Then I'm in too. Someone has to keep an eye on her."

Chuck chuckled. "I'll stick to dry land and guard the towels."

As the meal wound down, the group lingered, reluctant to break the camaraderie. Stories were traded Joe recalling dives off Florida, Bill sharing programming misadventures, Bob recounting a near disaster on a road trip in Texas. Laughter rolled, easy and free, binding them tighter as companions.

Finally, Rubin's voice cut through the chatter, warm but firm. "Friends, it's late. Tomorrow will demand strength and focus. Let's rest."

They rose, thanking the staff, and drifted back toward the elevators. Emily fell in step beside Errek once more.

"Goodnight, Indiana Jones," she teased softly.

He chuckled, shaking his head. "Goodnight, Emily."

Back in their rooms, the city lights glittered outside like stars fallen to earth. The sea whispered against the shore, a lullaby for those who sought treasure, history, and perhaps something even more elusive connection.

And tomorrow, the Mediterranean would offer new mysteries, waiting beneath the waves.

Chapter 12: Fishing for Treasure?

The morning sun shimmered across the Mediterranean, the water a calm, inviting blue as the group gathered at the docks. Excitement buzzed in the air; today wasn't just another dive, it was the first real chance to combine their spearfishing adventure with the possibility of uncovering long-lost treasure.

Rubin had arranged everything, and by the time they arrived, a sleek **35-foot cruiser** was already waiting. Its white hull gleamed against the sunlight, and three crewmen bustled about, readying equipment. At the stern stood **Captain Eli Horowitz**, a weathered man with a strong jawline and eyes that betrayed decades of experience at sea. He smiled warmly as the group approached.

"Welcome aboard," Eli said, his Hebrew accent noticeable but clear. "This is the *Galilee Star*. She's smaller than my other vessel, but for what we're doing today close to shore and near the wrecks she is perfect. She has two small cabins if anyone needs to rest, and the galley will take care of your catch. My men will help with the fish, fillet them, and pack them in ice."

Joe looked around approvingly. "This is more than big enough, Captain. Looks solid, and she's well kept."

Eli nodded with pride. "We keep her in good condition. The waters today are calm, visibility about 18 meters. Perfect diving weather. You'll have about two hours of air in your tanks, but remember ascend slowly. Even though we won't be more than forty meters deep, safety is everything."

Avi clapped his hands together, unable to hide his enthusiasm. "All right, everyone, gather around. Let's review the hand signals. Thumbs up everything is good. Palms flat stop. Finger pointing down means we descend. Hand slicing across throat means end dive, time to surface. Stay within sight of your partners." He moved through the signals quickly, and the group mimicked them until everyone was comfortable.

Emily stood near the rail, adjusting the straps on her gear, her blond hair tucked into a neat bun. "I've done plenty of dives for films," she said, "but this is the first time I'll be spearfishing."

Her bodyguard Tom, tall and broad-shouldered, stayed close. "Don't worry, Miss Wycliff, I'll be right there."

She shot him a playful glance. "Call me Emily, please. And don't hover too much I can hold my own."

Chuck, the larger of her two guards, shook his head. "I'll stay topside. The sea and I don't mix."

The others laughed lightly, easing some of the tension.

Within minutes the engines rumbled to life, and the cruiser glided away from the harbor. The coastline of Acre receded, its ancient walls etched sharply against the sky. The captain pointed toward the north. "The wreck we're heading to lies just past the ruins of the northern palace. About seventy feet of timber once made up the hull, though much has decayed. Still, the site is known for good fishing."

"Good fishing and maybe a few surprises," Joe said quietly, patting the waterproof pouch that held his metal detector.

It didn't take long barely five minutes before Eli throttled back and the wreck appeared beneath the surface, faint outlines visible in the crystal-clear water. A broken mast jutted upward, a ghostly finger pointing toward the sun.

"All right," Avi said, taking command. "Masks on, tanks tested. Thumbs up if your system is working."

One by one, everyone signaled readiness. Spearguns were checked and handed around, with Avi and Joe giving a final crash course on aiming and reloading. Then, in practiced unison, they sat on the rail and fell backward into the sea.

The water enveloped them like silk, cool but not cold, weightless compared to the heavy air tanks on their backs. Visibility was superb fish darted in schools, shimmering silver as they caught the sunlight. The wreck loomed below, resting quietly as though time itself had paused.

Joe descended first, motioning Bob and Errek to follow. He leveled his spear at a trio of mackerel gliding by. Steadying himself, he squeezed the trigger. The spear shot forward, striking a three-pounder squarely. The fish thrashed violently, but Joe reeled it in with practiced ease. He turned to the others, grinning behind his mask, and gave a triumphant thumbs up.

Bob chuckled through his regulator. "Show-off," he muttered, though no one heard.

Inspired, Errek scanned the area. Two mangrove snappers swam close, curious but cautious. He steadied his hand, aimed carefully, and fired. The spear found its mark in the larger fish's belly. The snapper bucked and pulled, dragging Errek a few feet before he wrestled it under control. Beside him, Bob took a shot at the smaller snapper but missed, the spear slicing harmlessly into the sand.

Errek gave him a thumbs up as he secured his catch to a stringer on his belt. Bob shook his head, reloading with determination.

From the other side of the wreck, Penny and Bill had their own success. Both nailed decent-sized snappers, their faces glowing with excitement as they displayed the fish. Avi hovered nearby, watching over them with a mix of pride and caution.

"Good start," Avi signaled, pointing toward the wreck's bow.

They drifted closer to the remains of a cabin, its timbers splintered but still forming an eerie outline. Bob spotted movement inside a hulking shadow sliding across the darkness. He steadied his spear, crept forward, and with a quick exhale, fired.

The spear slammed into the gills of an **eight-pound grouper**. The fish convulsed, dragging Bob deeper into the wreck, knocking loose rotted planks as it fought. For a moment, it seemed the grouper might win, but with a final effort Bob held his ground, reeling it in until the struggle ended. Exhausted but triumphant, he lifted the fish, showing it to the group.

Errek, meanwhile, had noticed something glinting faintly in the debris Bob had disturbed. He swam closer, brushed aside a layer of sand and algae, and uncovered **two gold coins**. His heart leapt. He quickly slipped them into his pouch, casting a glance at Bob who was too busy securing his grouper to notice.

Not far away, Emily and Tom hovered near a gaping hole in the wreck's side. A massive grouper easily fourteen pounds emerged, circling slowly. Emily's eyes widened. She steadied her spear, aimed, and fired.

The fish exploded into motion, yanking her forward like a ragdoll. She flailed, trying to hold steady as the spear line cut through the water. Tom swam in immediately, grabbing the shaft and helping to restrain the thrashing fish. Together, they subdued it, finally dragging it toward the surface. Emily surfaced briefly, removed her regulator, and shouted, "I got it!" before diving again, exhilarated.

When she rejoined the group underwater, Avi gestured for her to follow him. Near the broken planks where the grouper had burst through, a metallic glimmer caught his eye. He motioned to Emily, giving her the chance to retrieve it. She swam in, tugged gently, and emerged holding a **tarnished silver chain** nearly two feet long.

She cradled it like a prize, eyes wide, before Avi pointed them both upward. They surfaced together, Emily bursting into laughter as she pulled off her mask.

"Look!" she exclaimed, holding the chain aloft. "Actual treasure!"

The others surfaced shortly after, hauling their catches aboard. The crew whistled in admiration at the fish, but all eyes were on Emily's chain.

Avi examined it, nodding slowly. "This isn't just any trinket. Silver, likely Crusader-era. This ship… it may have been carrying more than just cargo."

Back on deck, the group gathered in a semicircle around the find. Joe pulled the detector from its waterproof pouch and powered it on. The device whined briefly before settling. He waved it over the chain, and it pinged sharply.

"Silver frequency," he confirmed. "She's real."

Emily's smile could have lit the whole harbor. "You mean to tell me I've just found my first piece of treasure?"

"You sure have," Bob said, clapping her on the shoulder. "And with style."

Her cheeks flushed with excitement. "This is the most thrilling thing I've done in years. You don't know how long I've dreamed of something like this. Since reading *Treasure Island* as a girl, I've wanted to find something hidden, something lost." She hugged each of them, lingering longest with Errek, who smiled awkwardly but didn't pull away.

Avi raised his hand. "Remember this is only the beginning. Where there's one coin, one chain, there may be dozens more.

We'll need to come back with Rubin and the IAA tomorrow. This could be the find of a lifetime."

The group exchanged glances, their excitement tempered with awe. The sea had just whispered its first secret, and it promised more.

The excitement from Emily's chain and Errek's coins hadn't yet settled when Avi signaled the group for another descent. They had only scratched the surface, and the wreck promised more. Bob, determined after his earlier miss, reloaded his speargun with a fierce glint in his eyes.

"Time for round two," he muttered into his regulator, mostly for himself.

They slipped back beneath the surface, bubbles trailing upward as they descended again toward the broken skeleton of the ship. The water shimmered with streaks of light cutting through the blue, casting shifting patterns across the timbers.

Bob hovered near the midsection of the wreck. Movement caught his eye something massive, lurking just beyond the shadows. His pulse quickened. Slowly, a **giant spotted grouper** emerged, easily four feet long, its thick body swaying as it turned. Bob steadied his spear, inhaled slowly, then fired.

The spear shot wide, scraping past the grouper and embedding itself deep into the decayed wooden floor. The fish bolted, vanishing into the shadows. Bob cursed, tugging at the line. But the spear was stuck immovable. He pulled again, bubbles escaping in sharp bursts of frustration.

Joe noticed his struggle and swam over, signaling with his hand: *hold still*. Together, they grasped the shaft, but it wouldn't budge. Joe motioned toward the wreck, pointing down into the debris. The spear hadn't just pierced wood it had struck something harder.

Bob hesitated as Joe gestured for him to follow inside. The wreck's interior loomed dark and tight, beams broken and leaning, but curiosity outweighed caution. They squeezed through the gap, fins brushing against splintered planks. Inside, the dim light revealed layers of sand, seaweed, and collapsed timber.

Joe's flashlight beam cut through the gloom. There, half-buried in the sediment, was a **chest**. Ancient, encrusted with coral and barnacles, its iron fittings fused with centuries of salt. And Bob's spear was lodged firmly into its side.

His eyes widened. He pointed frantically at the chest, then at Joe, who gave an emphatic thumbs up. Together, they cleared away debris, cutting at the reef that had grown around the box. Joe's carbon blade worked quickly, slicing stubborn strands until the chest finally shifted.

It was heavy much heavier than expected. They braced themselves, each gripping a side, and began hauling it toward the opening.

Outside, the others were patrolling the wreck. Emily and Peny nsifted through sand near the stern while Avi hovered with the detector. The device chirped repeatedly, marking spots, but all heads turned as Bob and Joe emerged, dragging the chest.

Eyes widened behind masks. Emily's hand flew to her mouthpiece, muffling a gasp. Avi swam closer, eyes gleaming with recognition. He touched the chest, nodded, and gestured urgently upward.

As they prepared to ascend, Bill noticed something glinting among the disturbed debris inside the wreck. He swam in quickly, curiosity piqued. There, entangled in the timbers, was the **skeleton of a man**.

The bones were yellowed with age, draped in tattered remnants of fabric that clung like seaweed. Beside the ribs, half-buried, lay a **sword** encrusted with barnacles. Its hilt still bore faint traces of ornate design, dulled by centuries underwater. A faint gleam of metal, perhaps once polished silver, winked beneath the growth.

Bill gingerly pried it free, careful not to snap the brittle remains. As he lifted it, something small slipped from the skeletal hand a ring, golden and inset with a dull red stone. He scooped it up, slipping it into his pouch before leaving the skeleton in peace.

When he rejoined the group, sword in hand, Penny's eyes widened. She pointed at the relic, then clasped her hands together in awe.

Errek gave her a look: *Later we'll study it together.*

Meanwhile, Joe, still buzzing from the discovery of the chest, noticed movement again. The **giant grouper** was back, circling just outside the wreck. It was larger than anything they had yet caught, easily thirty pounds or more, its speckled sides shimmering.

Joe steadied his spear. The fish circled closer. Then, with a flick of its powerful tail, it darted in. Joe fired, the spear striking cleanly through the gills. The fish bucked violently, dragging him forward, thrashing with explosive force.

Bobby swam in quickly, gripping Joe by the arm to steady him as the grouper fought, crashing against the wreck, breaking more timbers loose. The struggle was fierce, but slowly the fish tired, its thrashing slowing. Together they wrestled it toward open water.

The commotion had stirred up more debris, revealing yet more hidden objects within the wreck. But for now, they had all they could handle.

Joe and Bob secured the grouper, then turned back to the others. Penny and Emily were waving, signaling that their bags were full coins, chains, and smaller artifacts collected near the detector's signals. Avi hovered close, carefully marking the most promising spots for future exploration.

The chest was still the greatest prize. Bob and Errek clung to its handles, straining with its weight. Tom, Emily's bodyguard, swam down to help, gripping the embedded spear and lending his strength. Inch by inch, they rose together.

The ascent was slow and deliberate, bubbles swirling around them. Joe swam nearby with the monstrous grouper, guiding it upward. Penny and Emily carried their bags, while Bill clutched the sword. Avi brought up the rear, detector in hand, eyes constantly scanning the depths.

Breaking the surface was like stepping into another world the roar of the boat's engines, the shouts of the crew, the rush of air. Hands reached down immediately to haul the chest aboard, the wood groaning as it scraped against the deck. Joe's grouper was pulled up next, drawing wide-eyed whistles from the crew.

Masks came off, regulators spat out, and laughter erupted relieved, joyful, almost disbelieving.

They collapsed on the benches, exhausted. Bob leaned back, chest heaving. "I just… speared… a treasure chest," he said between breaths. "I'll never live that down."

Joe laughed, clapping him on the back. "Best shot you'll ever miss."

Emily pulled off her gloves, cradling the silver chain in her lap. "You don't understand," she said, her voice trembling with excitement. "This is the most exciting day of my life. I actually found treasure."

"You and me both," Errek said, opening his pouch to reveal the two gold coins. "Looks like we all struck gold today."

The captain and crew crowded around, eyes wide. Eli whistled low. "That chest alone could be priceless. You don't even know what's inside yet."

Rubin's instructions echoed in Errek's mind: *Don't open it until we're all together.* He nodded firmly. "We'll wait. It wouldn't be right to pry it open without Rubin. For now, it stays sealed."

Joe ran the detector over the chest, and it screamed with signals gold, silver, and perhaps more. "Whatever's in there," he said, "it's big."

Avi, his expression a mixture of pride and wonder, leaned against the rail. "You don't realize it yet, but you may have just uncovered one of the Crusader's lost ships. Tomorrow, when we dive again with Rubin and the IAA, everything will change."

For now, they turned to more practical matters. The fish haul was laid out mackerel, snappers, and three massive groupers. The crew weighed the largest, announcing the final tally aa 31.4 pound grouper, a new record for Joe and 30 pounds of snapper and mackeral. The men grinned, already imagining the feast.

The chest sat in the center of the deck, dripping seawater, its ancient wood steaming faintly under the sun. No one could take their eyes off it.

Emily touched its surface with reverence. "I've dreamed of this since childhood. Reading *Treasure Island*, I used to imagine stumbling upon a chest like this. And now..." She trailed off, overwhelmed, and hugged each of them in turn. When she reached Errek, she lingered just a moment longer, her smile warm and knowing.

Bob elbowed Bill with a grin. "I think our coach just got himself a fan."Bill smirked. "More than one, maybe."

The cruiser glided back toward the harbor, the sun beginning its slow descent. Spray from the bow sparkled in the golden light, and the deck was alive with laughter and excited chatter. The chest sat in the center of the boat, water streaming from its seams like tears, while the monstrous grouper lay in pride of place, its size still astonishing everyone.

Emily leaned against the rail, eyes still wide. "You don't understand," she said softly, her British accent wrapping around the words. "This is the day I've dreamed of since I was a girl. Treasure, real treasure."

Joe grinned, adjusting his gear. "And a thirty-pound grouper. That's not bad either."

Bob stretched his arms, proud of his unlikely "shot." "Don't forget who speared that chest. Best miss of my life."

Errek shook his head with a laugh. "We'll be hearing that story for the rest of the trip."

As the boat eased into its berth, Ahmed was waiting with the van, a grin plastered across his face as he saw the chest being hauled off. "Looks like you all had some luck," he said, eyes darting between the dripping box and the pile of fish.

"You could say that," Errek replied.

The crew filleted the catch with practiced hands, setting aside portions for the hotel kitchen. Joe carried the ice chest to the chef, who nearly fainted at the size of the grouper. "Fresh fish like this, gentlemen, is a feast," the chef said. "We'll prepare grouper, snapper, and sea bass tonight. Falafels and hummus too, if you wish."

"Perfect," Penny said, exhausted but smiling. "We'll be ready in an hour."

Rubin was already waiting in the hotel's private room when the group arrived with their haul. His eyes nearly popped at the sight of the chest.

"You weren't exaggerating," he said, rushing forward. "This... this could be monumental."

Emily stepped forward shyly, holding out the silver chain. "I found this," she said.

Rubin clasped her hand warmly. "Miss Wycliff, you've given Israel a gift today. You may keep that chain as a token, but the world will remember your name as part of this discovery."

Her cheeks flushed with delight.

Bob and Joe set the chest on the table, its silver latch still sealed tight. The room hushed as Rubin ran his fingers over the wood. "French design," he murmured. "Twelfth century. A Crusader's chest."

Joe retrieved his knife and carefully slipped it into the gap, prying gently. The latch creaked, ancient metal protesting. Everyone leaned closer, breath held. After tense minutes of cautious work, the latch finally snapped free. Together, they lifted the heavy lid.

The sight inside silenced the room.

Gold coins, thousands of them, shimmered in the lamplight, their surfaces catching fire in the glow. Silver coins spilled between them, and nestled among the glittering mass were gems rubies, sapphires, and diamonds, each one throwing off flashes of red, blue, and white. At the very top lay a ruby-studded ring, still gleaming despite centuries in the sea.

Emily gasped, hand over her mouth. "It's... it's like a dream."

Penny clasped her hands together, whispering, "Lord, thank you."

Joe let out a low whistle. "Two thousand gold coins at least. And that's just what we can see."

Rubin quickly began cataloguing, his practiced eye taking inventory. "Two thousand three hundred gold pieces. A hundred and forty silver. Twelve stones, three to six carats each. This… this is royal treasure."

Bill exhaled slowly. "This changes everything."

They laughed, they hugged, some even cried. Emily threw her arms around each of them, saving Errek for last, where she lingered just a moment longer. He gave her a quiet smile, one that needed no words.

"You're rich," Rubin said finally, his voice heavy with both awe and duty. "And Israel has a find for the ages. We'll announce it at a press conference on Monday. For now, the chest goes into the hotel vault. Guards will arrive in the morning."

The group nodded, still in disbelief.

Dinner that night was nothing short of a celebration. The grouper was grilled to perfection, its tender meat served alongside fresh snapper and sea bass. Platters of hummus, falafel, and warm lachtkas filled the table. Chuck, the hulking bodyguard, devoured his plate with gusto, earning a laugh from everyone.

Emily raised her glass of champagne. "To treasure, to friendship, and to adventures still to come."

"To treasure," they echoed, lifting glasses, cokes, and Dr. Peppers alike.

The night wore on with laughter and stories, the weight of discovery settling slowly over them. For all of them, it was a day that would never be forgotten.

The private dining room carried the soft aroma of grilled fish and baked bread, but no one was thinking about food anymore. Their eyes were still locked on the chest, now sitting open under Rubin's careful supervision. The coins gleamed like captured sunlight, the gems scattering prisms across the table.

Rubin's hand trembled slightly as he catalogued each item, but his voice was steady. "What you have found," he said, "is not just wealth. It is heritage. This chest… these coins… they tell a story of a people fleeing, of treasure carried away in desperation. And thanks to you, it is preserved."

Emily leaned forward, her silver chain still draped across her wrist. "It feels almost too much. I just wanted adventure, a taste of something real. But this this is history."

Penny nodded, her eyes shining. "And providence. We've seen with our own eyes what most people only read about in books."

Joe cleared his throat. "Rubin, what about the scrolls? The jar we found earlier what did it hold?"

Rubin smiled faintly, as though he had been waiting for the question. "Inside the jar was a scroll, and within that, a letter attributed to Matthew. Portions of his Gospel Sermon on the Mount, the first thirteen chapters, and fragments from chapter twenty-three to the end. Scholars have already dated it to around 40 AD."

The room fell silent.

Bill blinked. "Forty AD? That makes it the earliest known copy of a New Testament book."

"Yes," Rubin confirmed. "It mentions Barnabas and even Saul of Tarsus Paul, before his transformation. It also references Mark as a follower of Christ from childhood. The implications are… extraordinary."

Penny whispered, her voice reverent. "That would change everything we know about the early Church."

Rubin straightened, looking each of them in the eye. "You have done what even seasoned archaeologists have not. You've opened doors we didn't even know were there. The IAA is indebted to you, and so is Israel. Your reward will be substantial, but beyond that we want you as part of our permanent staff. You may not be archaeologists by training, but your knowledge, ingenuity, and courage have proven invaluable."

Joe chuckled. "I just wanted to test my detector. Didn't expect it to make us ambassadors."

Rubin smiled warmly. "Ambassadors of the IAA that's exactly what you are now."

Bob, still wiping fish oil from his fingers, leaned closer to the table. "So what happens to all this?" He gestured toward the chest.

"As per our agreement," Rubin replied, "half of the coinage's value goes to you. Specific artifacts, like the sword, dagger, and certain Hebraic objects, must remain with the museum. But I will see that each of you keeps something a coin, perhaps, and a share in the value of the gems. The gold and silver chains those are yours. Consider it both a reward and a reminder of this day."

Emily's eyes brightened. "So I may keep the chain?"

"Yes," Rubin said with a nod. "And Israel will honor you as one of the discoverers. You may not be an archaeologist, Miss Wycliff, but your name will be remembered alongside theirs."

She laughed softly, still in disbelief. "From Hollywood scripts to real treasure hunts… I think this is my best role yet."

The group shared a glance excitement, disbelief, and gratitude mingled in their expressions. Errek's voice broke the silence. "And tomorrow?"

Rubin placed his ledger down firmly. "Tomorrow, you return to the wreck. But you won't go alone. Four of our expert divers will accompany you, using two of your detectors. They will search the inner decks, while you remain in the safer open areas. Whatever they find, you will share in its value. A third, at least. And I promise, there will be more."

Joe whistled low. "So today was only the beginning."

"Yes," Rubin said. "And Monday, there will be a press conference. The world must know what has been discovered and who discovered it. You have given Israel one of its greatest treasures."

Emily's hand brushed Errek's as she spoke softly. "I think we've all found more than we came for."

Errek met her gaze, but said nothing.

The backroom of the hotel restaurant had grown quieter, though the laughter and music from the main hall still drifted faintly through the heavy doors. The long table was now covered with plates of fresh fish, steaming bread, and bowls of hummus and falafel. But scattered among the food lay relics ancient swords, rings, coins that seemed more suited to a museum display than a dinner setting.

Rubin carefully examined the smaller items they had brought from the wreck. He held up the sword, its blade blackened with age, coral clinging stubbornly to its edge. "This," he said, "is likely from the twelfth century. A crusader's weapon, once wielded in desperation. With proper cleaning, it will tell us more its craftsmanship, its origin. Already, it has value beyond gold."

He set the sword down gently and reached for the ring. The ruby glinted even beneath centuries of corrosion. "And this… perhaps a signet ring. It once sealed letters, decrees, maybe even carried authority in battle. Now, it speaks to us across time."

Emily leaned forward, eyes wide. "It's like touching the lives of those who came before. Not just treasure, but stories."

Penny smiled, pleased at her words. "Exactly. Every artifact is a voice from history waiting to be heard."

Joe tapped the chest still sitting half-open at the far end of the table. "I keep thinking about how close we came to missing it altogether. If Bob hadn't misfired, we wouldn't have found the chest wedged in the reef. Funny how mistakes turn into miracles."

Bob chuckled sheepishly. "Guess I'll take credit for that one, then. Maybe I'm better at spearing treasure than fish."

Errek grinned but added in a more serious tone, "It feels like we're being led. Call it luck, call it providence but there's something bigger at play here."

Rubin looked around the table, his gaze lingering on each of them. "You must understand, discoveries like these reshape how the world sees Israel. Not only do they strengthen our heritage, they remind us of the stories woven through these lands the stories of faith, of struggle, of hope. You are part of that now."

He folded his notes and set them aside. "Tomorrow, the dives will continue. The IAA divers will go deeper into the second ship, with your detectors. It may hold more than we can imagine. And when this is done, we will bring your story before the world. You have become witnesses of history and friends of Israel."

The room fell into a warm silence. Each of them felt the weight of Rubin's words, the responsibility and the privilege.

Emily raised her glass water for her, as the champagne remained mostly untouched. "To today," she said softly, "and to tomorrow. To treasure, to history, and to friends."

The group clinked glasses, smiles spreading across tired faces. For all the exhaustion, the salt still lingering in their hair, and the ache in their muscles, there was an undeniable glow of triumph in their eyes.

Bob leaned back with a satisfied sigh. "You know," he said, "this might just be the best fish dinner of my life."

And as the night stretched on, laughter and stories filled the room. Tomorrow promised more dives, more discoveries, perhaps even greater treasures. But for now, they were content resting not just in the luxury of the hotel, but in the knowledge that they had truly become part of history.

Chapter 13: The Treasure Hunt Dives

The aroma of grilled fish filled the air as the group gathered in the hotel restaurant, their bodies weary but spirits soaring from the extraordinary finds of the day. The golden shimmer of treasure was still fresh in their minds, but tonight was about camaraderie, celebration, and reflection.

"Well," Errek said as he slid into his seat, "let's eat. We've earned it. Fresh red mullet straight from the sea and luck still on our side. Maybe tomorrow will be just as good."

Emily, already seated with her two towering bodyguards, smiled as she removed her sunglasses. "Thank you again for letting me join the dive. I can't go tomorrow conference obligations but tonight, dinner with you all is non-negotiable. It would be an honor."

"We're the honored ones," Joe said, lifting his water glass. "You held your own out there. Not every celebrity dives headfirst into the Mediterranean and comes out with treasure."

Emily chuckled and pulled the silver chain from her handbag, running her fingers over the tarnished links. "It's already precious to me. Not because it's ancient or valuable but because I found it while just being Emily, not 'Emily Wycliff.' That alone was worth everything."

Rubin arrived moments later, having secured the treasure in the hotel's private vault. He gave a small nod to Errek. "All secured. We're good for the night."

"Perfect," Errek replied. "And speaking of treasures…"

He reached into his satchel and handed Emily a small velvet pouch. "Your silver chain is safe, and here's a gold coin from the same site. Twelfth century, give or take. Might have belonged to a merchant or a nobleman."

Emily's eyes widened. "I… I can't accept "

"You can," Rubin interrupted gently. "And you should. Besides, we've got plenty to go around."

She accepted the pouch, smiling with a blend of gratitude and awe. "Thank you. I'll get these framed. And in return…" She pulled out a small notepad from her purse. "Autographs. For Gal and Levi, right?"

Bob leaned over excitedly. "Yes! My neice and nephew. They'll go crazy. And, uh, could you sign one for me too?"

"Of course," Emily said, scribbling names. "Actually, I'll have personalized photos sent to the front desk by morning. One for each of you autographed and maybe a short note. You've all given me one of the best days of my life."

Tom and Chuck, the towering, always-stoic bodyguards, tried to melt into the background but failed miserably due to their sheer size. Errek looked up at them and said, "Hey fellas, don't think we forgot about you."

He handed them each a couple of silver coins and one gold coin apiece. "You were part of the team today."

Tom blinked. "Seriously? We just stood around making sure nobody messed with Emily."

"You stood around *with* us," Rubin corrected. "That counts."

The bodyguards, visibly touched, broke into unexpected smiles and gave both Errek and Joe massive bear hugs.

The table exploded in laughter.

Later, the group gathered in Errek's room, laid out on the beds and lounge chairs, the day's excitement still lingering in every breath.

Joe ran a hand through his salt-dried hair. "I can't even begin to guess how much everything is worth. Two thousand coins, silver chains, a gold chain… not to mention what we *gave away*."

Errek leaned back, arms behind his head. "Does it really matter? We found it. We logged it. The IAA gets their half, we get ours. What matters is we *did* it."

Joe grinned. "Still, I'm hoping that second ship tomorrow holds something juicy."

Bill, leaning against the doorway, added, "I'd bet on it. The sonar scans show it's better preserved. Three decks, larger build. Could've been a real merchant vessel or something royal."

Penny chimed in from the couch. "I'm just excited to get a look at what the IAA brings up. Between us and them, this is going to be one for the record books."

Errek turned to Emily. "You sure you can't join us tomorrow?"

She sighed. "Conference meetings morning and afternoon. A gender rights panel, followed by a closed-door cultural preservation discussion. No way out."

"But you'll meet us in Jerusalem?" he asked.

"Absolutely. I'll be there in three days. And I still owe you that walking tour."

Rubin winked. "And maybe a few more gold coins, if we're lucky."

"I'll bring cookies," Emily grinned. "I make a mean pistachio shortbread."

Errek chuckled. "Deal."

By 10:30 p.m., the group had broken up to return to their own rooms. Rubin reminded everyone to be ready by 7:30 a.m. sharp.

"Tomorrow is the real deal," he said. "We've got the IAA team joining us, and the second ship is deeper more dangerous, but possibly richer."

Bob stretched. "What's the depth?"

"About 100 meters," Rubin answered. "Clear visibility, maybe 10 meters max. You'll be down there 30 to 40 minutes. The ship has decompression rooms and dive showers. First class all the way."

Errek nodded. "We'll go in teams again. Joe, Bill, Avi, and I can rotate with IAA divers. Bob and Penny can rest or join light swimming."

Penny shrugged. "I may take photos from above. I think I've earned a short break."

Everyone laughed.

Errek turned serious. "Let's rest. We leave at 8:30."

The next morning arrived with a quiet sense of determination. At 7:15 a.m., most of the team was already in the lobby. They quickly grabbed muffins, bear claws, and quarts of milk from the buffet.

Rubin arrived with the security van. "Everything is loaded," he said. "Ship is waiting at the harbor. Dive gear is checked and packed. Let's make some history."

Ahmad pulled up moments later in the familiar blue Mercedes van. He grinned. "Shall we?"

"Let's roll," Errek replied, climbing into the passenger seat.

As the vans pulled away from the hotel, the mood was a mix of calm, excitement, and tension. Today was no longer casual exploration it was a coordinated dive operation with professionals. And the sea had not yet revealed all of its secrets.

Emily's autographed envelope had been left at the front desk. Inside were 15 signed photos one for each team member, personalized with small notes like: *"To Joe, a real-life explorer"*, *"To Bob, who made me laugh all day"*, and *"To Errek, the best kind of leader quiet, kind, and brave."*

He pocketed the photo and smiled.

Yes, today would be a day worth remembering too.

The salty wind whipped across the deck as the cruiser cut smoothly through the Mediterranean waters. The sun had climbed higher now, glinting off the rippling waves like scattered diamonds. Spirits were high, but beneath the excitement, each of the friends knew this dive was different. Today was no longer just adventure it was coordinated exploration with the **IAA's maritime team**, a step deeper into history.

Rubin clapped his hands once, drawing everyone's attention. "Alright, team. We're about twenty minutes from the first site. It's a smaller wreck likely a supply vessel. Our IAA divers will handle the internal sweep with two of Joe's detectors. The rest of you Joe, Errek, Bob, and Bill you'll run perimeter sweeps with the other two detectors. We'll cover more ground that way."

Joe gave a small grin. "Guess that means we're the fence around the yard. Sweep wide, sweep slow."

"Exactly," Rubin nodded. "Be thorough. Even scraps of chain mail or broken hilts are valuable when logged properly."

Penny leaned against the railing, adjusting her mask strap. "I think I'll stay topside for this one, maybe take a swim later. Yesterday was enough for me."

"Fair," Errek replied. "You've earned it. Besides, someone needs to keep Rubin company."

"Ha," Rubin chuckled. "I'm perfectly fine babysitting from here."

With tanks checked, masks snug, and signals reviewed, the first dive began. The team slipped backwards off the boat one by one, the cool embrace of the Mediterranean swallowing them whole. Immediately, the world transformed. The roar of the waves gave way to muffled silence, only the hiss of oxygen through regulators breaking the stillness. Shafts of light pierced the water, guiding them downward.

The wreck came into view quickly. What remained of the ship was broken but recognizable rotting timbers, a collapsed mast, and gaping holes in the hull. The Mediterranean had claimed it centuries ago, yet traces of its story clung stubbornly to the sea floor.

Errek and Bill took the side closer to shore, while Joe and Bob drifted outward toward deeper waters. Each carried one of Joe's advanced detectors, their blinking lights sweeping across the sand.

Bill gestured to Errek, pointing at a scatter of dark shapes just a few meters ahead. They descended closer, detectors humming. A sharp ping echoed through Errek's headset. He pressed the detector against the sand and began brushing gently.

Something metallic glimmered back.

A small corroded sword emerged, its blade eaten by centuries of salt but its hilt still ornate. Errek lifted it carefully and tucked it into their mesh bag.

Bill, meanwhile, was crouched over a different patch of seabed. His detector sang steadily as he unearthed a gold necklace, twisted but intact. Next to it were two coins, their inscriptions faded but unmistakably Roman. He held them up, eyes wide behind the mask, and Errek gave him a triumphant thumbs-up.

They continued, sweeping another ten yards. The detector pinged again, and this time the find was a thin length of gold chain, still gleaming despite its years below the surface. Errek coiled it carefully into their bag.

By the time they regrouped, they had filled half a satchel with treasures three coins, a necklace, the chain, and the small sword. Not a fortune, but more than they had dared hope so quickly.

Out beyond the wreck, Joe and Bob worked methodically. The deeper waters were darker, but visibility remained good about ten meters across. Their detectors gave off occasional beeps, most of them false signals, bits of iron or splintered nails scattered across the sand.

Then Joe's device gave a strong, steady tone. He signaled Bob, and together they dug into the sand, uncovering a bent strip of chain mail. Not glamorous, but significant. A soldier had once worn this, centuries ago. They bagged it carefully.

Moments later, another ping. Bob knelt, brushing away the silt, and uncovered a cluster of five coins nestled together. They shimmered faintly in the light. Roman silver, perhaps, though one looked distinctly different its faint etching hinted at a crusader's cross.

Bob held it up, eyes wide. Joe gave an enthusiastic nod.

By the time they turned back toward the wreck, they had recovered several more small items: another corroded strip of armor, a bronze buckle, and a chain fragment. Modest, but each piece another fragment of history pieced back together.

The two groups met midway and ascended together, breaking the surface with bursts of spray. They clambered back onto the deck, pulling masks off and exchanging grins.

"Not bad," Joe said, spreading their finds onto the table. "Five coins, chain mail, some odd bits."

"And we've got this," Bill added, laying down the necklace, chain, sword, and coins they had recovered.

Rubin examined everything closely, eyes shining. "Well done. This alone is worth a tidy sum for the museum and more importantly, it adds to the historical record. The ship's story is becoming clearer."

As they sipped water and rested, Avi and the IAA divers surfaced. Their bags clinked heavily as they were lifted aboard. From within spilled a cache of items: two ornate swords, several daggers, nearly fifty loose coins, and most impressively a small chest, half the size of the one found the day before.

Rubin crouched immediately. "Careful. Let's open this in the conference room below."

The chest creaked open under careful hands. Inside gleamed two hundred coins gold and silver mixed alongside a gold signet ring. The kind of ring worn by commanders or nobles.

Gasps spread across the group.

"Now that," Rubin said reverently, "is a find."

The cruiser's engines hummed steadily as it moved further out to sea. The horizon shimmered under the midday sun, but anticipation below deck was heavier than the air outside. The smaller wreck had been fruitful, yet Rubin made it clear the second wreck was the true test.

"This one lies deeper," Rubin explained, tracing a finger across a nautical chart spread on the table. "Nearly one hundred meters down. Visibility is good, but the pressure there isn't forgiving. Our divers will lead the way inside. You'll work perimeter sweeps as before, unless instructed otherwise."

Joe adjusted his mask strap, his voice firm. "A hundred meters means slower ascents, extra caution. No cowboy moves today. We stick to signals, we stick to time limits."

Bob let out a nervous chuckle. "Guess that means no chasing giant groupers this time?"

"Exactly," Joe replied, though the grin behind his regulator betrayed excitement.

Sliding once more into the sea, the divers descended slowly. The water grew darker, the sunlight thinning with every meter. Regulators hissed steadily, a chorus of controlled breaths echoing in the silence. At around eighty meters, shadows loomed ahead the outline of a much larger vessel, its skeletal frame jutting from the seafloor like the bones of some great beast.

As they adjusted their lights and steadied their descent, movement flickered in the edge of the gloom. Two sleek barracuda hovered near the wreck, their silver bodies catching what little light filtered through the water. A moment later, a darker shape glided just beyond the beam of Joe's wrist lamp—broad, deliberate, and unmistakable. A shark.

For several long seconds, no one moved. The divers tightened formation instinctively, keeping their signals slow and deliberate. Joe raised his hand, pointing toward the shadow, then gave the "hold steady" gesture. The barracuda swam closer, circling once before darting away, while the shark lingered near the torn hull of the ship, as though guarding it.

Errek's heart pounded in his chest. One wrong move, and their dive could turn catastrophic. But after an agonizing minute, the shark drifted off into deeper darkness, uninterested. Joe exhaled a controlled stream of bubbles, signaling calm. The team slowly resumed their sweep, tension still thrumming through the water around them.

Rubin's words echoed in their minds: *deeper, more dangerous… but richer.* They all understood now exactly what he meant.

Errek's pulse quickened. *Three decks… still mostly intact.* He signaled to Joe, pointing at the yawning breach in the hull. Joe raised a hand *that's for the IAA divers.* They acknowledged and peeled off toward the opening, lights strapped to their wrists cutting thin beams through the dark water.

Meanwhile, Avi and Bill moved toward the stern, while Joe and Errek began their sweep along the starboard side.

Avi's light flickered across a mound of collapsed timbers near the lower deck. Something metallic caught his eye. He motioned for Bill to help clear the debris. Together, they pried loose a drawer half-buried under the wreckage. With effort, they opened it. Inside lay a collection of objects:

- A gold signet ring, its crest still faintly visible.

- A pearl necklace, surprisingly intact.

- Two fine gold chains, tangled together.

- A small, corroded box that clinked faintly when shaken.

Bill's eyes widened behind his mask. He gave a slow, emphatic thumbs-up. They bagged the items carefully before resuming their sweep.

Nearby, Joe and Errek worked their way around the bow. Their detector whined steadily until Errek uncovered seven gold coins lodged between stones. Joe found something heavier a short dagger, its hilt wrapped in fabric long since turned to sludge, but its blade still intact enough to gleam in the light.

The four regrouped just outside the wreck, their bags already heavy. They shared a quick glance, the kind of wordless conversation divers know well: *We've struck something big.*

Bill tapped his watch and motioned upward. It had been nearly forty minutes. They began their slow ascent, careful and deliberate. Bubbles trailed toward the surface, a fragile ladder back to safety.

Breaking through, they hauled themselves aboard, collapsing onto the deck in near-unison.

Rubin leaned forward as the group emptied their bags onto the table in the conference cabin. "Well? Show me."

One by one, the items gleamed under the electric lights: the signet ring, the pearl necklace, the twin gold chains, the dagger, and nearly a dozen coins. Then Bill set down the small corroded box.

"Let's see what secrets you hold," Rubin murmured. He fetched a knife and carefully pried it open. The lid gave with a groan, revealing a cache of gold coins perhaps a hundred in all alongside a small bar, unmistakably gold, and several scattered jewels.

Everyone froze, staring in silence.

Rubin finally spoke, his voice hushed. "Gentlemen… this is extraordinary. That ring is a royal signet. The kind reserved for commanders or noble bloodlines. And this box it alone is worth a fortune."

Joe sat back, shaking his head in disbelief. "And that was just the lower level. We haven't even seen what else is inside."

Rubin closed the box gently. "No, but we will. The IAA divers are still at work on the upper and middle decks. Whatever they find, combined with this… will rewrite what we know of this ship."

The deck of the cruiser was alive with energy. Everyone leaned over the table in the conference cabin, still marveling at the box of coins, jewels, and the royal signet ring that Joe and Errek's team had uncovered. The hum of the ship seemed to fade as the group exchanged glances that were equal parts disbelief and exhilaration.

Rubin was still scribbling into his ledger when Avi, who had remained on deck, raised a hand. "They're coming up," he said, his voice carrying urgency.

Moments later, the IAA divers broke the surface in pairs, bags slung over their shoulders. Their wetsuits glistened as they climbed aboard, handing up their finds with an almost reverent care. The crew helped haul the heavier satchels, each clinking faintly with the unmistakable sound of metal striking metal.

The first bag opened revealed a trove of personal items ornate rings, bronze cups, and fragments of daggers encrusted with sea growth. The second bag spilled over with coins, gold and silver mingled in a shining cascade across the wooden table. Gasps filled the room.

"Good Lord…" Bob muttered under his breath.

One diver, removing his mask, explained in halting English: "Skeletons. Many. Still lying where they fell. We… we took only what was loose." His eyes were wide, the weight of history heavy on him.

Rubin placed a gloved hand over the pile. "You did well. These belonged to soldiers, sailors, maybe even nobles who died here. And now their legacy resurfaces."

The third bag was more shocking still. Inside were two ornate swords, their hilts inlaid with faint traces of precious stones, and a scimitar with a golden filigree handle that glittered even under its crust of corrosion.

"By heaven," Avi whispered. "That's not common loot. That belonged to someone of status… perhaps even a Marmuk commander."

Finally, the fourth bag was brought forward. Everyone leaned closer as Rubin carefully opened it. Nestled inside were several small wooden boxes, remarkably preserved by the sea. The first opened easily, revealing nearly three hundred gold pieces stacked like miniature suns, alongside about two hundred silver coins.

The second box contained something rarer still: a collection of signet rings, each etched with crests long forgotten, their surfaces dulled by time but unmistakably noble.

Rubin's voice shook slightly. "Gentlemen, you are looking at a fortune. But more than that, you are looking at *history*. These rings tie us directly to men who commanded armies, who shaped the Crusades themselves."

The group sat in awed silence, broken only when Joe exhaled a low whistle. "So between us and the IAA divers…" He gestured toward the amassed finds. "We've uncovered thousands of years of history, and if I'm not mistaken millions of dollars in treasure."

Rubin nodded gravely. "Yes. And yet what matters most is how this will deepen our understanding of those turbulent centuries. Still…" His lips curled into the faintest smile. "I imagine the rewards for your group will be substantial."

Rubin began cataloguing swiftly, dictating aloud as he went:

- 2,450 gold coins (combined finds).

- 350 silver coins.

- 3 ornate swords, 2 daggers, 1 scimitar with filigree handle.

- Several chains, including one silver and multiple gold.

- Jewelry: rings, pearls, necklaces.

- A small bar of gold, weighing close to a pound.

- The royal signet ring.

"Altogether," he concluded, "this represents one of the largest maritime recoveries in Israeli history."

Bob let out a laugh that sounded equal parts nervous and exhilarated. "So… we're rich, then?"

Rubin chuckled. "Perhaps. But more importantly you are now *legends*."

The divers slumped into their seats, fatigue finally catching up with them. Sweat and seawater mingled on their brows, their muscles aching from the strain of deep diving and heavy lifting. Yet the exhilaration was undeniable.

Errek leaned back, staring at the ceiling. "I keep telling myself this is real, but it feels like we've stepped into a storybook. Treasure chests, royal rings, sunken ships it's like living in *Treasure Island*."

Emily's absence was felt, her laughter and energy missing from the day's dive. Penny glanced at the finds and whispered, "She'd have loved this."

Rubin smiled. "There will be time to share the story. And when you stand at the press conference, remember you did more than find riches. You connected us to our past."

The room went quiet, each of them lost in thought, imagining both the warriors who once fought and died aboard the wreck, and the lives that would now be touched by these discoveries.

The ship rocked gently as the sun sank lower on the horizon, bathing the deck in amber light. The treasure lay neatly catalogued in boxes and velvet-lined trays, guarded by two crewmen and an IAA official who would transfer it later to secure storage. The group, exhausted yet still buzzing with adrenaline, began to drift toward their cabins for showers.

"Two stalls at the end of the hall," Rubin reminded them. "First come, first serve."

"I call it!" Errek shouted with a grin, sprinting down the corridor like a kid racing for the best bunk. Laughter erupted from the others, breaking some of the tension still coiled tight from the dive.

Hot water poured over aching muscles. For Errek and Joe, the showers felt like luxury after nearly an hour underwater. They emerged fifteen minutes later, toweling off, their faces relaxed for the first time since surfacing.

"What a day," Joe said, shaking his head. "From fish to treasure chests to royal signets. I almost don't know how to process it."

"You don't," Errek replied. "You just let it sink in. And tomorrow… we might do it all over again."

When they rejoined the others, Penny and Bob were playing a friendly but competitive game of Rook. Bill and Avi entered soon after, still dripping, each carrying small finds from their dive a pair of cups, a dagger, and a handful of coins. Rubin added them to the tally with meticulous care, every artifact treated like sacred scripture.

Rubin finally sat back, removing his glasses, his ledger thick with notes. "Gentlemen," he said, his voice both tired and triumphant, "what you've recovered between yesterday and today is unparalleled. Nearly 2,500 gold coins. Hundreds of silver. Rings, necklaces, weapons of high value. The scrolls alone… priceless."

Bob leaned forward. "So what does that mean… in numbers?"

Rubin smiled. "In raw gold and silver value? Tens of millions. In historical and antique worth? A billion dollars, perhaps more. But your portion, by agreement, will still be life-changing."

The group fell silent, the weight of his words settling in. Wealth had never been their goal, but the reality of it still dazzled.

"And remember," Rubin added, his tone softer, "the museum gains not just coins, but stories. Stories that would have been lost beneath the waves forever. That is your true legacy."

Later, in the quiet of his cabin, Errek dialed Arthur. His voice carried the fatigue of the day, but also the spark of boyish excitement.

"Arthur, you won't believe this," he began.

Arthur chuckled through the receiver. "Try me."

"We found scrolls… coins… over two thousand pieces of gold, Arthur. And a chest. A royal chest filled with jewels, rings, even a gold bar. The IAA catalogued it all. You'll get your return, and then some."

There was silence on the other end, then a sharp exhale. "You're not joking."

"No joke. And there's one more dive tomorrow at Caesarea. Who knows what's waiting there."

Arthur laughed, half in disbelief. "You've outdone Treasure Island, my friend. Just promise me you'll stay alive to tell me the full story."

"I promise," Errek said, smiling as he hung up.

The group gathered once more in the mess, plates of fresh fish laid out before them: grouper, sea bass, snapper, each prepared with local spices that mingled with the salty air. They ate heartily, the fatigue of the dive giving way to laughter and stories.

Penny teased Bob about missing his first shot at a grouper. Joe reenacted the moment Bobby's spear had lodged into the chest, sending the table into uproarious laughter. Even Rubin, usually so measured, chuckled until tears rimmed his eyes.

At one point, Errek leaned back, looking around the table. "You know, this might be the best vacation of my life. The Promised Land, the biblical sites... and now this. Treasure hunting with friends."

Penny raised her glass. "To history. To friendship. And maybe just a little treasure."

Glasses clinked, the sound ringing like a promise into the night.

As the meal ended, Rubin stood once more, his serious tone returning. "Tomorrow we go to Caesarea Maritima. It will be different. The wrecks there are older one Roman from around the 3rd–4th century, and another Marmuk treasure ship from the 12th century that sank in a storm. Both lie just off the harbor in shallow water. In fact, these sites are legendary. In recent years 2015 and again in 2017 divers in this very bay discovered Israel's largest-ever treasure hoards: thousands of gold coins and artifacts from the exact same wrecks we'll be exploring. The IAA normally restricts dives here to scientific teams, but tomorrow, with our detectors and clearance, we have a rare chance. It's dangerous, too. The wrecks are scattered, twisted together by centuries of storms, and predators like barracuda and reef sharks still patrol the waters. Yet the potential is staggering. Every storm uncovers new layers, and history shows that fortune is waiting beneath the sand. We have your detectors and hope to do well. Less explored, but perhaps less forgiving. It will be our last great dive before Jerusalem."

Bob stretched, suppressing a yawn. "One more day, huh? Then we go back to being regular folks."

"Regular?" Bill scoffed. "We'll never be regular again. Not after this."

The group filed off to their cabins, the hum of the ship lulling them toward rest. Outside, the sea shimmered under the moonlight, holding secrets still yet to be uncovered. Tomorrow, they would plunge back into its depths.

But for now, they slept dreaming of gold coins, ancient scrolls, and the thrill of history resting just beneath the waves.

They woke up early that Sunday morning and checked out after loading the luggage, equipment, and all the treasure into Rubin's trunk. It was an hour's drive along the southern coast to Caesarea Maritima. An ancient port of the Roman Empire about an hour from tel Aviv. The time passed quickly as they anticipated the ancient city and its wonders. Bill and Penny elected to tour the city and take pictures, while Avi, Bob, Errek, and Joe would go treasure hunting.

There was a wreck a mile out and two wrecked ships that had sunk from storm damage less than a hundred meters out. People had seen gold coins shining in the sand, and Rubin said that after a diver turned in 30 gold coins, the IAA placed it off-limits except for fishing, but they had permission.

The boys boarded Eli's ship and set out to sea. The first stop was an old shipwreck a mile and a half out, over 100 meters deep a 75-foot Roman ship sunk around 400 AD. The sonar showed a huge hole in the hull, which could provide easy access for the IAA divers, while the gang would sweep all around the ship. It was a simple dive: a slow descent until they hit the floor, then working their way around, one team going one way, the other the opposite. It was straightforward.

Each had about five pings. It was a discouraging dive; they found a total of 10 gold coins, 10 copper coins, and 11 silver Roman coins, along with two gold chains, one silver chain, and some bits of armor. The divers brought up two bags of weapons and a small chest containing rings and about 50 gold and silver coins. A good find, but nothing great.

Meanwhile, Bill and Penny were having fun. They ran five laps on the Hippodrome, took pictures, and moved on to the amphitheater for more photos. They were just enjoying the old town walking, taking pictures of statues, and buying a souvenir or two. The guys would be amazed, pretending to race chariots.

As the IAA boarded, they headed to shore where the two wrecks lay side by side, tossed and turned by time: a Roman ship from the second century and the Marmuk merchant ship around 1200 AD. As they dropped anchors in 15 meters of water, Joe said, "Am I imagining things, or is that 12 pieces of gold right on the seabed?" Joe said, "I'll get those right now," and quickly grabbed and bagged the 12 gold coins, handing them to Rubin.

He turned to Bob. "You're with me. We'll take the far ship and work the perimeter until we get between the two ships." Avi said, "Okay, me and Errek will take the near ship and meet you in the middle." "Are the IAA divers coming?" "No, they're not needed."

They jumped in, and each group started from offshore, working toward land. The pinging was consistent, most less than a foot deep. By the time they met at the shore side, they had recovered about 50 gold coins, and Errek had 10 Roman silver coins since they were working the Roman ship. Joe and Bob were doing much better. They realized the Marmuk side was obviously a treasure ship. They had gold coins and gold chains.

Rubin had said, "We are expecting big things. It is believed the Marmuk ship is a treasure ship based on spearfishers finding gold coins in the sand all the way to the beach." They went all the way to shore and found 10 more gold pieces and spotted seven lying on top of the sand. "This is crazy."

They briefly took off their masks, and Joe said, "I think you work the middle debris, and Avi and I will swim to the deep side, work there, and meet you in the middle." It was agreed. As they swam the 80 feet to the north end, Joe and Bob were busy sifting through debris, finding items.

Avi and Errek started working toward shore. They picked up a nice three-foot gold rope, and occasional pings. About 10 feet in, they hit a really strong ping. Errek removed debris and found eight gold coins together. Still, it kept pinging. Errek got his little pick and delicately removed debris until he struck something solid. He dug all around, and it was a chest with the lid torn off. They had to dig the chest out.

"Can we get this up?" "Well, it's maybe half full, the rest scattered." They gingerly picked it up, made it to the ship, and left Bob and Joe to their fun.

As they got to the ship, the divers helped get the big chest on board. "This is barely holding together." They dumped the chest on the big table. "Good grief, that is a lot of gold and some silver. It's not quite as much as I thought," Rubin said. They started counting, as did Errek and Avi. After several minutes, there were 1,979 gold pieces and 3,012 silver. "Now that is huge," Rubin said, smiling from ear to ear.

Joe and Bob had found seven more gold pieces but decided to enter the torn hull. They saw a broken desk, and in a crevasse in the ship, they saw a porcelain little chest. They tried to remove it, angering a conger eel that slithered partially out. "Patience," Joe said. He pulled out his carbon knife and sliced around the angry eel, trying not to aggravate it. Joe nodded. They waited five minutes, and the eel went back into its hole. They pried the chest out and made a hasty exit. They noticed a few things deeper in the ship and decided to call it a day.

They headed back to the ship with their bag and porcelain box. They made it aboard, put the porcelain box down, and emptied 53 gold pieces and three gold chains. Rubin was smiling. "Do you know what this is? A porcelain chest. More it's a Sultan's box." He opened it: 40 pieces of gold and three big gold rings, one with about an 8-carat ruby, and a copper box. Inside was a small, fully intact copper scroll, protected by the case.

"These three rings are worth about $50,000, the other two maybe $13k each. This scroll box is an incredible artifact. Can we have Penny read it?" "Yes, I would love that, because this scroll is excellent."

They called Bill and said, "We'll be on deck in 15 minutes." "No problem, we've got great pictures, but you must see the Hippodrome—it's magnificent." "No problem. We're going to clean up, see you in 30, and we'll eat and head back to Jerusalem."

They quickly bathed, put on their hiking clothes, and made shore at 12:30 pm. Bill and Penny were waiting, with Almad in tow. They came out, helping Rubin load up everything. Rubin said, "I know a place. Follow me." Soon they were at a nice little restaurant almost across the street from the Hippodrome.

As they piled in, Penny asked, "How did you guys do?" "Not good," Joe said. "Really? I'm sorry," Bill said. Then Joe smiled. "We found 2,500 gold pieces, some gold chains, expensive rings, and this."

Rubin pulled out the porcelain chest and the copper box. Penny said, "I've seen one of these—it's a Sultan's chest." Rubin pulled out the copper box. "It's a Muslim prayer scroll. Just a simple daily prayer a typical prayer, but very, very rare. A Muslim would pay anything for this." They put it back and said, "Well, we've got treasure packed."

They ordered lunch hummus and red mullet ate and then followed Penny and Bill to look at the amazing Hippodrome, like a full stadium with about 12 rows around. "This is amazing. I didn't know these still existed," Joe said. "I can imagine the chariot races they had here."

They then left and started heading home. Soon they were in Tel Aviv and saw the airport, which felt like déjà vu, flying in. An hour later, they were back at the Hilton.

Chapter 14: Jerusalem and an Enchanting Walk

The hum of Jerusalem at dusk was like no other city. The muted golden light washed over the ancient walls, blending old stone with the modern bustle of cars and voices outside the hotel windows. Inside, the group was unwinding after another long day. Rubin, ever the practical guide and mentor, broke the quiet first.

"You all might want to consider getting some proper clothes for tomorrow's press conference," he said, adjusting his glasses as if to emphasize his point. "And something light for walking the city khakis, shirts like the locals wear. Trust me, you'll thank me later."

"If you insist," Bob replied, shrugging but smiling, as though he already knew the rest of the group would follow Rubin's advice.

Soon enough, they were moving toward the hotel's fashion boutique, curiosity overtaking reluctance. The shopkeeper, a cheerful woman with sharp eyes for detail, measured them quickly, pulling out fabrics that seemed designed for the climate. Lightweight khakis, neatly pressed shirts, soft polo tops, and even a few semi-casual suits appeared in their hands before long.

"I just want something semi-casual," Bob said, trying on a shirt in a soft neutral shade. "Nothing too fancy. Something light and comfortable. I don't want to roast tomorrow."

"That works for me," Bill added, nodding approvingly as he felt the airy fabric of a khaki pair.

Rebecca, with her natural flair, chose a modest but elegant dress in pale cream. "If you're all going to look sharp, I'm not being left behind," she teased.

The group admired themselves in the mirrors, laughter bouncing through the store as they adjusted collars and tested fits.

"Man, these clothes feel so much lighter than the ones we packed," Bill said, stretching in his new trousers.

"I know, right?" Bob chuckled. "Feels like I shed ten pounds just changing into these."

Bags in hand, they returned to their rooms, each quietly pleased with their finds. After a short rest, they reconvened around six, making their way down to the hotel's Americana Restaurant for supper with Rubin. The room buzzed with energy waiters moving briskly between tables, the faint sound of a piano echoing from the far corner.

As they sat, Errek's gaze drifted across the room. In the private section, Emily was just finishing a meal with her team. Even from a distance, she carried herself with a mixture of poise and weariness, her beauty softened by the casual tilt of her smile.

"How did your speech go?" Errek asked when she noticed them and came closer.

"A success," she replied brightly. "I'm relieved, honestly. And tomorrow... well, I speak in the evening. Which means, she hesitated just long enough to let the anticipation build "I'll have most of the day free. What about all of you?"

"We've got a press conference at one," Errek said, steadying his tone, though his heart picked up speed. "After that, we're free as well." He paused, then took the leap. "Emily, would you like a private tour of the Holy Sites with me tomorrow? After the conference."

Emily's face lit up, surprise giving way to something warmer. "Oh, I would like that very much." She tilted her head, eyes gleaming with playfulness. "Will the entire entourage be tagging along?"

"Maybe just Tom walking ten feet behind us," Errek joked.

She laughed softly. "Well then, Tom, it's a date."

Tom, sitting a short distance away, looked up, expression unreadable before breaking into a chuckle. "I suppose it is."

"Wonderful," Errek said, trying not to show too much excitement.

Emily excused herself for a few minutes, promising to rejoin them soon. As she walked away, Joe and Bobby exchanged a quick glance before giving Errek subtle fist bumps under the table.

"That's our boy," Bobby muttered, grinning.

At another table, Penny had been watching quietly. She leaned toward Bill with a smirk. "I think our boy finally did it he asked his dream girl out."

"Well, I hope she didn't turn him down," Bill whispered back.

"Not a chance. She likes him," Penny said firmly. "You can see it in the way she lights up around him. Honestly, he's one of the only guys who treats her like a normal person. She needs that." Her smile softened. "I'm happy for them. Even if she is a little younger than him."

Bill chuckled. "Sometimes, Penny, I think she's more mature than he is. Don't say anything though he's coming back."

As Errek slid into his chair again, Bobby leaned forward. "So? How did it go?"

"She said yes," Errek replied simply, though the grin tugging at the corners of his mouth betrayed him.

"Well, that's great," Joe said. "Now, dress smart for walking. Maybe that light blue polo and get yourself a pair of nice sunglasses while you're at it."

Errek laughed, letting the teasing wash over him. "Okay, okay. Now let's order some grub."

They enjoyed a light supper matza ball soup for some, grilled fish for others. The conversation was easy, laughter frequent, and beneath it all ran a current of excitement. Tomorrow held weight: the press conference, yes, but also the promise of a walk through Jerusalem with Emily.

For now, though, they settled into the evening's rhythm. The day had been long, and tomorrow was bound to be even more so, yet each of them carried an unspoken sense that something special was unfolding not only for their discoveries and reputations, but for Errek's heart as well.

After supper, the group strolled back through the softly lit corridors of the hotel. The air smelled faintly of citrus and lavender from the lobby's floral arrangements. Guests passed by in crisp suits and flowing dresses, but the team was focused on their own rhythm of camaraderie and routine.

"I think I may hit the treadmill," Bill said, stretching his arms as if warming up already.

"Rook at 8:30 still sound good?" Errek asked, turning to the others.

"Perfect," Bob replied. "But first, gym time. I feel lighter I want to prove it on the scale."

"I'm in," Bobby said, his grin betraying the competitiveness still buzzing beneath his easygoing manner.

Together, the men changed into gym clothes and headed downstairs. The fitness center wasn't large, but it was well-kept: rows of treadmills, racks of dumbbells, and mirrors that doubled the appearance of space. The hum of machines blended with upbeat music piped from hidden speakers.

Bobby stepped on the scale first, leaning forward to check the dial. "Two-fifty!" he announced, pumping his fist triumphantly.

"Nice," Errek said, stepping up next. He watched the needle swing and land precisely at 205. "I thought I felt lighter." He exhaled with satisfaction. "First time in forever I've been at that weight. Bill, at five-foot-nine and naturally slim, didn't even bother stepping on the scale. "Lucky to break 140 on a good day," he joked, shaking his head.

As they traded places on the treadmills and weight benches, Penny wandered into the gym quietly, curiosity pulling her toward the scale. She stepped on, checked the reading, then hopped off with a subtle pump of her fist, a small gesture of triumph. She caught Errek's eye across the room and gave him a sheepish grin.

"Six pounds lighter," she confessed later, as they regrouped. "Almost catching up with you, Errek."

"You'll always be ahead of me, Penny," he teased.

Back in the room, they gathered around the small table to set up for Rook. The familiar ritual brought them together in a way that no gym session could the shuffle of cards, the playful arguments over bidding, the laughter spilling into the night.

"Two-fifty," Bobby repeated proudly as he arranged his hand. "That number has been taunting me for years."

"Two-oh-five and a 38-inch waist," Errek added. "Feels surreal."

"You're almost as thin as me, dear," Penny teased Bill before nudging him with her elbow. "Oye, dingo," she added playfully in her accented lilt.

The room filled with chuckles. Bobby leaned in, eyes gleaming mischievously. "So... you and Emily going to smoochie-kiss tomorrow, or what?"

"I wish," Errek said, shaking his head but smiling. "Just a nice walk. If sparks fly, then they fly."

"We'll see," Bobby said, raising an eyebrow knowingly.

Conversation drifted toward the basketball tapes Errek had picked up earlier. He fanned them out on the table like treasure maps.

"These guys are serious," Bill said, examining one of the cases.

"They look like playoff contenders," Joe remarked. "Better than starting from scratch."

"Maybe," Errek replied. "But I need to see for myself."

After a few more hands of Rook, they called it a night around 9:30. The others drifted back to their rooms, but Errek stayed behind, slipping the first tape into the player. The flickering images of a recent playoff game filled the small television screen.

He leaned forward, elbows on his knees, eyes tracking every movement on the court. Notes piled quickly in his lap: rebounds missed, defensive lapses, strengths in guard play, weaknesses in the post.

"These top two teams are destroying us at the rim," he muttered to himself. "Our point guard is one of the best in the league, our three can score, but no rebounding. We need a bigger, stronger forward who can crash the glass."

He paused the tape, scribbled furiously, then resumed. Sayid came to mind his size, his rebounding, his sheer physicality. Not as tall as the opposing power forwards, but stronger, hungrier, more dependable. "He could actually help us. We'd be better with him."

The game continued, showing flashes of brilliance from the current roster but also glaring gaps. "Our post is good, but he needs help. A stronger small forward could turn the tide. Fourteen points and three rebounds won't cut it against these teams. My guy could give us seventeen and six, easy."

The analysis consumed him. He scrawled arrows and percentages, weighing options, imagining scenarios. The more he wrote, the more excited he grew. It wasn't just numbers it was the thrill of strategy, of building something bigger than himself.

By the time he switched off the TV, nearly midnight had come. The room was quiet, the city outside hushed save for the occasional honk of a distant horn. He leaned back, exhaustion tugging at his eyelids, but his mind still humming with plays and lineups.

He thought briefly of Emily her laughter at supper, the way her eyes had lit up when he asked about the walk. Tomorrow wasn't just about basketball or press conferences. Tomorrow was about something else entirely, something far more personal. With that thought warming him, he finally let sleep take him.

The following morning dawned quietly, but inside the hotel there was a current of anticipation running through the group. The press conference loomed large an event none of them had ever imagined being part of when they first stepped foot in Israel.

Errek woke late, around nine, to the sound of faint city traffic outside the window. The room was empty, his brother already gone. He poured himself a cup of coffee and set up another tape from the championship series, notebook open beside him.

The game unfolded on the screen, two of the league's powerhouses clashing in a battle that highlighted exactly what Jerusalem's squad lacked. Errek scribbled, muttering under his breath: "Rebounding, rebounding… we're losing the glass every possession. Point's strong, three is good offensively but no boards. Local post at 6'8" decent but not dominant. We need physicality inside."

Sayid's name returned to his mind again and again. "Not quite as tall, but stronger. He could hold his own. Pair him with a scoring forward who rebounds… that changes the whole dynamic." His pen moved quickly, mapping scenarios, jotting down possible rotations.

By 11:30, he set the notes aside and joined the others for brunch. The group gathered in the dining area, sunlight spilling through the windows onto their table. Plates were filled with eggs, cheeses, warm pita, olives, and steaming mugs of coffee.

"Sleep in, coach?" Bobby teased.

"Yeah," Errek admitted. "But I got in another game tape. Learned a lot. Our weaknesses are glaring, but they're fixable."

Joe raised an eyebrow. "Already sounding like it's your team."

"I don't know about that yet," Errek replied. "But I'll be ready if the offer's real."

They lingered over brunch until noon before heading upstairs to rest. Just as Errek returned to his room, Bob met him at the door.

"Rubin left a message," Bob said. "Lobby at 12:45 for notes with him and Eli. Shouldn't take long."

At the appointed time, the group assembled in the lobby. Rubin was waiting, his usual energy tempered by the formality of the day. He motioned them into a small conference room where Eli was already seated with a folder of notes.

"Friends," Rubin began warmly, "today is important not just for you, but for us at the Antiquities Authority. You've done remarkable work, and the world will hear about it."

Eli adjusted his glasses, speaking with calm authority. "I'll open the conference, thank the Authority's team, and highlight your contributions. Then Errek, you'll speak brief, but enough to introduce everyone. Joe, you'll detail the technology. Rebecca, you'll discuss the scrolls. Bill , the language software. Afterward, we'll take questions."

"Keep it natural," Rubin added. "Speak from the heart, as you always do. That's why people listen."

They nodded, nerves buzzing under the surface. None of them were strangers to responsibility, but a global press event was something else entirely.

When they finally entered the main conference hall, the sight was overwhelming. Television crews from Israel, the U.S., and Britain lined the back wall. Reporters filled rows of chairs, pens and recorders ready. Cameras flashed as they took their seats at a long table facing the crowd.

"Good grief," Joe muttered, leaning toward Bob. "Wasn't expecting this."

"Don't worry," Bob whispered back. "Errek's a talker. He's got this."

At the podium, Eli rose, his voice firm and measured. For ten minutes he spoke, weaving a story of discovery and collaboration. "These friends of the Israel Antiquities Authority are true heroes," he declared. "Because of their skill and ingenuity, we recovered more than 5,000 pieces of gold and silver chains, rings, signet seals, cups, daggers, and more from shipwrecks off Acre and Caesarea Maritima."

Reporters scribbled furiously. Cameras clicked in rapid succession.

Eli continued, his voice carrying conviction. "Normally, we advise people to leave artifacts untouched, but these explorers possessed technology beyond our reach sonar and metal detection devices far superior to our own. Developed by Professor Joe Smith, these tools uncovered treasures hidden six feet beneath sand and debris. They have changed what is possible."

The praise rolled on, highlighting Errek's biblical knowledge and leadership, Penny's linguistic expertise, Billl's groundbreaking translation software, and Bob's inventive problem-solving. Each name drew attention, each contribution woven into the larger narrative.

Finally, Eli concluded: "They have proven themselves not only gifted but faithful friends to Israel and to history. And so I now present to you, Errek Johnson."

A swell of applause filled the room. Errek rose, heart thudding, and walked to the podium. He gripped it firmly, steadying himself as the lights glared down.

"We never expected any of this," he began, his Southern cadence lending warmth to the words. "I came here out of a love for biblical history, to stand where Scripture comes alive. To imagine, to relive, to share it with my friends. What we found… was beyond imagination. But the real treasure is the faith and friendship binding us together."

He glanced at his companions, pride flickering in his eyes. "Joe is a genius inventor. Penny's devotion to ancient languages brings the past to life. Bill used her expertise to create a translator that bridges barriers. My brother Bob well, he's always been an out-of-the-box thinker with a deep love for Scripture. I just had the joy of bringing us together."

He paused, letting the words settle, then gestured toward his friend. "And so I'd like to introduce Professor Joe Smith."

Joe stood, straightening his jacket as he moved to the microphone. His opening words drew chuckles "I really just wanted to scuba dive in the Dead Sea" before he launched into details of his devices, their precision, and the dives themselves. He credited Avi Breslin and the Dead Sea Divers, recounting how a misfired spear at Acre led to the discovery of a treasure chest. The reporters leaned in, captivated by the mix of serendipity and science.

When Penny spoke, her calm authority silenced the room. "I am simply a student of ancient languages," she said modestly, though everyone knew her expertise was far from ordinary. She described identifying Aramaic and Hebrew fragments, her work transcribing texts on-site, and her dream of continued collaboration with both the British Museum and the IAA.

Bill followed, demonstrating the translator's potential. He recounted conversations with locals where every word shifted seamlessly from English to Hebrew and back again. Laughter rippled through the hall as he quipped, "It even works when Bobby starts talking too fast."

Finally, Penny turned the stage back to Errek, who closed with words of gratitude: "We are blessed beyond measure to stand here. Blessed by Rubin, Eli, and the IAA. Blessed by this land. May we continue to learn, to preserve, and to share its treasures with the world. Shalom, and God bless Israel, America, and Great Britain."

Applause thundered across the room.

Then came the questions sharp, probing, sometimes skeptical. "So one of the greatest finds in decades came by accident?" a reporter asked.

"Yes," Joe replied without hesitation. "And you can thank Bob for being a bad shot." Laughter erupted, the tension breaking.

"What compensation are you receiving?" another pressed.

"That's between us and the IAA," Errek said firmly. "But know this: what we value most is the preservation of history."

Another asked about the scrolls. Penny leaned forward, her tone reverent. "One is a fragment of Matthew, dated around 40 A.D. earlier than any known copy. Another letter suggests Mark was present as a boy during Christ's ministry, the one who brought the loaves and fishes. These are not just priceless artifacts they are affirmations of faith."

Gasps rippled through the hall. Reporters exchanged wide-eyed glances, scribbling furiously. The weight of the revelation hung in the air like incense.

As the conference closed, Rubin leaned toward Errek, whispering with a grin, "Well done. You handled that like a veteran."

Errek exhaled, relief washing over him. It was over or rather, just beginning.

The conference ended with a swirl of cameras and handshakes, the group filtering out into the hallway, flushed with relief. Reporters still shouted questions, but Rubin and Eli deftly handled them, shielding their friends from being overwhelmed.

As they stepped aside, Rubin clapped a firm hand on Errek's shoulder. "So, my friend," he said with a knowing grin, "are you interested in the Jerusalem coaching job?"

"Without a doubt," Errek replied, the answer leaving his lips before he could even second-guess himself.

"Excellent," Rubin said, his smile widening. "We'll talk more later. But for now I think you have a date."

The grin that spread across Rubin's face was matched only by the spark of nervous excitement in Errek's chest. Emily had been waiting quietly at the back during the conference, her expression glowing with pride as he spoke. Now she stood near the exit, sunglasses perched on her head, her presence luminous in the bustle of the hotel.

By two o'clock, Errek was in the lobby, dressed in his new light khaki shorts, a soft blue polo, and a pair of simple sunglasses. He felt more casual than he had in weeks, and yet strangely more nervous. The elevator doors opened and Emily appeared, stunning in khaki shorts, a fitted dark blouse, and a wide-brimmed hat that framed her face perfectly. She carried herself with effortless grace, but when her eyes met his, she smiled like any ordinary woman excited for an afternoon walk.

Behind her, of course, loomed Tom massive, steady, dressed down from his usual formality but radiating the unmistakable "don't try anything" aura of a professional bodyguard.

The three of them stepped into the waiting car and soon were heading toward the Garden of Gethsemane. The ride passed with light conversation, the air carrying both excitement and a trace of nervous silence.

As they arrived, Errek led them into the garden's quiet, shaded paths. The ancient olive trees stood sentinel, their gnarled trunks witnesses to centuries of prayer and anguish. The church nearby shimmered in the midday sun, its golden mosaics glinting like divine fire.

"Here," Errek said softly, "is where Jesus prayed before He was arrested. The very ground we're walking on is steeped in His sorrow and His strength."

Emily gazed around, her expression softening. "It feels… peaceful. Sacred. Like the air itself carries His prayers."

They found a bench beneath an olive tree. For a time, they simply sat, talking about life, about faith, about the unexpected turns that had led them both here. The conversation drifted easily her films, his coaching, their shared love of history. Slowly, though, Errek felt his heart pounding louder.

Finally, he drew a steady breath. "Emily… I need to tell you something. You're beautiful. And I've had a crush on you since the moment I saw you. I'm older, and I'm not always bold about romance. But I couldn't keep it to myself any longer."

Her eyes softened, a smile curving her lips. "I kind of figured," she admitted with a light laugh. "Penny hinted at it. And… I like you too, Errek. You treat me like a normal person. Not like a celebrity. Not like someone to impress. Just… me."

Her hand lifted gently to his cheek, and before he could react, she leaned forward and kissed him soft, unhurried, a kiss that carried both promise and relief. When she pulled back, her voice trembled slightly. "See? I really like you too. You're the kindest man I've met."

Errek's world seemed to spin. His chest tightened with something that was both joy and disbelief. "Is that a good thing?" he asked, almost afraid to hope.

"It's the best thing," she whispered.

They rose together and wandered deeper into the Old City. She pointed at the golden onion domes of the Russian Church of Mary Magdalene. He showed her the Chapel of Ascension, where tradition said Christ's footprints marked the stone. They passed through St. Stephen's Gate, pausing where the first Christian martyr was stoned, then stopped at the Pools of Bethesda where Roman columns still stood guard over waters once believed to heal.

"This," Errek said as they stood at the edge, "is the start of the Via Delarosa."

Her eyes lit up. "The Way of the Cross? I've always wanted to walk it."

"Then we'll do both routes," he promised. "The Catholic way, and the Protestant way near Gordon's Calvary. You'll see both."

Emily glanced at Tom, who gave only a bewildered shrug, and she laughed, slipping her hand into Errek's as they set off.

The narrow streets wound before them, the sounds of the market mixing with the solemnity of sacred sites. They visited the Church of the Flagellation, pausing in silence where Jesus was said to have been scourged. At Ecce Homo, the spot where Pilate presented Christ to the crowd, Emily grew quiet, her hand tightening around Errek's.

When they finally stepped outside Damascus Gate and followed the path toward the Garden Tomb, the air seemed to shift. The garden there was tranquil, blooming with flowers and echoing with birdsong. They stood before Golgotha's rocky face, the skull-like features etched starkly into the cliff.

"This," Errek whispered, pointing, "is where Joe and Bill found the scroll and letters. A fragment of Matthew. A letter proving Mark was there as a child, the boy who gave Jesus the loaves and fishes."

Emily's eyes widened, her breath catching. "That's… incredible. To be standing here where it happened."

They entered the tomb itself, cool air brushing over their skin. The small, empty chamber seemed to vibrate with holiness. Emily's shoulders shook as tears welled in her eyes. "Sometimes I doubt," she confessed, her voice breaking. "But standing here… it reaffirms everything. He lives."

Errek took her hand gently. "Through His sacrifice, we have forgiveness. Peace. Eternal life. That's the real treasure."

They emerged into the sunlight, hearts heavy with awe, before retracing their steps toward the Church of the Holy Sepulcher. There, amidst the crowds, they knelt together at the anointing stone and pressed their hands to the cold rock inside the traditional tomb.

As they left, Errek put an arm around her shoulders. "He loved you this much, Emily," he whispered. "And I only wish I could love you the same way."

Tears glistened in her eyes as she leaned into him. "You already do," she said softly.

The evening came with the quiet hum of the hotel settling down for the night. Errek spent the hours after the press conference in a haze of anticipation. He changed into light khaki trousers and a brown polo, still hearing Rubin's teasing reminder echoing in his head: *You have a date.*

Emily's women's conference had gone smoothly. She had spoken with confidence, the audience captivated by her reflections on equal rights and the role of women in society. Though the subject was different from the treasures and holy sites that filled Errek's mind, he admired her composure. Beneath the fame, she was a woman with conviction, someone who wanted her life to matter in more ways than a string of films and interviews.

By nine o'clock, Errek was waiting at the pool, his heart pounding like a drum. He stretched out on a lounge chair, staring at the water that shimmered under soft lights. A warm night breeze carried the faint scent of jasmine.

And then Emily appeared.

She wore a sarong that slid away as she approached the pool, revealing a sleek black bikini that caught the glow of the lights. Her hair tumbled loosely over her shoulders, her figure graceful and strong. For a moment, Errek was certain he had stepped into a dream.

"Let's swim a little," she said with a playful smile.

He followed her into the pool, nerves giving way to the cool embrace of the water. They swam lazily, drifting close, talking and laughing about the day. At one point, Emily cornered him against the edge of the pool, her arms circling his neck. She pressed her lips to his, and the kiss stole his breath away. For a heartbeat, he wondered if it was truly happening that his dream girl was here, in his arms, choosing him.

"You're amazing, Errek Johnson," she whispered between kisses. "Do you know that?"

"I care for you deeply," he admitted, his voice low, almost trembling. "I've been smitten since London, and through every letter since. You're beautiful, yes but more than that, you're kind and giving. You treat people with respect even when they expect you to be untouchable."

Her forehead rested against his, her eyes shining. "I like you because you're different. You're humble, gentle… and you see me as just Emily."

For a while, they simply held each other in the water, speaking quietly of dreams and fears. She confessed how her career consumed her, how the endless travel and expectations left little space for a real life. He told her of coaching, of the opportunity Rubin hinted at, and of his longing for a home grounded in faith and friendship.

"Let's go to the hot tub," Emily suggested softly. "I just want to hold you."

The water bubbled warmly around them, and they settled close, her head on his shoulder, his arms wrapped protectively around her. For a fleeting moment, the world outside ceased to exist. She whispered how she had dreamed of someone who would love her not for fame or beauty but for her soul. He whispered back that he had dreamed of someone who would let him love with patience and honesty.

But then, the evening shifted.

Emily grew suddenly quiet, her breath shallow. She pressed her hand to her forehead. "I… I'm feeling dizzy," she murmured.

Alarm shot through Errek. He helped her sit up, brushing damp hair from her face. Her skin was hot, flushed in a way that wasn't from the steam. "Emily, you don't look well. Let's get you out."

She tried to stand but her knees buckled, and she collapsed softly into his arms. Panic knotted in his chest as he lifted her from the hot tub, carrying her to a sofa near the cabana. "Stay with me," he urged, fetching a bottle of cold water and pressing it into her hands. She managed a few sips but still looked pale, her voice faint.

"This isn't right," Errek muttered. He scooped her into his arms once more and carried her to the elevator, heart hammering. The doors opened on the penthouse floor where Tom and Chuck sprang to their feet the moment he entered with Emily cradled against his chest.

"Something's wrong," he said quickly. "She nearly passed out in the hot tub."

They hurried her to the bed, where Errek laid her gently down and pulled a blanket over her. The hotel doctor arrived within minutes, his face grave as he examined the small bottles of pills Emily had taken earlier.

"These aren't the same," the doctor said, holding up two nearly identical containers. "One is her normal medication. The other… I'll have to test, but it could cause dizziness, fainting even heart strain."

The words hit Errek like a stone. His mind raced: *Had she been given the wrong prescription? Or something worse?*

The doctor checked her pulse and listened to her heart. "She's weak, but stable. Keep her hydrated, and let her rest. She should recover by morning."

Relief washed over Errek, though the worry still pressed heavily on him. He stayed by her bedside, holding her hand while Tom and Chuck hovered close. At one point she stirred, whispering, "I'm cold." He gently pulled off his t-shirt and slipped it over her, tucking the blanket around her shoulders.

"Rest," he said softly. "I'm here."

Her eyes fluttered open just enough to meet his. "I love you," she whispered, the words so faint he barely heard them.

His heart ached with a tenderness deeper than he had ever known. He kissed her forehead and whispered back, "I love you too. Sleep well, Emily."

By the time midnight approached, she was breathing evenly, asleep at last. Errek stood reluctantly, turning to Tom. "Take care of her. Let me know in the morning how she is. It wouldn't be right if I stayed."

Tom gripped his arm, his face uncharacteristically soft. "Thank you. You may be her suitor, but tonight you proved you're more than that. You're the kind of man she needs."

Exhausted, Errek made his way back to his room. The group was waiting, eyes wide with curiosity and worry. He told them everything how the evening had been wonderful until Emily had collapsed, how the doctor had reassured them, how he had stayed by her until she was safe.

Joe shook his head slowly. "You did the right thing. You cared for her. That means more than anything else."

Bobby smirked, trying to lighten the mood. "Yeah, but did you at least get a kiss?"

Errek smiled faintly, his thoughts still tangled in the memory of Emily whispering "I love you." "Yes," he said quietly. "And it was the most amazing kiss of my life."

Morning came quietly, though Errek had hardly slept. His mind had circled through the night, replaying Emily's collapse, the doctor's calm reassurances, and the whispered words she had left him with before drifting into rest. By the time dawn broke, he decided to slip out early for breakfast, leaving Bob still snoring softly in the next bed.

The dining room was nearly empty, the buffet just being replenished with fruit and bread. He filled a plate lightly, poured a glass of orange juice, and chose a quiet table in the corner, his thoughts heavy. He was unsure had he done enough? Had he said too much? Did Emily now see him as a protector, a friend, or something more?

A tap on his shoulder startled him from the reverie. Turning, he found himself looking up at Chuck, towering as always but softer in expression. "Miss Wycliff would like to see you," he said simply, gesturing toward the private dining room.

Errek's pulse quickened. He rose, setting aside his breakfast, and followed Chuck into the quieter section where Emily sat waiting. She looked fragile but radiant, her hair tied loosely back, dressed in casual travel clothes that were simple and disarming. On the table before her sat only tea and toast.

"Hi, Emily," he said softly. "How are you feeling?"

"Better," she replied with a small smile. "I was nervous last night, and I took my anxiety pills before coming down. I think the hot tub made everything worse. I'm so sorry if I scared you."

"Don't apologize," Errek said quickly. "You don't have to. I was worried, yes but more than that, I was honored to be there to take care of you. You're not just a movie star to me, Emily. You're someone I care for deeply."

Her eyes glistened with an emotion he hadn't seen before a mix of vulnerability and relief. "You know," she whispered, "I had the sweetest dream last night. I woke up and you weren't there. I felt… disappointed."

Errek shifted, struggling with the knot of emotions rising in his chest. "I couldn't stay. It wouldn't have been right. People would have misunderstood. More importantly, I never want to do anything that would hurt your reputation. I left because I wanted to protect you, even if it meant breaking my own heart."

Emily reached across the table and took his hand. "You respect me more than I respect myself sometimes. That means more than you can know."

He took a breath, steadying himself, and laid his heart bare. "I don't know what the future holds, Emily. But I know what I want. I want to be with you not for your fame or fortune, not because you're stunning, though you are. I want to be with you because of your kindness, your heart, and your spirit. Love isn't about proving yourself through passion it's about self-sacrifice, loyalty, patience. That's what I want with you. A commitment, built slowly, honestly."

Her lips trembled as she tried to smile. "You're amazing, Errek. I don't know if I'm ready for all that, but I want to be. You make me feel like I could be."

They talked quietly over tea, the minutes passing too quickly. Emily confessed she often felt used by the industry, by people who wanted her fame, or by those who wanted to claim her as a conquest. With Errek, she said, it was different. For once she felt like herself, not a commodity.

"You gave me the most beautiful day," she said softly. "From the garden to the old city, to the tombs and holy places… it was more than I ever dreamed. And then, last night even though I nearly ruined it you still treated me with care and patience. That means everything to me."

"You didn't ruin anything," Errek replied gently. "It was perfect, because it was real."

She leaned forward, pressing her lips to his in a kiss that was tender but filled with longing. "I don't know what will happen, Errek. But I do know this you are different. You're the kind of man I've been searching for without even knowing it."

He squeezed her hand. "Then let's just take it step by step. No rush. We'll figure it out together."

They sat for a moment longer, quiet, content in the fragile peace of the morning. Then Chuck returned, reminding Emily gently that her car would leave soon for the airport. She stood reluctantly, shouldering a small bag, and turned back to Errek one last time.

"You look good in my t-shirt, by the way," he teased softly.

She laughed, the sound bright and real. "Comfort over glamour today. Besides, maybe no one will even notice me this way."

"You'd look beautiful in anything," he said simply.

Their final hug lingered. Emily whispered against his ear, "I'll think of you. Always. Maybe I'll come back at Christmas. Maybe sooner."

And then she was gone, her guards escorting her out through the quieter exit reserved for VIPs.

Errek remained in the private room, both elated and heartsick, feeling the absence of her presence already. Tom appeared at the door and gave him a firm nod. "She cares for you, more than you realize. You're the best man she's met, Errek. I'll remind her of Bethlehem at Christmas. For her sake, I hope she finds her way back to you."

When Bill and Penny arrived minutes later, they found him still staring at the empty seat across from him. "She respects you," Penny said gently. "And she cares for you. Sometimes that's all you can ask for at the beginning."

Joe, ever the blunt friend, clapped him on the shoulder. "You did right, my friend. You acted like a true gentleman. Whatever happens, that matters more than anything."

Errek nodded slowly, his heart heavy but full. He knew this was only the beginning whether of a love story or just a treasured memory, time would tell. For now, he held onto one truth: in Jerusalem, he had not only touched history but also glimpsed a future he had never dared to hope for.

Chapter 15: Tunnel Tour and Some Hidden Tunnels

After returning to our rooms, we decided to rest for a while, the events of the past few days still fresh in our minds. The adrenaline of treasure hunting, diving, and unexpected discoveries had left us both exhilarated and exhausted. So, in the comfort of our hotel suite, we spread a deck of cards across the table and spent the late morning hours playing friendly games, teasing one another, and sharing inside jokes.

"I'm not hungry," Bobby muttered as the others suggested ordering lunch.

"You at least need some juice," Bill reminded him, "Stay hydrated. Rubin's coming soon, and something tells me he's got big plans."

Right on cue, Rubin appeared, his presence commanding yet warm, as always. His eyes held the spark of a guide who lived to uncover the hidden secrets of his homeland.

"Friends," he began, "this afternoon we will venture into the ancient heart of Jerusalem. I've arranged a tour of the Pool of Siloam and several connected tunnels. These are not just any tunnels; they are a bridge to our past, carved by kings and preserved by faith. First, the Siloam Tunnel it was Hezekiah's aqueduct, channeling life-giving water from the Gihon Springs directly to the Pool of Siloam inside the city walls. It was both a marvel of engineering and an act of faith during the Assyrian siege."

We leaned forward, captivated. Rubin continued, "From there, we can follow the underground bridge that runs along the lower aqueduct leading into the Western Wall tunnels. This will bring us to chambers rarely understood by outsiders ancient cleansing pools, underground synagogues, massive vaulted spaces, remnants of markets and stores, all built beneath Jerusalem's living city. The visible Western Wall you know is but a fraction of what lies beneath. While most pilgrims see 150 feet, in truth, the Wall stretches nearly 1,500 feet underground."

"Wait," Penny interrupted, eyes wide. "You mean there's practically an entire hidden city beneath the Wall?"

"Exactly," Rubin replied with a knowing smile. "It is like walking back into the First and Second Temple periods layer upon layer of history. You will see the Holy of Holies site beneath, the closest point to the original Temple, preserved in sanctity. And tonight, after our journey, I have made reservations for all of us at a remarkable little place called *Under the Arches*. It's the only functioning restaurant hidden within the tunnel system an unforgettable dining experience."

We nodded eagerly, buzzing with anticipation. Rubin, noticing our casual attire, added, "One piece of advice: wear your hiking boots. The Siloam and City of David tunnels still run with water in places. The stone floors can be slick, and you'll want steady footing. As for dinner, a nice polo and walking shorts will suffice. Tonight will be a blend of exploration and reverence."

With our plans established, we organized our belongings and methodically placed water bottles, cameras, and flashlights into our backpacks. Rubin's enthusiasm was contagious, and though some of us had grown used to his historical detours, we knew that with him every stone had a story.

The cab ride from the hotel to Gihon Springs was filled with chatter. The streets of Jerusalem bustled with their usual mix of pilgrims, shopkeepers, and tourists. The golden hue of the afternoon sun bathed the city, reminding us again why this land was called holy by so many.

Soon we arrived at the entrance to the ancient tunnel system. The faint trickle of water echoed from within, its steady rhythm beckoning us forward. Rubin pointed to the narrow stone archway carved thousands of years ago.

"This," he said reverently, "is where Hezekiah's men began their task. Imagine two teams of workers, starting at opposite ends, chiseling through solid limestone with nothing but crude tools, until by faith and persistence they met in the middle."

We stepped inside, the cool dampness immediately enveloping us. Shadows danced against the rough-hewn walls as our flashlights flickered across centuries-old stone.

"It's larger than I expected," Joe remarked, brushing his hand along the wall.

"The tunnel runs about 580 meters," Rubin explained. "And near its middle is an inscription ancient Hebrew etched into the stone. It describes the moment the workers heard each other's voices echoing through the rock as they broke through, completing the waterway."

Sure enough, halfway through the tunnel, Rubin stopped and shone his light on a smooth section of the wall. Penny stepped closer, her eyes scanning the faint yet deliberate carvings.

"Well?" Bob asked impatiently.

She squinted, then smiled. "It's the Siloam Inscription. It says the tunnel was cut so the waters would flow into the city, safe from the enemy outside. King Hezekiah did not want Sennacherib and his Assyrian army to have free access to the springs. Two groups started from opposite ends and met here. Think of it two tunnels meeting precisely in the middle without modern tools. It's incredible."

We stood in silence, humbled by the ingenuity of a people whose survival depended on such faith-driven engineering.

Rubin continued, his voice reverberating in the stone chamber. "Later, other tunnels were built channels from Solomon's Pools to the Temple, possibly even chambers designed to hide sacred treasures. Some believe Solomon himself constructed emergency vaults beneath the Temple for times of siege."

Bob chuckled softly. "Sounds like exactly the kind of place someone would hide the Ark of the Covenant."

Rubin nodded knowingly. "Many have thought the same."

We pressed on, our footsteps splashing softly in the shallow stream that still flowed beneath us. Despite the damp chill, there was an odd serenity here, as though time itself had paused to preserve the faith of Jerusalem's kings. Each step seemed to carry us deeper not just into stone, but into history itself.

When we finally emerged from the narrow Siloam passage, blinking against the sunlight, it felt almost surreal. For nearly half a kilometer we had walked in the footsteps of ancient kings, the cool water soaking our boots, the weight of history pressing close. Yet Rubin's eyes gleamed this had only been the introduction.

"Now," he said, gesturing toward the ascending path that wound through the old City of David, "we make our way to the Western Wall tunnels. There you will see another side of Jerusalem one hidden beneath centuries of conquest, rebuilding, and prayer."

The short walk from the Pool of Siloam to the entrance of the Western Wall tunnels took us past neighborhoods brimming with both modern life and ancient echoes. Shopkeepers called out in Hebrew and Arabic, selling spices, bread, and souvenirs to bustling crowds. Pilgrims from every corner of the globe thronged the alleys, clutching Bibles, rosaries, or small prayer books as they headed toward the open plaza of the Western Wall.

Rubin led us past the familiar courtyard of the Wall, where men in black hats and women in scarves pressed hands and foreheads against the massive stones. "This," Rubin explained, "is the Western Wall most of the world knows. But what lies beneath is larger and far older. To understand the Temple Mount, you must see the foundations beneath it."

We followed him through a discreet entrance. Immediately, the noise of the courtyard vanished, replaced by the quiet, steady coolness of underground air. The tunnel opened into a passage lit by soft golden lamps, casting long shadows along ancient stones so massive that even modern machinery would struggle to lift them.

"These are Herodian ashlars," Rubin explained, running his hand reverently across a block that stood nearly fifteen feet high and weighed hundreds of tons. "This one stone alone is estimated at over 500 tons. We don't know exactly how Herod's builders moved it into place. But what you're seeing here is part of the original retaining wall of the Temple Mount. The Western Wall above is but the tip of this enormous foundation."

We walked on, the corridor stretching endlessly. The sheer scale of the underground wall stunned us; it seemed impossible that such stones could have been cut, hauled, and set in place two thousand years ago. Bob, ever the practical one, whistled softly. "Herod didn't think small, did he?"

Rubin chuckled. "Not at all. He sought to impress the world, and he succeeded. What you are walking through is the hidden backbone of Jerusalem."

The passage widened into vaulted chambers. Rubin explained that these had once been markets, ritual cleansing pools, and storerooms. Some were so vast that, illuminated by modern lights, they felt like cathedrals carved from stone. Arched ceilings rose above us, the craftsmanship both Roman and distinctly Judaic, layered together through centuries of rebuilding.

"This underground city is almost like strata of history piled upon itself," Rubin said. "Herod's expansions, Hadrian's reconstructions, medieval additions all interwoven. Above your heads lies today's Old City; here below lies its skeleton."

Our steps echoed as we approached a quieter section of the tunnel. The air grew cooler, stiller, as Rubin raised his hand for silence. "Here we approach the place Jews call *HaKotel HaKatan* the Little Western Wall believed to be the closest accessible point to the site of the Holy of Holies from Solomon's Temple and later the Second Temple."

We paused, awestruck. The space felt charged, as though the very air vibrated with centuries of whispered prayers. The stones here seemed older, more worn, their smooth surfaces polished by countless hands. Rubin placed his palm gently against the wall, his voice soft.

"This is as near as any of us may come to the Holy of Holies. According to tradition, it lies just beyond this point, under what is now the Dome of the Rock. In ancient days only the High Priest could enter once a year, on Yom Kippur, to atone for the people of Israel. Yet even here, generations of Jews have prayed, believing their words pass closest to God."

One by one, almost instinctively, we reached out and placed our hands upon the wall. None of us spoke; words seemed too shallow in this moment. The silence was not empty it was full, like a chamber resonant with the prayers of millennia.

Finally Penny whispered, "It feels alive. Like the stones themselves are breathing."

Rubin nodded. "Many say the same."

We moved deeper into the tunnels, passing niches where archaeologists had uncovered mikvehs ritual baths used by priests and worshipers before ascending to the Temple. Rubin pointed out a staircase that once led directly from these pools upward, perhaps used during the days when Jesus himself walked Jerusalem.

"It is humbling," Joe murmured, "to think He may have passed through these very passages."

The tunnel eventually opened into a cavernous chamber lit with warm lamps and filled with rows of chairs. Rubin gestured broadly. "This is the underground synagogue, established so worshipers could pray in proximity to the Holy of Holies. It is one of the most sacred places within the tunnels."

We sat for a few minutes, letting the weight of the place sink in. The sound of distant prayers drifted faintly from above, blending with the hush of the underground.

Then Rubin's voice broke the stillness. "There is more to see, and someone I want you to meet. A friend of mine he has ventured into sections of these tunnels few others have dared to go. He has stories you will not soon forget."

We rose and followed him deeper, our anticipation growing. The path ahead seemed to promise both mystery and revelation, as though each turn of stone would unveil another secret of Jerusalem.

Rubin led us deeper through the maze until the narrow stone passage opened into a warmly lit chamber where tables were set beneath graceful arches. The low hum of conversation, the aroma of fresh bread, roasted meats, and spiced vegetables filled the air. We had arrived at *Under the Arches*, the famous restaurant nestled within the Western Wall tunnels.

"This is the only true restaurant down here," Rubin explained, a satisfied smile playing on his lips. "A place where ancient stone meets good food. Tonight, we dine and learn."

We were ushered to a long wooden table, polished smooth from years of use. The vaulted ceiling above gave the impression of eating inside a medieval hall. Candles flickered beside electric lamps, casting golden reflections on the stones that had stood since the days of Herod.

Plates were soon laid before us hummus drizzled with olive oil, warm pita bread, falafel, lamb skewers, roasted eggplant, bowls of lentil soup, and small glasses of pomegranate wine. The flavors were rich, earthy, and grounding, tying us to the land as much as the history surrounding us.

As we were eating, Rubin rose and waved toward the entrance. A man entered tall, with a salt-and-pepper beard, wearing a simple button-down shirt and a kippah. His eyes carried both intensity and humor, the kind of gaze belonging to someone who had seen things most would never believe.

"This," Rubin announced, "is Dr. Levi Cohen. Archaeologist, historian, and, some say, a bit of an adventurer."

Levi shook our hands firmly, his grip strong, his presence commanding. "Shalom, friends. Rubin tells me you're curious about these tunnels and about the ones that are not on the public tours."

We nodded eagerly. Penny leaned forward, unable to hide her excitement. "Are there really sealed tunnels under the Dome of the Rock?"

Levi chuckled softly. "Ah, the question everyone asks. Yes, there are sealed tunnels. Some were closed centuries ago, others deliberately blocked by authorities who feared what might be found or what conflict might be ignited by their discovery. I myself have traced two passages that approach the Temple Mount foundations. One was walled off by Ottoman builders. The other " He paused for effect, letting the silence linger. " the other ends near a chamber long rumored to be connected with Solomon's treasure vaults."

Our forks froze midway to our mouths. The words "treasure vaults" hung in the air like electricity.

"Of course," Levi continued, "archaeology deals in facts, not rumors. Yet sometimes, rumors contain shadows of truth. Herod expanded and rebuilt much, but older chambers still lie hidden beneath. Priests in Hezekiah's and Josiah's time knew of secret storage rooms. And as you can imagine, if something precious something like the Ark itself needed to be concealed, the tunnels beneath the Temple would be ideal."

Joe leaned in, his voice low. "Have you ever gone inside one of those sealed places?"

Levi's eyes glinted. "Once. Briefly. I will not say too much now, but I have seen carvings and chambers that do not appear on any modern map. They whisper of secrets still buried."

Bob shook his head, half in awe, half in disbelief. "It sounds like something out of an Indiana Jones movie."

"Truth often sounds like fiction," Levi replied. "But the stones beneath your feet are very real. And Thursday night, when the tunnels are less watched, I can show you places few have ever walked."

A hush fell over the table. We could almost feel the weight of what was being offered a glimpse behind the veil of history, into the forgotten arteries of Jerusalem itself.

Finally, Bill broke the silence. "What if the Ark really is down there?"

Levi's voice grew more solemn. "If the Ark rests beneath the Temple Mount, then no power on earth can claim it by force. It belongs only to the God of Israel. But seekers through the centuries from Crusaders to Ottomans have tried. Perhaps one day it will be revealed. Perhaps not. But to walk those hidden passages is to touch the edges of that mystery."

Dinner continued, though our minds were hardly on the food anymore. The thought of hidden chambers, sealed passages, and the possibility no matter how faint that we were standing within reach of something holy and world-changing sent chills through us.

When we finally rose from the table, Rubin clasped Levi's hand warmly. "Thursday at six, then. They are ready."

Levi nodded. "Bring your courage. The tunnels are patient, but they do not yield their secrets easily."

We stepped back into the lamplit corridors, our hearts racing. It felt as though we had just been entrusted with a secret larger than ourselves, a key to mysteries buried beneath Jerusalem for millennia.

We returned to the hotel, the ancient stories of the tunnels still echoing in our minds. Yet the moment we stepped into the lobby, the world of archaeology gave way to the glare of modern celebrity. Errek's phone buzzed with a message from Emily.

She had just landed back home, her voice urgent in the text. *"Darling, I need to speak to you. There's been trouble. Call me when you can."*

Errek excused himself and dialed immediately. Emily's voice trembled between anger and exhaustion. "Do you know what happened the moment I stepped off the plane? Paparazzi everywhere. They had photographs of me in the morning wearing your T-shirt. Not the evening, not the late-night hours we spent talking but the morning. Do you see what this means?"

Errek's brow furrowed. "Emily, I left your room just before midnight. The only time I saw you again was at breakfast. That photo doesn't make sense. Send it to me."

A few seconds later, the image appeared on his screen. A slant of light fell through a shade, clear proof that it was morning. He shook his head. "This isn't from when I was with you. Someone staged this, or at least timed it to make it look like more than it was. Did your management know about us meeting?"

"Yes," she admitted. "They knew. They always want to control the narrative. My bodyguards were there that morning. One of them is in the picture. And then, as if on cue, my managers arrived around seven. Now I'm wondering if they orchestrated this whole thing feeding the story to the press just to stir up attention for my next film."

Her words carried both frustration and resignation. "It's exhausting, Errek. I'm not sure I can fight this anymore."

"Emily, listen," Errek said firmly. "Tell the truth simply. Say I was a family friend, that I loaned you a shirt because you were cold and feeling unwell. People can say what they want, but you know and I know there's nothing scandalous here."

There was a pause, softer now. "Thank you, darling. For having my back. Even if the world doesn't see it, I do."

When Errek rejoined the others, they were gathered in the lounge, drinks in hand, their laughter echoing in contrast to the heaviness of the call. He shared the story quietly, and the group responded with sympathy and indignation.

"Sounds like a setup," Bobby muttered, shaking his head. "Classic publicity stunt. They probably thought you'd react and create more buzz. But you handled it better than they expected."

Penny leaned in, her voice protective. "Errek, you've done nothing wrong. And we all know it. Emily knows it too. Just stay steady. Don't let them pull you into their game."

Bob laughed wryly. "Yeah, the only court you take advantage of is the basketball court." The tension lifted for a moment, and the group chuckled.

Still, the situation weighed on Errek. The night's revelations in the tunnels, the dinner with Levi, and now this swirl of paparazzi drama it all collided in his mind like two worlds refusing to stay separate. He glanced at his friends, grateful for their loyalty. Whatever storms lay ahead, at least he wouldn't face them alone.

The following morning brought a welcome change of pace. After the heaviness of the tunnels and the uneasy phone call with Emily, we decided that a day of rest and lighthearted fun was in order. The suggestion came quickly Tel Aviv. The beaches, the shopping, the chance to blend into the ordinary life of Israel's bustling coastal city sounded like the perfect escape.

We rose early, grabbed a quick snack, and by 8:45 were on the road. The drive carried us past clusters of modular homes, their sharp lines softened by the desert's golden haze, and through stretches of Middle Eastern houses with their flat rooftops blending into the landscape. Slowly, the desert yielded to the sprawl of a modern city, its whitewashed buildings gleaming beneath the rising sun. Tel Aviv rose before us, vibrant, alive, promising everything Jerusalem was not noise, fashion, sand, and sea.

Penny's eyes lit up as she pressed closer to the car window, already imagining the shops, while Bill leaned back with the resigned look of a husband who knew what was coming. Errek chuckled quietly; some adventures were timeless, and the shopping instincts of a determined woman were one of them.

When we reached the beach, the sand greeted us like warm silk beneath our feet. The waves rolled in steady rhythm, blue-green and endless, their spray catching the light in diamonds. We spread our towels, rubbed on sunscreen, and for a while, the group simply lay there in silence, soaking up the sun. Bobby stretched luxuriously. "This is life," he declared.

Soon, laughter broke out as the group trickled toward the water. Joe and Bill strapped on snorkeling masks and drifted into the waves, disappearing beneath the surface, while Errek and Bob followed a few minutes later, splashing like children. Penny joined them, shrieking as the cold water wrapped around her legs. The morning unfolded in carefree joy water fights, playful dives, and drifting in the Mediterranean as if nothing else existed.

By noon, hunger called them back. Bobby, rubbing his arms, grimaced. "I think I'm getting sunburned, lotion or not. And I'm starving." His eyes lit on a golden arch almost comically close to the water. "McDonald's. Perfect."

Inside, the group laughed at Bobby's order. "Fish sandwich with cheese, extra tartar sauce."

The clerk gave a solemn shake of the head. "Sir, we do not put cheese on fish. It is against kosher law."

Bobby blinked. "You've got to be kidding me. Cheese and fish go hand in hand."

"No, sir. It is a sin," the clerk replied, expressionless.

Errek snorted, trying not to laugh as Bobby backtracked. "Fine, just give me two fish sandwiches with extra tartar and a Coke."

They ate quickly, savoring the strange blend of familiar fast food in an unfamiliar context. "Good," Bobby admitted, "but still needs cheese."

Shopping followed, and while Penny attacked it with purpose, the men treated it more like a scavenger hunt. Errek and Bob found new tan waterproof shoes, comfortable light pants, and embroidered shirts. Joe and Bill found local clothing perfect for the climate. The conversations were light, peppered with jokes about gifts for fiancées, girlfriends, and family back home.

Joe lifted a small jewelry bag with a grin. "Got her a gold necklace. Might as well spoil her a little."

"And I suppose you can afford it now," Errek teased.

Joe laughed. "True. Between treasure and contracts, I'd say life's not too bad."

Errek admitted he had bought Penny silk gloves and scarves, while she, in turn, had gifted him a silver Jerusalem cross necklace. Their quiet exchange did not go unnoticed by the group.

The afternoon slipped away, sun and city weaving together into a memory of ease, before the group finally returned to Jerusalem. But the day still held surprises. It was Bob's birthday, though he had forgotten to mention it in the rush of events. Joe quietly called the hotel from the restroom, arranging a chocolate cake and a steak dinner in the conference room. Meanwhile, Errek had already secured a special gift: a top-tier cell phone with a powerful camera and global compatibility.

That evening, after Penny and Bill returned from another round of shopping, the lights of the conference room clicked on and the chorus of "Happy Birthday" rang out. Bob froze, wide-eyed, as the massive chocolate cake gleamed with its inscription: *Happy 41, Bob.*

Presents followed Bill and Penny with DVDs and a gift card, Joe with a folded bill tucked slyly into Bob's hand, and finally Errek, handing over the carefully wrapped phone. Bob tore the paper and whistled low. "Now this is something. Thank you, brother."

Bill leaned in eagerly. "I'll show you all the tricks tomorrow. This thing can do everything but make coffee."

Laughter filled the room as the evening stretched on with steak, baked potatoes, and stories shared.

But as the celebration wound down, another thread emerged. The hotel staff approached Errek, informing him that the basketball directors he had met before were waiting in the lobby. Nervously excusing himself, he walked down to find two women and three men, one of them the very man he had spoken with at the under-16 game.

They gathered in a private room, tapes spread out, discussions flowing quickly. Errek spoke with clarity, outlining the team's glaring weakness rebounding and the need for a small forward who could crash the boards. He detailed strategies, player evaluations, and adjustments in practice structure. By the time he finished, the directors exchanged approving glances.

"Mr. Johnson," one of them said, "you have a gift. You see the game not just for what it is, but for what it could be. We would like to offer you the position of head coach for our Pro A team."

The offer was clear: $70,000 salary, bonuses for playoffs and championships, housing, a car, and the option for his brother to join as assistant coach. Sayid, a trusted player-coach, could also be added. The directors' faith was evident.

When Errek returned to the group later that night, his face carried both joy and awe. "I took the job," he announced simply. "Looks like I'm staying in Israel a while longer."

Cheers rose around the table, Rubin included. Yet beneath the laughter and clinking glasses, a new seriousness settled. They still had the tunnels to explore, mysteries to uncover, and perhaps treasures yet untold. But for now, there was contentment the kind that comes when past and future briefly pause, allowing the present to shine.

After the birthday celebration wound down and the laughter gave way to tired smiles, the group gathered around Rubin once more. He had brought with him not only his excitement but also a large folded diagram, worn from use and marked with careful notes. He spread it across the table, the paper covered with winding lines, dots, and shaded blocks that seemed more like a labyrinth than any simple map.

"These," Rubin began, tracing with his finger, "are the known tunnels of Jerusalem. Here are the chambers that have already been excavated, and here " his hand shifted to the shaded areas " are the ones that may still exist, though no one has entered them in centuries."

The group leaned in, eyes widening as Rubin spoke.

"We must concentrate on the areas near the Western Wall and beneath the Temple Mount. These tunnels, particularly near the Holy of Holies, are rumored to have been used to conceal treasures, even sacred artifacts. The Ark of the Covenant, if it was ever hidden in Jerusalem, could be somewhere in one of these chambers."

Bob gave a low whistle. "The Ark. That's aiming high."

Rubin nodded gravely. "Perhaps. But the clues point here. Hezekiah built tunnels for water, yes, but he also may have created hidden chambers for protection. If the Levites needed to move the Ark to preserve it from Babylon, this would have been the only possible place. We cannot prove it but the possibility alone makes it worth exploring."

The group absorbed his words, each one weighing the magnitude of what lay before them. Joe tapped the map thoughtfully. "What about access? Aren't some of these tunnels sealed off or restricted?"

"They are," Rubin confirmed. "Particularly those leading under the Dome of the Rock. That area is highly sensitive controlled by Muslim authorities, and any movement there is closely monitored. But Thursday night provides a rare opportunity. Friday is their holy day, so activity will be lighter. I've arranged discreet access around six-thirty in the evening. We'll eat first at the restaurant 'Under the Arches,' then begin exploring once the crowds thin."

"Sounds like a plan," Errek replied, though his voice carried both excitement and a trace of caution. "What do we need to bring?"

"Everything charged and ready," Rubin instructed. "Retractable detectors set to maximum sonar, solar watches, hand tools, flashlights. And be aware: oxygen levels in the smaller tunnels may be lower than expected. Wide chambers will be safe enough, but some of the narrow passageways could be dangerous."

Penny leaned back, frowning. "Collapsed tunnels, low oxygen, earthquakes in the past... sounds like a recipe for trouble."

Rubin gave a small smile. "Yes, which is why the Israel Antiquities Authority is selective about who enters. Normally the IDF escorts explorers away from sealed or unstable sections. But with careful planning and discretion, we may have a chance to examine places others have only whispered about."

Bill studied the map, pointing to one particular shaded tunnel. "What about this one, about fifty yards beyond the Holy of Holies area?"

Rubin's expression grew thoughtful. "That one has long been closed. Some believe it runs directly beneath the Temple Mount, under the Dome itself. Its existence is disputed, but records suggest it once connected to chambers Solomon built beneath the Temple as storerooms possibly for treasures."

"And possibly for the Ark," Bob said quietly, the words hanging heavy in the air.

"Yes," Rubin replied. "If the Ark was not carried away, if Jeremiah did not remove it elsewhere, then the most logical explanation is that it was hidden here, in these very chambers. But remember, this is theory. Legends and whispers mix with history."

The group nodded solemnly. Even so, the thought that they might be standing on the brink of uncovering one of the greatest mysteries of faith sent a ripple of energy through the room.

Joe clapped his hands together. "Then it's settled. We're going prepared. We'll bring the detectors, the tools, and the courage. Thursday night we go in."

"Agreed," said Rubin. He began folding up the diagram carefully, as though the fragile paper itself held the weight of history. "One last reminder: we must be discreet. If word spreads that we're searching for the Ark, not only will the authorities intervene, but we may also stir political unrest. Our work must be as silent as the tunnels themselves."

Bob gave a mock groan. "And let's hope we don't stir up an earthquake while we're at it."

Joe chuckled. "Way to jinx us, Bob."

The group laughed, but the humor did not erase the gravity of what they were about to attempt. Each of them knew, deep down, that Thursday's journey would not be an ordinary exploration. It would be a step into the unknown, into history, and perhaps into legend.

That night, as they finally retired to their rooms, the city of Jerusalem seemed to breathe beneath them a city layered with secrets, waiting for the right hands, and the right moment, to reveal what had been hidden for centuries.

Chapter 16 The Tunnel of Doom

What a day, Errek thought. I get a dream job here in Jerusalem and can stay here at the condo. I like it here two good restaurants, a gym, and a rooftop pool. This is nice. Just got to see what Bob wants to do. It would be great working here with him, but what do we do with our home back in Alabama? I am happy. Lord, I just pray that I can help my players and see if I can win. This is actually a much better team than my others. I was starting with almost nothing except my last team here. Then there is Emily… maybe there is hope that my dream girl will be mine. But I am more apprehensive about the tunnels than even the scuba diving for treasure. What if we can find it? I cannot touch it, but I want to prove Bible history is real history. Plus, I am doing my thesis on the Ark, so it would be awe-inspiring. I am just a bundle of nerves. Maybe just going to the hot tub and relaxing will help me, so I can sleep.

"Well, guys," Errek said, "I am going to the hot tub, and then if you like, we can play some Rook."

"I could use a good hot tub," Bob said.

So, they left to go to the room and get their swimsuits for a nice time in the tub. Bob and Errek went to the tub, and soon the rest of the group joined them.

"You seem nervous, Errek," one of them observed.

"Yes," Errek admitted. "Just thoughts of what if we find it. It is kind of overwhelming. Today was a fun, relaxing day, and now I am nervous as a cat. My mind is racing about something we may never find."

"Just relax, Errek, and pray," Bill said. "Put tomorrow in God's hands. You should be relaxing. I mean, you got a great job coaching a pretty good team, and you put up a great plan to improve them.

You got this. The Lord has blessed you, and He will continue to be with you. Just keep Him first, like you tell us and your Bible class."

This gave Errek some comfort. It took him an hour to get to sleep, but he fell asleep and had a dream telling him: *seek and you shall find, and knock and the door will be opened for you.* These were the last things he remembered as he woke to the sunshine through his windows.

Bob was already awake, and it was after 10 a.m.

"Well, you must have had a good sleep," Bob said before Errek rose from bed.

"No, had a weird dream," Errek replied. "All I remember was the Bible verse: 'Ask and ye shall receive, seek and ye shall find, and knock and the door will be opened for you.' That is all I remember."

"Well, I am going down in about an hour to eat brunch. I've just been playing computer games."

"Well, that is your new cell?"

"Yes, and I love it. Thank you. I cannot wait to get full internet; just playing games, and the camera is great."

"Make sure your old phone is charged before we head to the tunnels. I figure since we eat at the restaurant at 6:30, maybe we can get there and just look around a few minutes to be more acquainted with the main tunnel. Have you seen the rest of the team?"

"Yeah, Bill and Penny had breakfast and were at the gym. Joe I have not seen yet. I may just relax in the pool and go eat lunch or go to the gym for a few minutes."

The day slowly passed. The group had lunch, went back to the room for rest, and to check their equipment.

"We must go in light and not be too noticeable," Errek instructed. "Just simple picks and shovels, the translators, our solar watch, and one small retractable metal detector that fits in my backpack."

"I am just taking a couple of thermoses with ice water," Bob said.

"I think we all are. Joe, I can put a thermos for you since you have the tools," Errek offered.

They left to go to the Western Wall at 4:30; it was another bright, sunny day.

They soon found the entrance to go down to the Western Wall tunnel.

"Not many people here today," Joe observed.

"That is good news. Looks like a synagogue service is going on," Bill replied. "I am going to the ground level by the stairway."

He managed to take a few pictures. "Bill, moved behind us," Errek said. "There is supposed to be a tunnel behind us at ground level."

"Yeah, I can see it. Check it out right quick."

Bill disappeared into a dark corner. He snuck into the tunnel; it angled down and toward the wall. It went for about five meters but was sealed shut as if an earthquake had collapsed it—the wall was actually only at the lower tunnel chamber. He backtracked and quickly reported his findings.

"The tunnel, about four feet by seven feet, ended possibly right below the base of the Wall, but it was sealed solid," Bill said.

So, one of the alternate tunnels was a dead end. The next main one was following the tunnel wall about fifty meters from them, maybe twenty yards past the Under the Arch Restaurant.

"Let's try to see that one next," Errek suggested.

"Okay," Joe agreed. "Let's maybe sit outside the synagogue and listen to the rest of the service. Let's turn on our translators."

They casually made their way there.

"Is it me, or are there fewer lights as you get further past the synagogue?" Bob asked.

Slowly, the big chamber narrowed. They saw the tunnel and went to enter but were stopped by an IDF soldier.

"Sorry, you cannot enter. It is forbidden. It goes under the Temple Mount and is sealed. Sorry."

Well, that was disheartening.

"There has to be something there, or they would not protect it," Errek muttered. "Looks like this tunnel exploration is doomed."

"May I just go five feet forward and use my little device?" Joe asked the soldier. "You can watch."

He stepped forward and saw the tunnel was blocked, but there was an opening about two feet under the seal. Very interesting, he thought.

"Well, let's go eat at The Arch," he said to the group.

Dejectedly, the group left to meet Rubin and eat.

"Hey, Rubin," Errek said as they sat down. "We hit the two main caves off the Wall. One on the west side ended with it sealed, maybe by an earthquake. The seal might be right under the base of the wall. The other had IDF guarding the tunnel about thirty meters east of here. They let Joe use his sonar—they didn't know what it was—but he said the seal is about two to three feet wide and there is open space behind it."

"Okay," Rubin said, thoughtfully. "Was not expecting that, but something must be behind there, five to seven meters under the Temple Mount, which is an area under dispute."

The waiter came to take their order.

"I want a nice Israeli meat dish," Bob said. "I like potatoes and hummus."

"No problem," the waiter replied. "You know, our wine cellar is pretty cool. You have to go down a few steps to a small seven-by-seven-foot chamber with a door sealing a tunnel, but we never go there. It is kind of spooky. We occasionally hear weird sounds. Almost like a light, cool breeze, but we are about sixty feet below ground, and it is below our floor here."

"Is the owner or manager here?" Errek asked.

"Of course, he is in the office."

"Our charts show a possible tunnel near here that may intersect with that, maybe," Joe mentioned.

Their food arrived, and about ten minutes later, the owner arrived. Rubin smiled.

"Yacub! I did not know you owned this great establishment."

"Yes, the food is great. I am honored," Yacob said, his eyes widening. "Is that Errek Johnson and company?"

"Yes, it is," Rubin confirmed.

"Should I call you Coach or Indiana Jones?" Yacob asked, laughing.

"Coach is fine."

"I am one of the sponsors for the Premier League and the Pro A team."

"Well, it is my honor. I think we can win it all."

"We can talk about that later," Errek said. "Well, we are exploring caves and tunnels, and we were hoping to find maybe the Ark or the missing utensils from the Temple."

"I see," Yacob said.

"We went to the tunnel about twenty meters from here, and it was sealed with IDF guarding it. Is there another way to see what is behind the seal?"

"Possibly. There is a tunnel by our wine cellar in my restaurant. Have you been in it?"

"I have been in it," Rubin said, "but did not go to the end. We put in a sealed door because we kept hearing noises and feeling a slight breeze. That should not happen about sixty-five feet underground. After that, I did not want to explore it, but you can if you like."

"It is weird," Yacob added. "The tunnel is very old, maybe even from Hezekiah or Josiah's time. It is about five feet wide and seven feet high. No lights after fifteen meters; you will need lights. It is cool with an unusual breeze at times—there should be none—and the oxygen level is a little less than where we are."

"Can you take us down and just make sure we return?" Errek asked.

"No problem. Good luck. Oh, you must try the dessert; I will bring it to you."

"Bring one for each."

"No problem. Dessert is on the house for my new coach."

"This might not be such a bad deal," Bob joked.

It was a delicious pomegranate and mixed berry mousse with pomegranate ice cream.

"Well, that was a great last meal," Bob joked again as they finished.

They followed Yacob through the kitchen down to about a ten-foot-squared room with metal surroundings, nice wine racks, and a big sealed door in the corner. He unlocked it, turned on the one light a few feet past the door, and said, "It runs at a slight angle toward the east. So, any guess how far from the Wall? Maybe twelve meters, but I think this may be below the Wall because my restaurant is right at the floor; this may be seven to nine feet below. But look at the wall."

"Yes," Penny said, examining it. "This has very old elements, well before Herod's time."

"Well, wish us luck," Errek said. "Guys, turn on your lights. Off we go."

"Well, at least this tunnel is a little wider than Acre," Bob noted.

"Yes, that is surprising," Errek agreed. "Two people can walk side by side with at least a foot of space and a decent ceiling."

"This is actually pretty well constructed," Joe said as he pressed a few buttons on his watch. "Well, so far, we have travelled twenty meters. We should be near the Wall. According to my watch, we are travelling southwest at maybe a fourteen-degree angle."

"Why do I almost feel a breeze?" Bill wondered. "Maybe it is a small gap from the wall with a breeze blowing down, and we barely feel it."

"Well, if this is under the Wall, we should be getting close," Errek said. What is that? I hear something he shined a light down and there was a big rat scurrying and disappeared where did it go. That was a big rat."

Well, it disappeared about a meter in front of us, Penny said. "I do not like rats and that was a big one."

Joe said, "Nah, I've seen bigger."

The group flashed their lights and saw a small tunnel that seemed to have been dug by accident right into the bigger tunnel we were in. Joe bent over and entered it is a dark tunnel but it is a dugout tunnel it gets a little bigger maybe a room I see something."

Ugh get off me, Aww there are nasty cob webs and I found our rat and something else. Hey, my light, my light. Guys, my lights gone out and I can't see anything please come help."

Joe said," I gotcha friend. He bent over and entered his light shining here I am." Hey, Errek, Come hear, we need more light." Joe said.

Errek entered and with both flashlights their situation illuminated. It appears that this used to be a hand dug tunnel heading upward, but it collapsed on itself and on these two skeletons one is half buried. Looking at the old torn cloth remains these were crusaders that were digging down from the temple mount hit on a smaller tunnel and maybe and earthquake or something and their man-made tunnel collapsed on themselves. We pointed flashlight up and it appeared that our rat buddy had gnawed his own little rout upward.

Rubin said, "try to uncover it see if there are any signet or tools we can recover."

So, we did, there is an old spade on the skeleton buried and a broken spade and decent dagger. They seem to be trying to excavate probably looking for ark. After a minute of metal detecting, they found a couple coins and worn-out silver ring Nothing earth shattering just looked like crusaders hoping to find hidden treasure on the Holy Mount and there cave collapsed.

The intrepid group back tracked back into the main tunnel that they were in carried on for about ten more meter narrowing until it appeared the tunnel had hit a dead-end.

"Bill, go ahead," Errek instructed.

"Guys, it doesn't dead-end; it turns left," Bill called back. "But I cannot see after three meters; it is dark."

"Hang on, we are coming."

"Well, this way is all black," Bill said, his voice echoing slightly.

Joe and Bill turned on their high-powered flashlights, the beams cutting through the profound darkness.

"Well, this is not on any maps," Joe observed, his tone a mix of awe and excitement. "But my guess is this could be below where the original Temple was."

"Is it near the Holy of Holies?" Penny asked, her voice hushed.

"I just do not know," Joe admitted. "But it could be one of Solomon's rumored hidden rooms to hide the Temple treasures or the Ark."

"It does not make sense," Rubin said, skepticism in his voice.

Errek and Joe laughed.

"It makes perfect sense," Errek replied.

The light from their flashlights was absorbed by the darkness ahead; it was not like the cave walls they had just passed through.

"This could be it," Errek said, his voice ecstatic and heavy with emotion. He moved to the end of the tunnel and pressed against the dark surface before them. It moved. "It is like a huge curtain covering something. A pretty heavy curtain, jet black. Very, very old and smelling of mold."

Joe pulled out his detector and switched it to sonar mode.

"Very big room," he announced. "Maybe ten meters deep." He changed the setting. "Putting it on metal mode now." The device immediately began beeping erratically. "Oh, it's beeping off the charts!"

"Okay, guys," Errek said, "see if we can pull this tarp down or if it is on a rod."

"No need to destroy anything," Errek and Rubin said in unison.

"I feel the side," Penny said, running her hands along the edge of the massive curtain. "Let's see if it slides."

It did, moving about five inches with a gritty, ancient sound.

"Well, let's try to squeeze through."

They worked and tugged, grunting with the effort, and finally got the curtain wide enough to enter the dark room. They all had to hold their flashlights up to squeeze through the narrow gap.

Once inside, Errek turned his flashlight beam onto the old curtain and the floor.

"Let's wait until everyone is safely inside, then turn on our lights together," he instructed.

They all shuffled into position in the impenetrable darkness.

"You ready?" Errek asked.

A chorus of affirmations answered him.

"Now."

They turned on their lights simultaneously.

"Oh, wow!" Penny gasped.

The beams illuminated cups, utensils, and treasures glinting in the dark.

"Some of this must be from the Temple," Bill whispered reverently. "Some maybe even Solomon's booty."

"But what is that in the corner?" Bob asked, pointing. "It is almost glowing. Looks like skins or something."

"This is in a disputed area," Rubin said, his practical mind cutting through the wonder. "This is a problem."

"Grab me a few coins and cups," Errek said.

"Well, these coins have a lion on one side and a Star of David on the other," Joe reported, examining one. "The cups are gold; some are silver and gold utensils. All perfect."

"Look at the ceiling," Bill said, shining his light upward. "Get our bearings. The ceiling is about twelve feet high but almost as if it was made of a black stone slab. This must be a secret room."

"Hang on," Joe said. "I am putting the detector in sonar mode again. Let's see how thick the ceiling is."

He extended the detector and held it over his head.

"It is a different texture than the ground or bedrock," he announced, "but at least five feet thick."

"Thick enough to hide from Babylonians or Romans," Errek concluded.

"Indeed. This is a monumental find. But how do we get this into governmental hands-on disputed ground?"

"Let's put some of these into my backpack before we search what is in the corner under the skins," Rubin suggested, his archaeologist's instincts taking over. He carefully gathered a few items and about fifty coins. "This should be enough proof. We do not need to take much, but this is extremely important for my museum and the IAA. Be careful. Also on opposite corner there looks like there is a long doorway. "He walked over and said interesting there is a stone step but its like it has formed a wall as if the steps removed and the lower room closed in for eternity.

"I am taking this backpack out," Rubin said, "We'll take out the thermoses so we have an empty backpack to put stuff in and I will take backpack to tunnel."

"Okay."

He slid out through the curtain with the pack, but suddenly the room started shaking.

"Rubin, throw in the backpack!" Errek yelled from the other side. "Guys, get out!"

But it was too late. A huge slab, as if by some unexplained mechanism, fell from above, sealing the entrance with a thunderous crash. They were trapped.

"Well," Joe said, examining the new barrier, "this slab is about ten inches thick and wide enough to Seel the five inside . It will take a while to pick our way out if we can."

"Okay," Errek's rattled voice replied, "let's explore to see if there is another way out!"

They heard a faint cry.

Joe smiled. "That is Rubin. Glad I gave him a watch."

Joe started writing a message on his watch: We are okay. Get help.

A reply came quickly: No problem. I will let Yakub know and call IAA. Just stay calm.

"Looks like bedrock or granite," Joe said, examining the slab. "We are stuck here, but we are going to look and see if there is another way out.."

They methodically searched the room's perimeter, their flashlight beams dancing over the ancient walls.

"We're saved!" Penny yelled from the north side of the chamber. "I found a second tunnel!"

They rushed over and shined their lights into the new passage, only to see that it was collapsed about three meters away.

"Okay," Errek said, his hope deflating. "I wonder if that is the one the IDF is guarding."

Penny yelled a few times into the blocked tunnel, but no reply came.

"It is 8 p.m.," Bill noted grimly. "The tunnels are officially closed except for the restaurant."

Meanwhile, Rubin retraced his steps in a panic and found Yacub.

"I think they found some of the Temple gold!" Rubin exclaimed, breathless. "And maybe the Ark! When I left with a sample, a huge slab fell from the ceiling, blocking them in. Look at this!" He showed the artifacts to the restaurateur.

"This is unbelievable," Yacub whispered, his eyes wide. "These guys are geniuses. Maybe they can figure it out. Call Eli and Benjamin. This is huge, and we need to get them out. Tomorrow is the Muslim rest day, so we need to do everything tomorrow. They may be stuck overnight, but we need strong diamond drills."

"Go back, Rubin," Yacub instructed. "Make sure they are okay. If there is one booby trap, there may be a couple more. Let's just hope they are not too bad."

"Well, at least they have four certified geniuses with them," Rubin said, trying to reassure himself.

"Yes," Yacub agreed.

Rubin went back to the sealed entrance and sent a phone message. He quickly got a reply: Second tunnel to room sealed. Think it might be the IDF tunnel.

"Makes sense," Joe's voice came faintly from the other side of the slab. "That is not as hard to get out."

"Let me work on that," Rubin said. "Just remain calm."

"No problem," Joe replied. "We are looking for a release mechanism. Also, we are going to remove the skins and see what is underneath."

"Well, make sure you do not touch what is under it if it is the Ark," Rubin warned, "or you will surely die."

"Errek told us that," Joe confirmed.

"I figured he would," Rubin said. "We will go to the other tunnel and check it out."

Back inside the chamber, Bob said, "Well, I am here. What is under the big animal skins or tarp?"

"Actually, if I am correct they are Manatee skins and may be fragile," Errek cautioned. "Best to slowly lift it. Whatever you do, do not touch what is under it."

Bob and Joe slowly lifted the heavy, ancient skins high enough to remove them.

A soft, ethereal glow and its overwhelming beauty instantly filled the room. They could see the intricate forms of the cherubim arched over the mercy seat. The whole room was illuminated by its divine light. Bill and Errek quickly took pictures before the light became blinding.

"Oh, my goodness," Penny breathed. "That is the Ark."

Then, a booming voice like thunder filled the chamber, sending Bob and Joe flying backwards as if struck by an invisible force. Errek and Bill tried to catch them but they all smashed into the big slab.

"Oh no," Bob grunted as he hit the ground. "Well, that's gonna will leave a mark," as he and his friends gradually lost consciousness.

Before they lost consciousness they all heard a booming voice that put fear through every fiber of their being They all heard a booming, thunderous sound that was not a sound, but a voice that resonated in their very souls. You will understand the Ark and its Glory, it said.

Everything went blindingly white, and then all became quiet. A profound silence filled the room as they slowly, one by one, lost consciousness. They became as dead people in a deep sleep.

They knew not how long they were out, but their bodies felt radiant. They felt different, as a sense of profound peace was over them. They thought they were dead as they slowly woke.

Bobby, as his eyes were adjusting to the light, said, "I don't think we are in Kansas anymore, Toto."

As they slowly came to, Errek asked, "Did you hear the voice?"

"Yes," they all murmured in reply. "We all heard it."

"I think… so I see you and the others and we are talking," Joe said, his voice full of wonder, "but this is beyond me. This has no logical explanation. Are we dead?"

"Well, let's take God at His word," Errek said, his faith solidifying the experience. "We must be where the Ark wants us to be."

"But where?" Penny asked, looking around at the unfamiliar landscape.

"A better question might be," Errek said, shading his eyes from a sun that was not Jerusalem's, "when are we?"

"This place is not Jerusalem," Errek stated, stating the obvious yet unbelievable fact. He looked down at his own body. "Just how long were we out?" He tried to shade his eyes from the sun. "And… these are clothing of ancient times we are wearing."

"I DON'T KNOW," Joe said, his voice a mix of awe and confusion.

"Could be ancient times," Errek mused, trying to rationalize the miracle. "Let's stay patient and figure this out. We're on a ridge partway up a desert mountain. This can't be a dream—five people can't share the same dream."

Where were they, when were they and how did they get there. The epic journey continues in Adventures in Biblical times.